THE COP

THE COP

SASHA WHITE
ALYSSA BROOKS
RENÉE ALEXIS

APHRODISIA

KENSINGTON BOOKS

http://www.kensingtonbooks.com

KENSINGTON BOOKS are published by

Kensington Publishing Corp.
850 Third Avenue
New York, NY 10022

All Kensington Titles, Imprints, and Distributed lines are available at special quantity discounts for bulk purchases for sales promotions, premiums, fund-raising, and educational or institutional use.

Special book excerpts or customized printings can also be created to fit specific needs. For details, write or phone the office of the Kensington special sales manager: Kensington Publishing Corp., 850 Third Avenue, New York, NY 10022, attn: Special Sales Department, Phone: 1-800-221-2647.

ISBN: 0-7582-1531-2

First Trade Paperback Printing: October 2006

10 9 8 7 6 5 4 3 2 1

Printed in the United States of America

Contents

SEX AS A WEAPON

Sasha White

1

He tried to control his heart rate as he drank in the vision of her. With feet planted wide apart in fuck-me stilettos that made his dick throb, and the stretchy rope he'd found in the closet hanging suggestively in her hands, she had him so excited he could barely see straight.

His wife was out of town visiting her family, and when he ran into this seductive woman in the lobby of his law firm he knew Lady Luck had just given him a gift. Her short blond hair framed a pale face with heavily lined eyes and full bright red cock-sucking lips that made him think of a Geisha. When her blue eyes had locked with his earlier, the invitation to have a drink together had flown from his lips.

Somehow, they'd ended up at his house for that drink, and now they were in his bedroom. Him naked on a straight-back chair, and her getting ready to tie him up before she rode him long and hard.

God! Just the thought of her climbing onto his lap and sinking onto his aching cock had him closing his eyes in anticipation. But then he couldn't see her anymore, and that was a true loss.

"Ready, handsome?" She leaned forward and brushed her lips across his cheek, her words flowing into his ear and racing down his spine. He looked down her dress, and the view of abundant breasts spilling over the lace cups of her bra had saliva pooling in his mouth.

How this woman had managed to get him worked up like a fifteen-year-old when he'd been feeling every one of his fifty-two years only an hour ago was beyond him.

"More ready than you can believe," he replied and placed his hands behind his back and gripped the rungs of the chair.

The light brush of her fingers against his arms had the fine hairs standing on end as he felt her wrap the rope gently around his forearms. She wrapped it several times, going closer to his wrists with each turn. There were some rustling noises and he felt soft plump flesh press against his arms. "Hurry up back there, would you?"

She finished with a gentle tug, and then put her hands on his shoulders from behind. "How does that feel?" she whispered in his ear.

He tested the restraint, surprised when he had no movement. There was very little pressure on his wrists and nothing cutting into his skin. He was almost disappointed there was no discomfort. "It feels fine, good. Now step around here, lift up that skirt and climb on for the ride of your life."

Vanessa Lawson let a wicked chuckle rumble from between her painted lips as she strode around the arrogant prick she'd just tied to the chair and headed for the west wall. It had been almost too easy to seduce him.

She ignored his sputter of surprise and the curses that should've turned the air blue as she opened the antique armoire there. Adrenaline pumped through her veins, but her hands were steady as she went straight for the safe hidden behind the hanging clothes, and pushed any lingering sexual thoughts out of her mind.

Edward Yardley was a decent looking guy. His hair was meticulous and he was in good shape for a man his age. However, his ego was even bigger than the erection standing proud in his lap at the moment, and that was what made her job so easy. When you knew what made a person tick, it was easy to get what you wanted from them. And there was no doubt that what made this man tick was the thought of a night of hot nasty sex while his new wife was out of town.

Sucking in a deep breath Vanessa keyed in the combination into the safe, only to let it out nice and easy when she saw that the idiot was too arrogant to change it after he divorced his first wife. Everything was just as she'd been told it would be. She pulled out three jewelry cases and a canvas bank envelope. After checking the envelope to make sure it contained the cash, she closed the safe.

Vanessa shut the door of the armoire and turned back to the red-faced man in the chair. She gave his still hard cock a hungry glance. It really was a nice one; too bad the guy was such an ass-hole or she might've given him the ride before she went for the safe. "Don't worry, handsome. I won't tell anyone how easy it was to get you to ask me to tie you up if you don't tell anyone I was here, period."

She sauntered from the room, leaving him with a wilting hard-on and a variety of lame threats flying fast and furiously from his thin lips.

2

Forty minutes later Vanessa strolled into the small thirty-year-old cottage style house she called home. Signing the mortgage papers on it six months earlier had been one of the proudest moments in her life. Not many twenty-six-year-olds owned their own house. Then again, she wasn't your normal twenty-something.

The house needed a bit of work, but it was clean and stable, and it was *hers*. That was what all that mattered.

She tossed the leather backpack that held the stolen goods, her wig and the makeup kit with her three pairs of colored contacts on the floor, and sank down on the faded futon she used as a couch. With a small sigh she unbuckled her heels then reached for the phone on the side table. Flexing her feet and stretching her toes, she dialed the familiar number and waited for her friend to pick up.

"I'm back," she said after a cultured female voice answered on the third ring.

"Was there any trouble?"

"Nope. In fact, it was ridiculously easy." Vanessa took a

deep breath and spoke her next words clearly. "But that doesn't change what I said before. That was the last time, Ophelia."

"Of course, Nessa. This last time was strictly a favor to me. I'm aware of that and I thank you."

Except the first one, they were all favors. She wanted to remind Ophelia of that, but she couldn't bring herself to be snippy with the woman she owed so much to.

What could she do? Friends did favors for each other, and Ophelia was the only person Vanessa considered a true friend. So when she asked for something, it was damn hard to say no. But, instead of dwelling on the topic, she made plans to drop off the goods the next day and said good night to her friend.

Vanessa pulled herself up off the futon and headed for the bathroom, stripping the slinky dress off as she went. As she undid her bra, she shoved all hints of loneliness aside and focused on the distraction that always worked. Sex.

The image of Yardley panting as he peeked down her dress came to mind. The fact that she'd gotten a bit of a thrill from his obvious desire reminded her it was time to find another lover. It was almost two months since she set John loose to find another, and while she didn't miss him and his neediness, she did miss the sex.

She really missed the sex.

"The Risqué Robber strikes again." Detective Kane Michaels threw a folded newspaper on his friend's desk. "Fucking reporters are gonna screw everything up."

Jackson Barrows was a good cop, and a good friend. And that was the only thing that kept Kane from smacking him upside the head when he looked up from the file in his hands with a gleeful smirk. "It's time to put on a collar and go hunting in the clubs, my friend."

"The only collar in my house belongs to Mystery." Kane ignored the smirk and dropped into the chair behind his own desk. He reached into his trouser pocket for a hard candy and popped it into his mouth, balling up the cellophane wrapper and flicking it at his friend while savoring the rich flavor.

"You still got that mangy cat?" Jack dodged the shot and picked up the newspaper.

"She's not mangy anymore. In fact, now that she's been in my loving care for a while instead of on the streets, she's got a shiny coat and a sweet disposition."

Jackson snorted. "Too bad you didn't have the same effect on women as you do on cats."

"If I ever found a woman I wanted to keep around she'd be purring happily in my lap the same way Mystery does."

The banter between the men was fast and smooth, second nature to them both.

"'An inside source says, "The woman who's committing these crimes is not only seductive to her victims, but damn talented with a rope."'" Jackson read out loud.

Kane switched gears as he flipped through the last batch of pictures from Yardley's crime scene. "With each robbery, the victim is bound in a different and more creative way. And even when she uses a silk tie or an electrical cord to bind them, there's never a mark or bruise left behind."

"That's not much to go on after four robberies in ten months." Jack shook his head and leaned forward to tap his pencil on the photo of Edward Yardley's bound wrists. "Tell me about these ones."

"These knots are a beauty. She used a twelve-foot section of climbing rope this time. Forearms and wrists were bound to the chair in such a way the guy didn't have a clue what he was getting into until he tried to stand up and realized that not only was he bound, but he was stuck there until someone else came along." He met his friend's gaze. "A clear example of Shibari."

"You're an expert on bondage now?"

"No, but I showed the crime scene photographs to a guy I found on the Internet, a bondage instructor, and he says it's so."

Jackson shook his head, smirk still peaking out from under his Fu Manchu mustache. "Did they lift anything from the rope?"

Kane heaved a sigh of frustration. "No hair or skin, just a piece of fiber. They're looking into it, but I'm not holding my breath."

"So you get to cruise the local adult playgrounds looking for a sexy babe that likes to get kinky, but isn't so kinky she's into pain, while I get to catch up on paperwork." He shook his head. "Want to trade?"

"Sorry, bud. But I didn't get myself shot in a drug raid, so I'm not stuck with desk duty. Although, I can't say I'm sorry you are since you seem to know all the right places to look for information on bondage knots and that's the only solid lead I have to follow, so far."

His blood heated and his frustration eased as the thrill of the chase ran through him. It was time to start digging deeper into the sub-culture of alternative lifestyles.

3

Kane was frustrated as hell.

In the past three nights he'd been through almost every club on the list of "adult playgrounds" Jackson had compiled for him. And he'd had absolutely no luck.

Sure, he'd met plenty of people dressed in leather and lace with Goth-style makeup and studded collars. A few of them, male *and* female, had even offered to tie him up when he'd hinted at an interest in bondage. But the feel had all been wrong. Something had been off.

He'd decided as a last ditch effort to try talking openly with the owner of the next club as a cop. Straight out.

Pretending to be into the lifestyle had gotten him nowhere, and after double-checking the knots and restraints from the Yardley photos he knew that the Risqué Robber wasn't just playing at bondage. The particular way things had been done had led them to learn more about bondage, and Shibari in particular.

He'd learned it was more than just tying someone up, or even the way the knots were done. It originated with the Japanese and is considered an art. With the restraints done in different designs meant to be effective, pleasing to the eye, and pleasing to the recipient, it wasn't something just anyone could do. And while RR wasn't binding the victim's genitals, as seemed to be a common thing in Shibari, she was certainly doing more than just tying them up.

The O Club was one of the last ones on his limited list. Jack had told him that the O stood for anything from "Orgasms" to "Oh My God!"

Great, just what he needed . . . a club that couldn't even decide what its name stood for.

He shook off his frustration and headed for the entrance.

"Sorry. We're closed to the public tonight, sir." A tall slim blonde dressed all in black stepped in front of the doors, stopping him. A female doorman—doorperson?

Kane smiled and flashed his badge. "I'd like to speak with the owner if he's here.

The woman's expression didn't change, but she stepped to the side and opened the door for him. Kane glanced at the man standing a couple feet away, also dressed in black, who was now speaking quietly into a two-way radio.

It was just after eight in the evening, and Kane hadn't expected the club to be busy, but finding it closed was interesting.

Kane stopped just inside the doors and let his eyes adjust to the dark room. Dull golden lights gleamed behind a long wooden bar that stretched the length of the room, making the various bottles of liquor sparkle and shine like a rainbow. The club was empty except for one guy behind the bar and a couple waitresses in skimpy, shiny black outfits seated there, all with their heads turned in the same direction.

A loud slap echoed through the air, followed by a slight moan, and Kane's eyes flew over the couches and overstuffed chairs that were arranged throughout the club to the far wall.

There, on a stage than ran the length of the back wall, was a naked woman bent over what looked like a padded sawhorse. Blond curls fell forward to obscure her features, but her tension was clear in the lines of her body. Yet, as he studied the scene, the tension somehow announced itself as excitement, not fear.

Kane watched closely as a shirtless man in leather pants hauled back his arm and smacked the pink cheeks of her rump with a paddle of some sort. A loud crack echoed through the club, and Kane realized just how quiet it was in the dark cavernous room. Unable to stop himself, he inched closer to the stage.

When a third person stepped out of the shadows cast by the dancers' cage at the end of the stage, Kane's mind went blank.

She was beautiful.

The woman was wearing the most basic clothes. Low-slung faded jeans with rips in the knees and a white ribbed cotton wife-beater tank top. Dark hair, with a tinge of red under the lights, was pulled back in a ponytail, which gave him a clear view of her features. Fair skin, dark brows, dark eyes and full luscious lips that, even from a distance, made his cock wake up and say hello.

Kane's blood heated as he watched her take the paddle from the guy's hand, step behind the naked girl and swing it.

Three times in smooth, even strokes, each swat landing on the girl's rump at a different angle. She handed the paddle back to the man in leather, then smoothed her bare hand over the girls flaming ass cheeks, talking to him the whole time.

She was teaching him how to spank that girl!

Blood raced south and Kane forced himself to think about hockey stats for a minute. It had been too long since he'd had a good fuck, and his body was suddenly making him very aware of it.

The woman in jeans talked softly to the guy, as her touch soothed the girl bent over the wooden horse. She leaned forward, placed a soft kiss at the base of the girl's neck and moved back.

Fighting to get his hormones under control, Kane watched her step down off the stage and sashay straight toward him.

"I'm Vanessa Logan, officer." Her husky voice sent a shiver down Kane's spine as she held out a pale hand with short, clear nails, no jewelry. No wedding ring. "I run The O Club. What can I do for you?"

4

Oooh, he's a cute one.

Vanessa gave herself a mental head slap and ignored the heat that swept over her as she shook hands with the cop. *Rein in your libido, girl. A cop is not the type of playmate you want.*

Vanessa cocked her head to the side and let her gaze roam over the man in front of her. With only a few inches on her five-foot-eight frame, she placed him at about five feet eleven. Not real tall, but she could tell he had a great body beneath that suit.

Wide shoulders filled out the jacket, a firm chest and flat stomach under a cotton button-up shirt, and the way his pants draped made it obvious he was in prime physical shape. It also made it obvious he was . . . interested in what had been happening on the stage. The fact that he didn't try to hide the slight lift to his zipper, despite his very man-in-charge demeanor, gave him points in her book.

It might be kinda fun to see exactly how he would react to *not* being in charge.

"I'm Detective Kane Michaels, Miss Lawson. I was hoping to speak to the club owner. Is he in?"

"*She* leaves the running of the place to me, so if whatever brings you here has to do with The O Club, then it's me you want to talk to."

He nodded and ran his eyes over her figure. Vanessa felt the heat of his gaze and fought the urge to prop her hands on her hips and thrust out her breasts. She knew she didn't look like a typical bar manager. She looked even younger than she was without her makeup on. Between that, and her naturally cocky attitude, most men . . . hell, most *people* underestimated her.

Normally she liked it when people did that; it gave her an advantage over them, but for some reason it nettled with this guy.

"Nessa!" Rob called from behind the bar. "O is on the phone. You want me to take a message?"

She glanced over her shoulder at the new bartender and smiled. He was a cutie, and so eager to please. She liked that in a man.

"Please do, sweetie. I'll call her back in a little bit." Nessa waved JJ over before leading the silent cop to a couple of low chairs and a table. "Let's have a seat shall we, detective?"

The waitress arrived just as they sat down and smiled flirtatiously at the cop. "What can I get for you tonight?"

She ran her eyes over him and licked her lips in a sassy way that left most men either crossing their legs, or drooling. But Vanessa was happy to see that Detective Michaels just gave her a quick once over, and asked for a soda with lime. When she left to fill their order, he didn't even bother to check out the girl's curved butt in her leather short-shorts.

Controlled was one thing, but the servers' uniforms weren't exactly sedate, and it was the first time she'd seen a straight man not react to them. Maybe he was gay?

"How can I help you, detective?"

"I'm looking for someone, a woman that's experienced with bondage, and I was told that I might find her here."

Vanessa's pulse jumped and her eyebrows shot upwards. She didn't bother to hide her surprise, but instead, deliberately gave him a reason for it. "Are you asking me to pimp for you?"

"What? No!" A slight flush crept up his neck, and a small kick of pleasure ran through Vanessa. Before he could speak again JJ was back with their drinks. She set a wineglass in front of Vanessa and turned to set the soda down.

Nessa watched as JJ flashed him a good deal of the cleavage bulging over her black leather bustier and winked at him. He didn't respond to the flirting, and when JJ stood up, she met Vanessa's gaze and shrugged as she sauntered away, hips swaying.

"As I was saying," he leaned forward, resting his elbows on his knees and staring at her earnestly. "I'm looking for a woman who's into bondage, Shibari to be exact. It's not personal, it's strictly for a case."

Vanessa's insides clenched in disappointment, then a surge of adrenaline whipped through her. A case, he was working a case. And she bet she knew which one it was.

Well, her Dad had always said a good defense is a strong offense.

"That's too bad, detective. I've a bit of experience with it myself and for a minute there I was imagining just how hot you would look restrained and awaiting my pleasure." She eyed his sedate suit and tie get-up, not bothering to hide the way her gaze lingered on the fabric stretched taut over his muscled thighs.

Heat flared in his gaze, but his expression remained blank. *Oooh, a reaction!*

Nessa's pleasure at his response was short-lived, when he said, "I just need a list of names of any female customers that are into that sort of stuff. Anyone who comes to mind that is particularly good with any type of rope or restraint, and who might not have a great fondness for arrogant men."

"I'm sorry, detective, but many people who live an alternative lifestyle tend to keep it private, and as manager of this club, I respect that." She set her drink down and stood up, hinting that the conversation was over. It was almost time to open the doors and she still needed to get things set up.

"Surely they're not that secretive if they hang out it clubs like this?" He stood up as he spoke, and remained close enough to Vanessa that she had to fight the urge to touch him. She just knew he had a fantastic body under that staid suit and her fingers were itching to undress him. She kept her eyes on his face and saw an answering awareness there.

He felt the pull between them, too. Self-preservation told her to ignore it.

"Some people wear masks to either hide their identity, or enhance the experience. Or both."

"Do you?"

"Do I what?"

"Wear a mask when the club is open, or when you're *playing*?"

She tried to keep her expression blank, but felt her lips tilt up at one corner before she replied, "We all wear masks, Detective. Some are just much harder to spot than others."

She met his gaze and tried not to think about her own secret identity. It was time to shift the direction of this conversation.

"Actually, with the exception of our monthly 'members only' nights, like tonight, The O Club is open to the public. Most of the nightly crowd isn't really into bondage enough that they'd even know what Shibari is. They just like to play at it. To pretend they're more adventurous than they really are." She'd meant to leave it at that, but when his intense gaze met hers, her mouth opened and words kept tumbling out. "Of course, if you're really serious about finding this woman, I might be able to help you out."

She tried to ignore the thrill that went through her at the way his eyes heated when he glanced at *her* cleavage before he replied, "Oh, I'm very serious about it."

He was definitely not gay.

A fire started low in Vanessa's belly. She licked her lips and let a taunting smile creep across her face. "Serious enough to embark on a little adventure of your own?"

5

Adventurous. I'll show her adventurous.

Kane watched her hips twitch as she walked away and wondered what the hell he'd just agreed to. Letting himself get goaded into doing something, anything, wasn't his normal style. He was no slouch when it came to action, but he wasn't usually so impetuous. All he'd wanted was a list of names.

Only the owner wasn't there. Vanessa Lawson was. And an invite to the private "members only" party that night was even better than a list of names. Yet somehow, he still felt that in the space of a ten-minute interview, that woman had chased him off-script in a big way.

Kane sat in his car and watched the entrance to the club. Since it had looked like it was going to be a long night, he'd left the club to grab a bite to eat; now it was just before ten p.m. and he was hesitating.

He should be in there. But the need to center himself, and remind himself why exactly he was going in there was strong. He wasn't going in there to flirt with a sexy woman, or to get laid. He was going in there on the hunt for a thief. A woman who manipulated men with the promise of sex to get into their houses, and into their safes. He thought about calling Jack. It might be good for another cop to know what was going down, and Jackson was a friend—he'd back him up.

But Kane never reached for his phone. Instead he popped another candy into his mouth and left his car to continue the hunt.

The security at the door recognized him and the male guard radioed inside before Kane was ten feet away. The bouncer stepped aside and held open the door for Kane, and he entered the club.

There were at least sixty people in there now. All dressed, or undressed, to the nines. Some had masks on, some wore next to nothing. Some of the men were shirtless; Kane even saw one who wore only leather chaps with thong underwear underneath. But most were dressed in dark suits or trousers, so he felt okay about not standing out.

The women were even more varied. Corsets, dresses, trousers, leather, latex and bare skin. Most had incredibly high heels on that brought the words "fuck me" instantly to mind, and Kane was having a hard time not staring. When a man walked by holding a chain leash attached to the diamond-studded collar of the woman behind him, Kane realized just how truly different this clientele was from the crowd he'd seen in the other bars.

He stepped deeper into the room and saw Vanessa Lawson through the crowd. And for just a second, Kane lost the ability to breathe.

She'd changed her clothes.

Instead of the ripped jeans and tank top of earlier, the young, attractive woman was now a devilishly sexy seductress. She had on black high-heel boots that went to the knee, a tight leather skirt and a plain white silk blouse that draped lovingly over her curves. She looked like a cross between a high-powered business-woman and dominatrix Barbie.

Her dark hair flowed down her back in thick waves that, when she turned her head to look at him, caught fire in the dim lights.

Their eyes locked and Kane forgot about everything but the sexual pull between them. She excused herself from the people she was talking to and strode toward him. His heart pounded and his gut clenched as his eyes followed the sway of her pert breasts beneath the silk. There was no way she was wearing a bra.

She stopped only inches away from him, leaned forward to brush her cheek against his, and whispered in his ear, "I need to know your name. Introducing you around as Detective Michaels sort of defeats the purpose of this little escapade, don't you think?"

He breathed deep and her scent went straight to his head. Clean and light, with a hint of feminine musk. Instantly, images of naked bodies writhing together on a sun-dappled bed filled his mind.

"Kane." He cleared his throat and spoke softly. "My name is Kane, Vanessa."

"Nice to meet you, Kane." Her lips barely moved when she spoke, the damp heat of her words floating over his lips. His fists clenched at his sides to stop from reaching up to cup her head and slanting his mouth over hers.

Vanessa looked up at him, dark eyes sparkling with mischief. "Are you ready?"

Was he ever! But somehow, despite the promises he saw in her gaze, he didn't think she meant ready to bend her over and sink himself in deep. "Ready?"

"To tell me exactly what it is you're looking for tonight, and why?"

Kane bit back a curse. "I told you what I was looking for," he said carefully.

Vanessa swayed closer to him, her fingers trailing down his

arm, the hard tips of her breasts brushing against him. "If all you're going to tell me is that you're looking for a woman familiar with Shibari, then I'm not going to be much help to you. Almost every female in here tonight is familiar with it to a certain extent." She stepped back and the loss of her nearness gave him a chill.

Before he could say anything he shouldn't about the case, a strident voice interrupted them.

"Well, Miss Vanessa. Where have you been hiding this one?"

"Marissa, how are you tonight?" Vanessa's voice was smooth when she greeted the newcomer, but Kane sensed a strong undercurrent there. He pulled his mind out of the bedroom and gave the woman a once over.

"I'm well, thank you," she replied.

With her hair pulled back in a tight bun to expose strong features, she was beautiful in a cold, meticulous way. Hungry blue eyes ran over him and his stomach roiled in response.

"Kane, this is Mistress DeVartan. Marissa, my guest tonight, Kane."

"Hello, Kane." She held out a hand tipped with lethal-looking fingernails. "Welcome. Switches don't usually intrigue me, but you're very attractive. If you've a yen to play, please come see me tonight."

After he dropped the cold hand and she'd walked away, he looked at Vanessa and raised an eyebrow. "Switches?"

"A switch is a person who can be either dominant or submissive in the BDSM world." She led him to the bar where he watched a shirtless guy in leather pants, a leather collar and a cowboy hat flip a bottle in the air before catching it upside down right over the ice-filled glass. "I figured you'd at least have done some research before showing up here tonight."

He did know what a switch was, but he figured she might tell him more if she thought he was ignorant.

He turned to face the woman next to him and ignored the

way his pulse jumped at her nearness. "And she thought I was a switch? Just from looking at me?"

"Marissa thinks she knows everything about everyone just from looking at them." She caught the bartender's eye before turning to him. A small grimace flashed across her pretty features. "Sorry, there's just something about that woman that I've never liked."

Kane could understand that. He hadn't liked her either, and the fact that Vanessa shared his opinion made him feel another link click shut on the connection he felt growing between them.

"What about you?" he asked. "Are you a switch? Or do you prefer to dominate men?"

She arched an eyebrow at him. "Do you really want to find out?"

"What can I get you tonight, Miss Vanessa?" The shirtless bartender leaned against the other side of the bar, interrupting them.

"Apple juice for me, please, Rob. You know how I like it. Kane?"

Kane stopped trying to read the woman in front of him and nodded to the bartender. "Whatever dark beer you've got on hand will be fine, thank you."

The bartender brought the drinks over, a bottle for him and a wineglass for her, and Kane watched his face light up at the smile Vanessa gave him. So he wasn't the only one affected so strongly by her.

She scanned the room and took a sip from her wineglass. Smart move, juice in a wineglass. It looked like she was drinking alcohol, but she wasn't.

He reached out and took the wineglass from her, setting it on the bar behind her. When he had her full attention he stepped closer. He planted his hands on the edge of the bar on either side of her, invading her personal space and pinning her between his body and the bar.

Her pupils dilated, and he almost groaned when her tiny pink tongue darted out and licked at her luscious bottom lip. When he was close enough to feel her breath panting against his lips he spoke softly, but firmly.

"I think you like to control everything around you. You're very young in years, but you're not innocent or naïve, by any means. You run this place, and the staff seems to like and respect you. That tells me you know what you're doing. But I bet when it comes to sex, you're not into games in the bedroom." He tilted his head and leaned closer, making sure his lips teased her earlobe with his next words. "I bet when the bedroom door closes you like to be a real woman. All slow and sensuous and warm and wet for the man lucky enough to see the real you."

Then he pressed his lips to the baby-soft skin behind her ear. He couldn't stop himself.

He felt the heat of her hand at his waist and his gut tightened. He pressed forward slightly, letting her feel his hard-on, letting her know just what she was doing to him. Her fingers dug into his back, and her eyes dropped to his mouth. Kane leaned forward—

"Ahem."

He froze. Suddenly the throbbing music of the club rushed into his ears and their surroundings slammed back into focus.

"Excuse me, Nessa." A soft feminine voice sounded behind him. "You're needed in the back room."

Fuck!

He felt her nod once at the girl behind him, and he stepped back, aching at the loss of her touch when her hand dropped to her side.

"I need to do some work," she said softly, without meeting his gaze.

"Okay."

He watched her take a sip from her drink and straighten her spine. The she graced him with a small smile. "Try not to get into trouble while I'm gone."

"Me? Trouble?"

She lifted her empty hand and patted his Beretta. "Just don't interrogate anyone. If you have any questions, remember, I'm yours at the end of the night."

Kane gripped the cold beer bottle in his hand and watched her hips twitch as she walked away, his dick pressing hard against his zipper.

She was his at the end of the night.

6

He was dangerous.

Not just as a cop, and a threat to her personal freedom. But as a man. She hadn't counted on that.

Nessa strode through the bar, a friendly smile pasted on her face as she nodded and waved to various members on her way to the back room. *Shit*. She didn't have a clue how to deal with Kane.

Growing up with a con man for a father had taught her how to read people, and how to manipulate them. It was what made her so good with the alternative crowd at the club. She never judged, and she understood the power and the lure of emotional and psychological manipulation.

But to have it turned back on her was scary.

Men rarely bothered to wonder what was beyond the image she presented. Most of them looked at where she worked, what she did, her demeanor, and they assumed she liked to be in charge in the bedroom, too. Or they went in the other direction completely. Assuming that she wanted someone else to take charge, that she would enjoy being dominated in the bedroom since she was in control of every other aspect of her life.

Never before had a man picked up on the fact that what she really wanted . . . was to just be seen as a woman. As an equal, or a partner.

Shit, shit, shit.

Suddenly, the game with him was no longer a game, and Vanessa realized that maybe, just maybe, this guy might figure things out.

Her pulse raced and she swallowed the panic that started to creep up into her throat. It didn't matter. None of it mattered because she wouldn't let Kane see any deeper, or get any closer. She'd just do what she was best at . . . and use sex as a weapon.

Things got busy and time flew. Vanessa worked the room, talking to everyone, making sure all was well and that everyone was behaving within the club's guidelines. Nudity was allowed, and there were always some subtle things going on in dark corners, but by and large, the members' nights were more social than sexual. They were a chance for people of like minds or libidos to meet in a safe environment.

She kept an eye on Kane as she did her rounds, and noticed that he stayed at the bar, chatting occasionally with Rob the bartender and anyone else who approached him. He was sticking to their deal. And it was a good thing so many women approached him.

Really, it was.

It didn't matter that every time she saw one of them lean in too close, or touch him, she wanted to bare her teeth and growl. What mattered was that with so many women approaching him, he was sure to find a suspect that wasn't her.

Throughout the night she made it back to Kane's side a few times. The first couple of times he was in conversation with regulars, and Nessa was happy to hear that his questions were normal. He wasn't interrogating the guests.

Just before one, she stepped up behind him in time to catch the words, "No, thank you," come from his lips in an almost tired-sounding refrain. The music was throbbing, the crowd was relaxed, and the sexual vibe was heavy in the air. It gave her a thrill to trail her hand across his back and shoulders in a possessive way while she watched the bare-breasted blonde with the red velvet mask and collar lower her eyes and back away.

Kane turned to her, and before she could say anything his hand cupped the back of her head and his mouth was on hers. A large strong hand settled on the small of her back and pulled her body flush against his as his tongue parted her lips and her surroundings disappeared.

He tasted like butterscotch. Smooth and sweet and tempting. Hard muscles flexed under her hands and she pressed against the hot body in front of her. Their tongues rubbed against each other, performing an ancient dance that her body ached to follow, and a small moan rose in her throat.

He pulled back slightly and rested his forehead against hers. She was pleased to see that his eyes were bright with passion and his breathing was just as rough as hers.

"I had to do that before we got interrupted again," he said softly, then pressed his lips to hers again.

When he pulled back again, she nodded and nibbled at her bottom lip, savoring the flavor he left behind.

He tasted like *more*.

Kane sat on a bar stool and watched as Vanessa said good night to the last of the club's patrons. It had been an interesting night, to say the least. He'd seen some things he never thought he'd see, and learned more than he ever really wanted to know about one of the city's top businessmen. He also really hadn't needed to know that one of his favorite hockey players liked to be led around on a leash and made to kneel so that his mistress could sit on him like a chair all night.

He shook his head and picked at the label on his beer bottle. He just didn't get where the pleasure came from with that, but to each his own.

"C'mon, boy. Spin that bottle, and don't spill!"

Kane glanced down the bar at Rose, one of the waitresses, as she taunted Rob. At least through the night he'd gotten to know the staff a bit better. He watched as the shirtless bartender flipped a bottle in the air, only to catch it upside down over the ice-filled glass on the bar.

JJ, the only other waitress still left there, hopped up on a barstool directly in front of Rob and joined in the jeering. "The only way I want you getting me wet is with your tongue, baby. Don't waste the alcohol!"

Laughter erupted inside him and Kane swallowed quickly so he didn't spit out his drink.

With a grand gesture Rob spun the bottle over his wrist, set it on the counter, and pushed two full glasses forward for the girls. Amid the waitresses' clapping and whistling, he removed his straw cowboy hat, revealing thick, wavy light brown hair that just brushed his shirt collar, and gave a deep bow. "Ladies. It was my pleasure to serve you."

"You want to serve me, baby, get on your knees."

"Enough, JJ." From beside him Vanessa's voice held laughter, but there was a clear warning there too. "Finish up your staff drinks and head home, guys. We can stock up before we open tomorrow."

Kane felt the touch of her hand on his shoulder and met her laughing gaze.

"Give me fifteen minutes to finish locking up and I'm yours."

7

Jesus. Did she deliberately say things like that to keep him hard? He knew she meant "all his" to answer questions. Didn't she?

Kane watched her walk through the swinging doors and into the back of the club with gritted teeth. She'd been teasing and taunting him all night. The overt sexuality and blatant come-ons from the over the top crowd in the bar hadn't tempted him at all. But every time his hard-on disappeared, she'd show up at his side again. She'd rub against him, or whisper something naughty in his ear, and his dick would salute her.

He felt the staff's eyes on him but he didn't look up. The urge to question them about their clientele was strong. Hell, he wanted to question JJ just to see how she reacted. With her sass and slight bitterness toward men, she was a good candidate for RR, but he had agreed to hold all his questions for Vanessa.

"So, who are you? Exactly." A cold beer appeared in front of Kane and he looked up to see all three staff members scrutinizing him.

"Thanks," he reached for the fresh beer and took a long pull from the bottle before answering them. "Just a friend of Vanessa's."

"Nessa doesn't have friends," JJ said.

Interesting.

"She does now," was his reply.

"Jane said you're a cop."

He nodded at Rose. Jane must be the blond doorlady. "I am."

"So what do you want with Nessa?"

He gave JJ a droll look and she smirked. "Oh, well, if you hurt her, cop or not, I'll hurt you."

Kane normally didn't take well to being threatened, and the look in JJ's eyes *was* a threat, but in this place, and this circumstance, he let it go. He was even strangely pleased to see that Vanessa did have friends, no matter what they said.

They went back to doing their cash-outs, and he sat silently, waiting for Vanessa to finish her paperwork. After about ten minutes, Rose gathered the cash from the other two and disappeared behind the swinging door. To the office he supposed.

She came back out, they all put their jackets on and said a casual goodnight as they walked out the door. Kane walked around the bar, checked to make sure the doors were secure, and still, Vanessa didn't emerge from her office.

So he went looking.

He pushed through the swinging doors and entered a short hallway. There was an open door near the end so he strolled down it, and perched his shoulder against the door jam of Vanessa's office.

Her head was bent over some papers on her desk, and, although she didn't look up, he knew she felt him there. The awareness that arched between them was too strong.

He should leave and save his questions for the next day, after he's had time to process what he'd seen, and his own impressions of the people he'd met.

Yet none of it mattered right then because all he wanted to do was touch her.

Without waiting for an invitation, he stepped into her office and closed the door behind him. Vanessa lifted her head and glanced at him but kept working, silent.

He shifted behind her at the desk and placed his hands on her shoulders. They were delicate in his hands, but tight. Adding a bit of pressure, he dug his thumbs into her back. The soft groan she released went straight to his groin and his dick stiffened, *again.*

Her shoulders loosened up, and he let his hands wander. The thin silk of her shirt only enhanced the softness of her curves as he cupped her shoulders and trailed his hands down her arms to press her hands into the desk and nuzzle her hair aside with his chin.

"You smell so good. Feel so soft and smooth under my hands, too." He pressed his lips to the soft shell of her ear.

"You're just horny after having half-naked women propositioning you all night."

Kane was glad to hear the hint of laughter in her voice. It was obvious this woman enjoyed teasing. "Ahh, but the woman I wanted to proposition me didn't."

She still didn't look at him, so he lifted a hand and pressed two fingers under her chin, leading her to look into his eyes. "That would be you I'm talking about," he whispered before kissing her.

He nipped and licked at her full lips until they parted and gave him entrance. She leaned back in her chair, her head cradled in his palms as he loved her mouth. His tongue darted in and out, dancing sensually against hers. Tasting her, teasing her the way she'd been teasing him all night.

His heartbeat picked up and his fingers sank into the thick waves of her hair. The air was warm and the yearning for slow sultry loving was strong. After watching so many people be so blatant and crass, all he wanted was to feel the soft skin and warm comfort of a true woman who desired him. And there was no doubt in his mind that Vanessa desired him.

With one sure movement he pulled her out of her chair and into his arms.

8

He leaned back against the desk, cradling her against him. They fit perfectly. Chest to chest, groin to groin and thigh to thigh. Her softness giving way to his hardness.

Arousal curled low in Vanessa's belly and started to spread outward. It felt so good to be held, to be kissed and cuddled, and to know that this man wanted her.

Yeah . . . he wanted her in more ways than even he knew.

Vanessa tore her mouth away from his. Closing her eyes and tilting her head back she reminded herself how she met him. Who he was, and *what* she was.

Kane wanted her all right. He also wanted to arrest her.

She couldn't let herself forget that. And she couldn't let herself forget that this man already had a good idea what she wanted. But at that moment, she wasn't too sure she cared about any of that shit.

She just wanted him, and the promise of the hard cock pressing against her.

His hardness was everywhere. His arms around her, his

hands in her hair, his lips on her neck. It was all making it very difficult to think.

Who needs to think, when you can take control?

Vanessa reached up and ran her fingers through the short pelt that covered his head. She gripped his head and pulled him back, so she could nuzzle her head under his chin. She licked up the side of his neck, felt the rasp of stubble against her tongue, and tasted the slightly salty flavor of man.

When his rumbling groan echoed through the quiet, it hit her right between the thighs. She rubbed against him, feeling the rigid length of his cock burn into her belly through their clothes.

Kane's hand ran down her back and cupped her ass, pulling her even tighter against him as their lips met again in an open-mouthed, hungry kiss.

Vanessa struggled to breathe, to think. Her breasts ached, bolts of pleasure zinging through her every time she rubbed against his chest. But it wasn't enough. The feel of him, the taste of him, that taste of *more*.

She reached up and tugged at his shirt buttons. Thank God he hadn't worn a tie. She pulled the shirt open, yanking it from the waistband of his trousers, and started nibbling her way over his almost hairless chest.

"Nessa," he groaned, his hands pulling her own shirt out of her skirt. "You're driving me nuts here."

"Good," she said, lowering herself to her knees. She undid his belt buckle and ignored his mumbled protests, ignored the hands that tried to get her back on her feet.

She needed to keep control of this. She needed to show him that he didn't see her as clearly as he'd thought. That she wasn't looking for some romantic, soft, sensual loving.

She focused on the fire running through her veins and the driving hunger for the taste of Kane. Leaning forward she pressed an open-mouthed kiss to the cloth-covered ridge beneath his zipper. Her fingers worked the belt out of the way and undid his trousers while she teased him through his pants. Then she gripped the waistband of both his trousers and his boxers, leaned back and looked up at Kane and slowly pulled them down to his knees.

When his cock sprang free, she gave a wicked smile at his groan. Kane had been blessed, and she was about to make him thank the gods for giving her plenty to play with.

She leaned forward and let her breath tease him. She saw his cock dance and twitch, as if it were searching for her mouth, reaching out for the warmth it knew was waiting for him. Her hands ran up and down his thighs, those lovely muscled thighs that had made her drool from the minute she'd met him. They were thick and corded with the muscle of a man who worked at staying strong. There was a light brown layer of fur that covered them. Softer than the hair of any man she'd met.

She put her hands between his legs and pushed them apart, widening his stance, then leaned in and licked her way up his inner thigh. She could hear his gasp and his panting breath echo in the quiet room, and her own fire burned hotter.

People were too fast when it came to sex, men were too fast. They needed to understand that the tease was almost as much fun as the payoff, and the better the tease, the bigger the payoff.

When her lips hit the top of his inner thigh, she nipped at the skin there and exhaled hotly over his balls before nibbling at the soft skin of his other thigh.

"Oh God, woman!" Kane's fingers tightened in her hair and she smiled against his skin.

Unable to refuse her own desire any longer, she nuzzled against the velvety sac and breathed in deep. Such an honest male primal scent, it fired her up inside and she squeezed her thighs together.

A loud cross between a sigh and a groan echoed through the room, and Kane's thighs trembled beneath her hands. She licked up the underside of his shaft and gave the shiny head a quick, hard suck that made his knees buckle for a second. Her insides melted and her pussy clenched when she relaxed her throat and took him as deep as she could, only to find that there were still a good couple of inches left.

Oh, yeah, he was blessed, and for that she was thankful.

She reached between his rock-hard thighs and cupped his balls, fondling and rolling them between the fingers of one hand while she used the other hand to squeeze his shaft in time with her bobbing head. She sucked him deep and pulled back, adding a little twist with her hand that soon had him gasping and pulling at her hair and shoulders.

"Vanessa, stop, I want you. Not just your mouth." His voice was strained and Nessa knew she had him. She had the control, and she needed to keep it.

She increased the suction and the pace. Kane's panting grew ragged and his taste grew stronger. Her pussy was clenching rhythmically, aching for attention, but she ignored it. She would take care of herself later.

"Damn it, woman!" Kane's hand gripped her shoulders and the next thing she knew he had her off her knees and seated on her desk. Her legs were spread wide and he was standing between them, his hard cock nudging against her nylon-clad thigh. "I want *you*, not just your mouth."

Then he swooped down and claimed her mouth, and any plans or resistance she had, fled. His tongue thrust deep in her mouth and his large hand shoved her skirt up. Then he tugged her forward until her butt was on the edge of the desk and only he was keeping her pinned there. She'd never been so damned happy she never wore underwear in her life.

When Kane discovered her nakedness, his groan echoed in her mouth and her fingers dug into his shoulders. He ran a finger over her slit and Vanessa spread her legs wider, unashamed of the wetness he found.

"Feel what you do to me . . . how much I love the way you taste, the way you feel?" She panted the words against his lips, her body writhing against him. "Fuck me."

Kane's cock found its way between her swollen pussy lips and nudged at her entrance. He gripped her hips and thrust deep, making them both gasp.

As he pumped his hips, he dragged his mouth away and nipped at her neck. She wrapped her legs around him, her hands clutching his ass, urging him on. Faster, deeper. This was no soft, sensual partnership, he was fucking her. Rutting like an animal with no care for his partner. And he couldn't stop.

Her moans and grunts urged him on. Soon her hands left his ass and she scraped her nails across his chest, leaving a trail of fire that made him growl in pleasure. She ripped her mouth away from his and nibbled at his neck, sucking and biting. He cupped her ass, tilted her hips and fucked her harder.

"Yes, yes," she chanted.

Her pussy clenched and he felt his balls tighten and pull up. He pumped harder, pulling back to look into her glowing eyes. Their gazes locked and he saw her lids drop, her lips parted and a long, low moan filled the room. Her legs tightened around him, her hips jerked, and hot wetness drenched his cock.

Her cunt milked him and he couldn't hold back. His cock swelled until it erupted inside her and pleasure exploded throughout his body.

9

"What are you looking at?" Kane growled at the scowling female on his bed as he strode naked into his bedroom, fresh from the shower.

The one-eyed furry thing just stared at him silently.

"Hey, it wasn't my choice to leave her after a good fuck, she *made* me go. Vanessa is not exactly an easy woman to win an argument against, you know?" He turned away from the cat and pulled a clean pair of boxer briefs from his dresser drawer. "And I did tail her when she left the club to make sure she got home safe."

Mystery stayed silent, watching him as he moved about the room getting dressed. He didn't know exactly what went wrong last night, but he was sure it wasn't the sex. He knew when a woman came, and Vanessa had pushed and pushed his buttons until he lost control. She'd liked it when he'd gone caveman on her, which was completely opposite of how he'd pegged her.

He could've sworn she wasn't into the power games he saw others at her club engaging in. His instincts had said she was putting on a front for all those who were there. That inside, she was just a woman wanting to be treated like a woman.

Then again, he wasn't into all the head games either, and he'd sure enjoyed their little bit of tug-o-war over who controlled their first time. He swallowed the last of his morning—afternoon now—coffee and gave himself a once-over in the mirror. He looked the same, yet, inside he felt different. Something inside him had shifted since the day before, and he wasn't sure he wanted to examine it too closely.

"Be good," he instructed the feline, and snatched up his keys on his way to the door. Time to go to work.

Kane spent the rest of the afternoon in court, testifying on a home invasion case that he'd closed months ago, but that the court was just getting around to dealing with. It was after five o'clock when he entered the station house and found Jackson gobbling down a greasy cheeseburger and fries.

"Eating that crap is not going to help your recovery process you know." He tugged off his tie, undid his collar and dropped into his chair.

"It's not going to slow it down either," he retorted. "Besides, I am recovered. It's the pencil pushers and insurance geeks who think I'm not street worthy yet."

Kane shook his head and pulled a protein bar from his desk drawer. The men ate in silence for a few minutes, until Kane snapped at Jackson. "What?"

"Have fun at the sex club last night?"

"I don't know that you'd call it fun. But I did find a person of interest or two."

"Yeah? Would one of them be the person who bit you?"

Kane's hand snapped up to his neck and the love bite that Vanessa had left. Damn it. He'd forgotten about that.

He let his hand fall and glared at Jackson. "Lay off."

"I thought you were a classy guy, Michaels. Didn't you know hickies went out when I was a teenager?"

"You're just jealous because the last woman to see your naked ass was the nurse who emptied your bed pan last month."

"At least she didn't want to spank me."

"That's not what happened. In fact—" He cut himself off before he became a complete idiot and asserted that he'd been the one in charge. "Forget it."

He picked up a case file and tried to get into some work. He tried to call Vanessa a couple of times that day. Each time he got her voice mail. He thought about calling the club later, or maybe dropping by. She'd turned down his invitation to spend the night, but she'd done it in such a way that he wasn't exactly sure what had happened. He'd been outside and in his car ten minutes after he'd pulled his pants up.

"Hey man, come on," Jack wheedled. "You couldn't expect me to let it go. Not when for the first time in the ten years I've known you show up not only with a bite, but that look in your eyes."

"What look?"

"The look that means some woman's got her claws into your brain. I've never seen it on you before, but I've seen it enough to recognize it."

"Your bitterness is showing. It wasn't like that."

Jackson looked at him. "Something about her has your shorts in a knot."

"It was nothing. Just a beautiful woman that got to me a little more than I'd anticipated."

"Yeah? Well, I'd be careful around that woman. The ones that can make your brain numb are the dangerous ones. Just ask Yardley and the other RR victims."

Damn it to hell. He was right.

10

A flash of flowing red silk caught Vanessa's eye and her hand stalled. Instead of pulling out the black flared skirt she'd been thinking of for work that night, her hand came away with the dress she'd worn the night she'd broken into Edward Yardley's safe.

She rubbed the rich texture of the material between her fingertips and came to a decision. She'd told Ophelia she was done, so why was she hanging on to the trappings of the Risqué Robber?

With fast and sure movements she gathered up the dress, the wig box from the top shelf of her closet, and the make-up kit from the floor. She shoved the items into an old backpack she'd pulled from under her bed, adding the outfits from the other robberies as well. It was past time for her to get rid of the evidence.

Things were chaotic, to say the least, at the club that night. Wednesdays were a busy night; the middle of the week, and people needed a small pick-me-up to make it to Friday. That usually meant alcohol.

She'd been in the club all afternoon, waiting for a workman to show up and fix the pipe that had sprung a leak under their beer cooler, only to be told to duct tape it until the next day.

Now she was working the bar next to Rob so he didn't have to rush. The last thing she needed was for him to slip on the wet floor and break a leg. When Vanessa looked up and saw Ophelia striding through the crowd, she squelched a sigh. She knew that look, and she wasn't in the mood for an argument with her boss.

When the perfectly coifed blonde stopped in front of the bar and smiled at Rob, he straightened up and waved Vanessa on. "Go on, Nessa. I'm all caught up and you don't want to keep this beautiful lady waiting."

Ophelia blew Rob a kiss and swept through the swinging doors to the back, ahead of Vanessa.

When they reached Vanessa's office, she waited until Ophelia was comfortable before dropping into the seat behind her desk. "That boy's a real charmer, Vanessa. It was a smart move, keeping the bartenders male."

"The male customers enjoy watching the go-go dancers, but we both know that females are happier with a little eye candy around too. Especially if the eye candy flirts with them."

When Vanessa had started working for Ophelia the only male staff members had been a couple of knucklehead bouncers who harassed the waitresses worse than the customers did. That had been eight years ago. When one of the bouncers had grabbed her by the ass as she was bent over cleaning a table, Vanessa had come up swinging, and gave the guy a broken nose.

That was when Ophelia had taken her under her wing, and started grooming her to run the club.

"What's up, O?"

"What makes you think something is up?"

"You never come by the club anymore unless you've got something important on your mind." Vanessa noted the worry in her friend's eyes. "Are you okay?"

The woman waved a manicured hand. "I'm fine. It's my friend I'm worried about."

A chill skipped down Vanessa's spine. "I'm sorry to hear that." She braced herself to hear O's request, on behalf of her friend, of course, that she help her get what was rightfully hers from a selfish ex-husband.

Vanessa was all for women getting half of what their husbands had in a divorce. Especially when said wives had supported the man while he went to school and built a business, only to get rid of their loyal wife in favor of a newer, younger version after they were rich.

Nessa used the skills her daddy raised her with to help Ophelia get what she deserved from a stingy ex out of loyalty to the woman who gave her a chance, and a home, when she so desperately needed one. The other three robberies had been favors for O, but that was it. She was done. She wasn't going to put herself at risk anymore for people she didn't even know.

"This friend of mine seems to have gotten herself into a bit of a pickle."

Vanessa nodded, and girded herself to tell Ophelia that if she cared about her at all, she wouldn't ask her do it again.

"She broke the law, you see, as a favor to me, and now there's a cop sniffing around her. I'm worried she's not seeing things too clearly at the moment."

"Me?" Surprise made her voice squeak "You're worried about me?"

"Of course I'm worried about you, Nessa. What do you think you're doing letting a cop hang around here?"

"What was I supposed to do? Chase him away and make myself look even more suspicious?"

"No. Talking to him was the right thing to do. But I was led to believe there was a bit more than talk happening?"

Her heart raced. She wasn't used to other people caring what she did. She'd grown up with only her father, moving around constantly, always leaving friends behind. When she was eighteen and showed up at The O Club looking for a job, she never thought she'd make a life out of it.

She thought of Ophelia as a friend, but she'd purposefully kept others at a distance. Warmth flooded her at the thought that Ophelia also felt the same way about her.

"It was sex, O. It's been a while and the man was hot. It was nothing more."

"You need to be careful, Nessa. I don't want you to end up like your father."

"Then maybe you shouldn't have asked me to do those extra *favors*," she snapped.

Silence fell over the room as the women eyed each other. Vanessa was the first to give. "I'm sorry. Yes, you asked, but I could've said no. Anyway, it's over and done with, and I'm *not* worried about Kane."

It was a lie. She was a bit worried. She was worried she'd never see him again. Or that if she did see him again, he'd be wrapping handcuffs around her wrists, and not in the "Let's get naked" sort of way.

"I am worried," Ophelia stressed. "Something must've led him here."

Restless, Vanessa stood up and leaned against the desk. "He came here looking for answers, but all he has is a hunch, and he doesn't even suspect me. Even if he did, I left nothing behind, and there is no way any of those men can identify me. Trust me, Ophelia. We're okay."

Three days. He gave her three days before he strode past Jane the bouncer and her male escort. He'd hoped she'd return at least one of his calls. But she hadn't, and his suspicion grew.

He'd gone into The O Club on Sunday night looking for a woman who was familiar with Shibari, and knew how to manipulate men into thinking things were their idea, and he hadn't realized it until the next day that that was exactly what Vanessa had done to him.

She hadn't tied him up, but she'd sure made him feel like everything from the first kiss in the bar to wild monkey sex in the office had been his idea.

He'd spent the whole night surrounded by the perfect suspect list, and never questioned one of them. Because of her.

It was exactly the type of manipulation he hated. It was exactly the type of manipulation that the Risqué Robber used to get her victims bound.

He'd thought about little else the past couple of days, even when he was working his other cases, he'd held out hope that his instincts hadn't been wrong. That she had truly been interested in him and his growing suspicions were only because he'd become a touch cynical in his ten years as a cop.

He'd really wanted her to call him. If she returned one of his calls it would go a long way toward easing his suspicions and proving that she'd wanted more than to just throw the cop off track. That she'd wanted him, as a man.

But she hadn't. And he wasn't going to wait any longer. He wanted answers, and he wanted them now.

It was early yet and the club wasn't too busy. There was a scantily clad girl in each cage on the edges of the stage, go-go dancers, he guessed. Rob was behind the bar and JJ was weaving her way through the thin crowd. There was a group of college-age guys near the stage, and a few single men in business suits scattered throughout the club. But Kane didn't see Vanessa.

He stepped up to the bar and met Rob's stare. "Is Vanessa here?"

"I'll buzz her for you."

Kane's hand blocked his from reaching for the phone on the bar. "Don't bother. I know where the office is."

He pushed his way through the swinging doors and immediately heard Vanessa's voice.

"I *know*, Ophelia. It's done, it's over with. You can stop worrying."

The ringing of her office phone muffled the other person's reply.

Kane stopped at her office door and took in the scene before him. Vanessa stood behind the massive desk, the phone to her ear and her back to the door. An older woman was seated in front of her. She wore a casual chic pantsuit, her blond hair sleek and classy, her make-up perfect. Yet he didn't get the snooty uptight impression from her that one would expect. An amazingly sexual vibe came from her when she met his gaze briefly. Especially for someone old enough to be his mother.

Vanessa's head swung around and their eyes met. "Yes, I see him. That's all right. Thanks, Rob."

So he'd called to warn her anyway.

"Hello, Vanessa." He greeted her.

"How are you, Kane?"

11

Vanessa's heart kicked in her chest and her mouth started to water. He looked even better than she remembered. But the look on his face wasn't exactly as welcoming as she'd have liked.

"I have some questions for you," he said from the doorway.

"Kane, meet Ophelia Wentworth, the owner of The O Club." She met Ophelia's bright blue gaze and gestured at the doorway. "Ophelia, meet Detective Kane Michaels."

"Detective Michaels, nice to meet you." Ophelia's voice was soft and cultured, not showing a hint of the tension Vanessa knew she was feeling. "You look very familiar, are you related to Anson Michaels?"

"He's my father, ma'am."

"Really?" A hint of laugher sparked in her voice. "And how does he feel about you being a police officer instead of joining the family firm?"

A small smile played at Kane's lips. "About how you'd expect, ma'am. I take it you know him?"

"Yes. The bastard is my ex-husband's attorney." She shot Vanessa a telling look as she stood up. "I should be going now."

Vanessa moved around the desk to give her friend a quick hug. "Thanks for coming in, O. I promise I'll make sure everything we talked about is secure."

There was worry in Ophelia's eyes when she stepped back from Vanessa. "I know you will, dear. Just please be careful."

"It was a pleasure to meet you, ma'am." Kane stepped aside so that Ophelia could exit the room.

When she was gone, their eyes met. Vanessa's stomach knotted and she waved him into the office. She needed to get things back on track. She had wanted to return his calls. She'd wanted it so much that she knew he was trouble. Not just to her physical freedom, but to her emotional freedom as well. Kane wielded more over her than the power of the law.

"You have some questions for me?" she asked.

"You said if I refrained from interrogating your customers you'd answer all my questions."

"So I did." She took a deep breath. "I'm sorry I haven't called you back. I'd planned to, but the time just never seemed right." Yeah, the timing of them even meeting had been all wrong. Why couldn't she have met him last year? Before her dip back into illegal activities.

Kane's face tightened and she knew that he, too, had doubts about exactly what was going on between them. Well, she'd never been one for beating around the bush, the best defense and all that. "Are your questions about your investigation then? Or about us?"

"Is there an us?" He arched an eyebrow.

"I'm not sure," she replied honestly. "Part of me would really like there to be, but I'll be honest, you scare me."

A flush crept over his cheekbones and he crept closer to the desk. "I'm sorry about that. You said you were all right, and I never meant to be so rough . . . I just sort of lost control."

Confusion drifted in her mind for a brief minute until a light bulb went on in her head.

"No! Not because of that. *That* was wonderful. I love the fact that I can make you lose control. You don't strike me as the type of man who lets that happen easily." She gave him a small smile.

God! She was such an idiot! What the hell was she doing even bringing this up? She was supposed to be chasing him out of her life. Not inviting him deeper into it.

"I'm not," he said as he shifted his stance. "So how do I scare you?"

Vanessa cringed inside. She'd opened up a can of worms there and wasn't sure how to close it up again. "Poor choice of words. I just meant . . . I'd like to get to know you better, but I'm not very good at this sort of thing."

"What sort of thing?"

"I don't do commitments or attachments very well." She bit her lip for a moment, trying to stem the flow of words that seemed to be coming from nowhere. "I live in the real world where the divorce rate is skyrocketing, and the marriages that are still together are unhappy ones. I believe more in sexual pleasure than loving satisfaction, yet . . . you make me imagine lazy Sunday afternoons curled up on together on the sofa watching movies."

There. She'd done it. She'd opened herself up to the rejection she knew was sure to come. He might be the only man that had ever made her feel more than a sexual attraction. But how could a man like him, from a high-class family of lawyers—yeah, everything she'd sensed about him had clicked into place when O had placed him as one of *those* Michaelses—ever fall for a woman like her?

A con man's kid that grew up to be a thief.

Kane's heart was beating triple time. She'd had thoughts of them together? In a relationship? Damn! He wasn't nuts then. There was definitely something strong between them.

But she still hadn't called him back. And he still felt the sting of manipulation.

He gazed into her eyes and forgot all about his suspects. "I don't know what's going on between us, Vanessa." He backed up from the desk and sat himself down in the chair there. "On Sunday night I thought there might be something there, too, but now I'm just not sure."

Her head dipped and she seated herself. Her posture was straight, thrusting her perky breasts out, making him highly aware of the fact that he'd been too out of control to even get a taste of them the other night. His dick twitched and he forced the right words out of his mouth. "I don't think getting involved personally right now is the smartest thing to do."

When she met his gaze again, her dark eyes were shadowed, and his chest tightened. He could've had her. She'd basically offered herself up to him, and he'd pushed her away because of his innate sense of suspicion. He could literally see her pulling away.

"I like you, Vanessa, but you're right. We really don't know each other. We need to slow things down for now." He rested his ankle on his other knee, which hopefully hid his reaction to her nearness.

"Okay," she nodded. She placed her hands on the desk in front of her and gave him a tight smile. "You said you had questions?"

He asked her about a few of her customers. How much she knew about them personally. Did she ever think they could be into illegal activities? When she replied she didn't think any of her club's members could possibly be the Risqué Robber, his surprise must've shown on his face.

"I do read the newspaper, Kane. When they mentioned the unique way the knots were tied and you showed up asking about female clients experienced in Shibari, it wasn't difficult to put together."

It was a smooth answer that made sense. So why did his gut tell him there was more to it than that?

"If you don't think the robber could be any of your members, what about your staff?"

Her face froze. "My staff? You think it's one of my staff?"

"Tell me about JJ." Fear flashed in her eyes and Kane's gut clenched. She definitely knew more than she was letting on.

Vanessa shifted in her seat, slouching back in the chair and folding her arms across her ribs. It was clear body language for "Back off," but the way it plumped up her breasts called him closer.

He looked away and thought about the shitty hockey game he'd seen the night before. When the blood stopped flooding his groin and started to flow through his system again, he looked back at her.

She was glaring at him. Not just a frown, but an actual glare. He quirked an eyebrow at her in question.

"Don't you dare think you can pin any of this on JJ. That girl has had enough troubles in her life, and I will fight you every step of the way."

"Whoa!" He raised his hands in a gesture of surrender. "I'm not going to pin anything on anyone unless they're guilty. I just want to know a bit about her background."

"JJ moved here six months ago from Toronto, where she left behind an abusive asshole of a husband. He followed her here, and last month he was arrested for assault, and I believe he's still in jail. JJ's had enough taken from her in life that she'd never turn thief."

"Then I guess I've hit a dead end here." He shrugged. *Unless you're RR.*

He thought it, but he couldn't bring himself to say it. He hated that the thought even entered his mind. "Listen, I heard about another private 'alternative' gathering at an underground club called Chains. Ever hear of it?"

He watched her shoulders relax and felt a bit of tension drain from his own frame.

"It's a small bar by the University. I've never been, but I've heard it mentioned."

"There's a private gathering there on Sunday night. I doubt I can get myself in. Are you still willing to help me with this investigation?"

12

Vanessa threw her hairbrush in the sink. *God! This isn't a date!* So where did the butterflies in her belly come from, and why wouldn't they go away?

Stomping into her bedroom, she looked at the outfit she'd laid out to meet with Kane. It was sexy, a bit demure for her, but that was good. She needed to look professional. She needed to look calm and cool, and not like she'd called him because she couldn't forget the way he tasted. Whether it was butterscotch or beer, musk or male, his flavor was burned into her taste buds, and the dream of a partner was burned into her heart.

At first she'd been upset when he'd left the bar the night before. Upset with herself for forgetting that she wanted to stay away from the lawman, and letting him know how she felt. Upset with him for choosing his investigation over her. She'd agreed to help him get into chains later that week, and that had been the end of it. But then her dreams that night had been full of his rock-hard body and promises of acceptance, of partnership.

He'd picked up on her deep-seated dream the first night

they met, and she couldn't forget that. She wasn't going to let him forget it either.

Whatever else was going to happen, she decided she wasn't going to give up the one man that had been able to read her. Not without a fight.

She glanced at the outfit again and headed for the closet. Screw demure. She wanted Kane, and demure wasn't going to get him.

It was just after two in the afternoon when she strolled into the police station. She was directed to an open room near the back of the building, and there she saw a half dozen desks covered in files, computers and paperwork. She spotted Kane near the windows with a tall, dark-haired guy whose face was covered by a long, unruly moustache.

She felt the heat of several gazes on her bare legs but the only thing that mattered was the way Kane's eyes widened and lit up when he saw her stop in front of him.

"Vanessa! This is a surprise."

"Is there somewhere we can talk?" She glanced at the guy next to him. Lean and mean looking in jeans and T-shirt, with visible tattoos on his arms; he had bright green eyes that looked sharp. Like they missed nothing. "Alone."

Kane tossed the file folder he'd been holding on a nearby desk and started down the hallway. "Follow me."

She noticed the way his trousers fell perfectly over his firm butt and wondered just how yummy it would look naked. It was round and muscled looking. Like something she'd really enjoy sinking her teeth into.

She gave her head a shake and fought to keep her hands from reaching out to pinch him. A second later he led her into a small room with a window that looked over the parking lot. There was a fridge, a coffee machine and a sink. A round table sat in the middle of the room and an overstuffed beige sofa was against the wall. A staff room.

"What can I do for you?" He closed the door behind him and turned to face her.

She reached behind him and flipped the lock on the door, then looked him right in the eye and grabbed him by the tie. With a quick tug she'd pulled him close enough so that her lips brushed against his when she whispered, "You can tell me how this makes you feel."

Then she kissed him. She licked at his bottom lip, tasted his breath as he exhaled sharply in surprise, then sealed her lips over his and snaked her tongue into his mouth. The sweet, seductive taste of butterscotch was strong, but soon she could only taste him. The unique flavor of man.

"Hmmm," he hummed in surprise. His hands gripped her hips and pulled her tight to him, where she could feel his cock growing rapidly.

She pulled her head back slightly and gauged his reaction. "Well?"

"I feel pretty damn good about it," he growled and tugged her close again.

She steered him to the sofa and pushed him down on it before climbing on his lap. "When you left yesterday, I thought that was it. That we'd had our chance and I'd screwed it up by not holding on to you when you gave me the chance that first night. Well, now I'm giving you the chance. Take me or leave me."

There was a brief struggle in his eyes before his fingers sank into her hair, and the words "Take you" flowed from his mouth to hers.

She grabbed his head and tilted it to the side, pulling her mouth from his and licking down the side of his neck. She nibbled on his earlobe and felt a shudder go through him.

His hands ran from her hip to her shoulders, then around her rib cage and up to cup her breasts. God she was glad she never wore underwear. His hands cupped the small mounds and her nipples pebbled against his palms. "More, Kane. I need more."

He groaned and tugged the neckline of her cotton top down, exposing her bare flesh to his lips. His hot breath feathered across her sensitive nubs a second before he sealed his lips around one nipple and suckled.

She cried out and ground her hips down against him. Her hands reached between them, caressing his cock through the material for a minute before finding his belt buckle.

Suddenly, Kane pulled away from her, his head back against the sofa and his hands holding hers still. "Stop," he gasped. "We can't do this here!"

"Why not?"

"This is a police station. I work here!"

"So what? We did it on my desk." Kane's eyes drifted shut and Vanessa's chest tightened. She needed this. She didn't know why she needed it so strongly, but instinct told her she needed to cement this connection with him.

He opened his eyes and lifted a hand to her cheek. His calloused fingertip stroked over her bottom lip and her tongue darted out to taste him. "I want you so much, Vanessa, but it should be in a bed. You're an amazing woman, and you deserve more than this. I want to strip you naked, lay you out and worship you the way you really deserve."

"I don't care where we are. I don't want fancy sheets and candlelight. I just want you. I want that man that lost control on Wednesday, the one that really showed me how he felt, and not just what he thought I wanted to see." She pulled his belt loose, and undid his pants. When her hand reached in and circled his hot hard cock, she leaned forward and pressed her lips to his. "I want you inside me now."

With a quick wiggle she rubbed the head of his cock against

her slit and they both groaned. Kane's hands tightened into an almost painful grip. One in her hair, the other on her naked hip under her skirt.

"Hurry," he commanded hoarsely. "Take me inside you. Show me the way home."

They met in an open mouthed kiss, all semblance of control gone the second Vanessa impaled herself on him and started to ride. The muffled sounds of people in the hallway disappeared as she rocked in his lap. She buried her head in his neck and breathed deep, inhaling the clean manly scent that held just a hint of musk. Whiskers were starting to sprout on his jaw, and she rubbed against them, the soft scrape making her feel primal. Marked by him.

He was so deep, settled firmly inside her. With every shift of her weight her clit rubbed against his pubic bone and shot pleasure bolts at the knot of tension low in her belly, making it bigger, stronger.

She panted against his neck. Trying hard not to be too loud. "More, Kane. So close. Harder."

As if he already knew everything about her body, he placed his open mouth against her nipple, sucked hard and reached a hand between them to pinch her clit. The knot of tension in her belly exploded, her thighs squeezed him, and her inner walls clutched at his throbbing cock.

"Oohhh." She dug her head deeper into his neck and cried out in pleasure as fireworks went off inside her. Just when she felt herself coming back down to earth, Kane thrust deep and hard, one, two, three times, until hot juice flowed from him to her. She wrapped her arms around him and held his head tight to her chest to muffle his own groan of release.

When all was quiet she leaned back to gauge his reaction to her whirlwind seduction. When his mouth curled into a slow, lazy smile, elation floated through her and she giggled like a schoolgirl.

"So, how is your day?" she asked.

A chuckle rumbled from him, and she realized it was the first time she heard him laugh, and her next words jumped from her mouth. "See me tonight."

"At the club?"

"I can usually leave for an hour or so as long as it's before ten. That's when things start to get busy. Meet me for a late dinner."

"Okay. I'll be there around eight-thirty." Kane's lazy smile spread into a boyish grin and Nessa's heart skipped a beat. "But I'll never make it if I don't get back to work now."

They disentangled themselves slowly. Kane tucking everything back in and doing up his pants while Vanessa fluttered her skirt to shake out any wrinkles and adjusted her top. When they were ready he placed a soft kiss on her lips, but said nothing.

No words were needed.

13

"You're thinking with your dick, buddy."

"Leave it alone, Jackson."

Kane knew it was too much to ask that Jack wouldn't comment on Vanessa's visit. Especially when he'd let it slip that morning about meeting her for a late dinner the night before.

The dinner had been great. They'd walked down the street and grabbed pizza at a small hole-in-the-wall place. Seated on the plastic stools at the chipped countertop, he'd felt himself falling harder for the woman next to him. Not only was she sexy as hell, she was intelligent and funny too. They'd spent the whole hour talking about everything and anything, except the past. She didn't ask about his family and he didn't ask about hers. There was none of the life history getting-to-know-you shit. It had all been about who they were now, not how they got to be there.

"You think because you've fucked her you know her? Kane, think about it. What do you really know about her?"

"She's an Oilers fan, and she's never tried to tie me up."

"I think she doesn't need to tie you up. She's already got you right where she wants you." Jack tossed a file in his lap and limped away.

With a heavy sigh Kane picked up the folder. What was his problem? He'd only gotten a glimpse at Vanessa the day before, and he had an instant dislike for her? It wasn't like Jack to judge anyone so quickly.

Kane flipped open the file and started reading, only to feel pain slice into his chest.

Vanessa Lawson had a record.

Vanessa's heels clacked against the concrete steps that led to the entrance to Chains. She'd called the owner the night before and he'd extended her an invitation, said he would put her name on the list at the door. When they reached the bottom of the steps there was a huge WWF look-alike in leather pants and a mesh T-shirt guarding the door. She glanced at Kane, humor tickling at the back of her throat, but when he met her gaze his eyes were quiet.

He'd been quiet ever since he picked her up, but she just thought he was apprehensive about facing another alternative crowd. But she couldn't kid herself anymore. Something was wrong. The connection she'd thought they had was gone.

"Vanessa, from The O Club," she told the bouncer.

He nodded his head and opened the door for them. Loud, throbbing music blasted up from even more stairs, making it hard to think. When she reached the bottom of the stairwell, it opened up into a large cavernous room. The basement bar was dark and dingy. The music was pulsating, and the crowd was mostly male.

It was then that she realized that the private night wasn't for a BDSM crowd, but a gay one. "I got you in the door, but I'm afraid I'm not going to be of much help with anything else. This isn't the type of crowd that will be open to me."

Kane's face tightened even more when it became clear to him

what she'd meant. His neck turned red, but that was the only outward sign of his discomfort.

"I see several women here. Let's have a drink anyway. I was told there'd be a bondage demonstration and I want to see who does it."

Kane's hand burned at the small of her back as he steered her toward the bar. The second they were there he removed it and she bit her lip. There was obviously something on his mind, something that made him pull away from her, and she wasn't sure what to do about it.

This was why relationships sucked. She'd pretty much laid herself out for him, and he'd closed her out. What was the point? The sex was good. Okay, it was great, but was it worth the pain that was creeping into her heart?

They sipped their drinks silently. A couple of guys eyed Kane boldly as they passed—he did look yummy in a black T-shirt that molded to his muscles, and loosely fitted jeans—but no one approached them.

Then a pretty redhead came over and asked Vanessa to dance. Kane's silent treatment was starting to piss her off, so she accepted the woman's invitation, and headed out to the dace floor without a word to him.

Vanessa closed her eyes, let the music roll over her. Her pulse pounded in time to the beat and she let herself go. In her mind she was dancing for him. She felt his gaze on her as she moved. When the redhead danced close and did a bump and grind against her hip, Vanessa turned away, but kept on dancing. She tossed her head back and closed her eyes, letting her own hands run over her body. Skimming her curves, cupping her breasts and dipping between her thighs suggestively. When she felt a female body press against her from behind she knew it wasn't the redhead. This body felt different. It felt good. It felt . . . erotic.

Another pair of hands started skimming her curves, hot

breath feathered across her neck and Vanessa's nipples hardened. Vanessa spun around and faced her dance partner.

She had long, blond waves, smooth skin and dark brown eyes that held a sexual awareness Vanessa had not seen in many people.

"Hi," she whispered.

"Hi," Vanessa replied.

They moved together perfectly. For the first time since she was teenager, Vanessa thought about another woman in a sexual way. She lifted her hands and placed them on her partner's hips, enjoying the feel of the supple leather and the way it hugged her hips. Her nipples ached and her pussy heated. She saw the blond move in, felt herself being pulled closer, and she let it happen.

Their lips touched softly. Breath mingled and tongues reached out, rubbing, dancing against one another.

The music changed, the beat shifted and the kiss was over almost before it started. Vanessa opened her eyes and gave the enticing blond a small smile. "Thanks for the dance."

She left the dance floor and walked toward Kane. He was watching her with glowing eyes that heated her hot blood to a boiling point and any doubts she'd had about him fled.

When she stopped in front of him, his eyes went over her shoulder and affection filled his gaze.

"Fancy seeing you here, Lexy," he spoke softly, but loud enough to be heard over the music.

Nessa turned sharply and saw that her blond dance partner had followed her off the dance floor.

"Kane, I wonder who's more surprised to be found here, me . . . or you?" A secret smile played at the blonde's full lips.

"You two know each other?" Something mean and green stirred to life deep inside Vanessa at their obvious affection.

"We've worked together on occasion," Kane said. "You working tonight, Lexy?"

"Yeah. Used to be a woman only had to worry about her man cheating with another woman. Not the case anymore, as I'm about to prove to a very unlucky lady." She glanced at Vanessa, but her question was for Kane. "You?"

"Yeah . . ."

Kane kept talking, but the roaring in Vanessa's ears drowned him out. She'd expected him to say no, or, at the very least, a little business, a little pleasure. But he hadn't even looked at her, and he'd said yes. He was working.

Everything slammed into place in her head then. The way he hadn't been able to find the time to see her in the last two days. The way he'd kept his distance from her all night. He hadn't even been able to touch her for any longer than was absolutely polite.

He was working the case. He was working *her*.

"Excuse me," she muttered and pushed past them.

She spotted a glowing red exit sign and headed for the back hallway. She had to get out of there. Now!

14

"Vanessa! Stop already." Kane caught up to her in the short hallway at the bottom of the stairs. She'd almost gotten away. "What's gotten into you?"

Her heart in her throat, she met his gaze. "You think it's me, don't you?"

His mouth snapped shut and he let go of her arm. Shit. This wasn't how he wanted to confront her. He hadn't even decided if he wanted to confront her. His hands clenched into fists at his sides, he wouldn't lie to her.

"You *are* very good at using your sex appeal to distract men from what they're really after."

"When have I ever tried to distract you from your case? I've only ever offered help!" A rosy blush started at her chest and rose up her neck and into her cheeks.

God, she was beautiful, even in her anger.

Heart pounding, he ignored the stirring in his groin. "You've distracted me from the moment I met you."

"If you think I'm the thief you're after, at least have the balls to admit it."

Her sneer cut through what was left of his patience. "All right. You are on my list of suspects. Right at the top, actually. And I'm not happy about it. You think I want you to be the thief? You think I want to arrest you and put you behind bars?"

"Why not? Since your only real interest in me is as part of your investigation, why not question me? Why not arrest me and try to put me away? Oh, right!" She threw her hands up and gave him a mocking look. "It's because you have *no evidence*."

He grabbed her arm before she could walk away and spun her around. When he had her back against the wall, he pressed the full length of his body against her. He cupped her soft cheeks in his hands and stared deep into the flames of fury in her eyes. "I haven't done any of that because I'm afraid of the answers. I don't *want* it to be you!"

He should've walked away right then, but he couldn't. So he kissed her.

His tongue thrust between her lips and claimed her mouth. Vanessa fought for control of her emotions and lost. Her anger turned to lust and she kissed him back.

Their lips met, their tongues danced, their harsh breathing blending, filling each other intimately. She pressed her body against his, reveling in the feel of his hardness against her softness. She reached up and ran her fingers through his hair, the feel of it silky and soft, a complete contrast the hardness of him. His hips pinned her to the wall, his cock teased her, taunted her. Made her ache to spread her legs and be filled.

She tore her mouth away. A whimper of want escaped, only to be followed by a gasp as Kane's mouth worked its way down her neck and his hands cupped her breasts. He tugged at the top of her satin corset and her bare breasts filled his hands. He tugged at her nipples and pleasure zinged straight to her clit.

He continued to roll one nipple between the fingers of one hand while he offered the other one up to his mouth. With no hesitation, he laved the rigid nub, then pulled it into his mouth and suckled.

Vanessa tossed her head back and forth; her body writhing. She ached to spread her legs, to wrap them around his waist and feel him grind against her, but he wasn't having any of it.

Kane was suckling, nibbling and licking at her nipples, first one, then the other, and he wasn't going to stop. She felt his hand slip under her skirt and snake between her thighs. "Yes!"

A long finger slid inside, and her pussy clenched. He pulled it out and entered her again, two fingers this time. Vanessa writhed against the wall, her eyes closed, her hands clawing at him, pulling him closer to her. He wiggled his fingers inside her and pressed his palm against her clit. He rotated it, sucked on her nipple, pinched the other and her body jerked, an orgasm ripping through her. Her juices flooded his hand and her thighs, yet still her insides spasmed. Wanting more. Needing to be filled. "Please," she gasped.

"Please what?" he demanded hoarsely.

"Please fuck her already, mate. I can't wait to see what's under that skirt," called an accented voice from the shadowed entrance to the hallway.

Vanessa grabbed Kane and held him tight to her. Their eyes met, and she saw murder in them. With a small shake of her head she reminded him where they were. "Leave it. We were putting on a show, let's just take it home."

She saw the struggle in him. Felt it in the tremors of anger that went through the arms holding her. She also felt when he got control of himself. He pulled her corset back up, covering her nakedness before he stepped back and offered her his arm in a courtly manner.

"Ah, mate, you can't tease me and leave me like that! I'll stay quiet. I promise."

Vanessa breathed a sigh of relief when Kane ignored the intruder and led her up the stairs and out the door.

They were silent during the drive to her house. The whole time she ranted to herself.

She shouldn't be doing this. She should've told Kane to fuck off. Yes, that's what she should've said. Instead she'd said, *let's go home*. Vanessa gave her head a shake. How stupid was she? She deserved whatever she got after this.

She looked out the window and listened to the rumble of the powerful engine as Kane turned on to her street. It had surprised her to see him pull up to her house in a sleek black Charger. It shouldn't have, though. Chargers were beautiful, strong cars. Powerful in a very subtle way. Much like Kane himself.

He wore his fancy silk suit, and had the clean cut good looks of a conservative businessman, but underneath . . . he was powerful . . . primal.

And a threat to her.

Yet there she was. Her mind racing as fast as her heart, her thighs sticky from the orgasm he'd given her, and the hunger for more urging her on.

15

"Are you coming in?"

She didn't look at him when she asked. He should say no. He knew that. It was completely wrong to get involved with a suspect. Fuck, it was time he stopped kidding himself. He was already in too deep with her to walk away.

All he could do was hope to hell he was wrong. That Vanessa and the Risqué Robber weren't one and the same, and that he wouldn't have to send her to jail.

"I thought you'd never ask," he replied and turned the car off.

He jogged around to open her door for her, but she beat him to it. Without waiting for him, she strode up the walk and climbed the three steps to the front door.

He watched as she fumbled with the lock and felt a surge of satisfaction that she was just as unnerved as he was by the whole thing.

She opened the door and entered the small bungalow-style house. He followed her, pulse racing, cock throbbing. He closed the door and gave the living room a cursory glance. He should take a closer look. There's a lot to be learned by seeing what a person surrounds themself with. But he only had eyes for the woman in front of him. She glanced over her shoulder and turned down a hallway, leaving him to follow once again.

She led him to her bedroom. He stepped inside and was surrounded by the scent of Vanessa. The clean womanly scent that he'd always associate with her. The big double bed was made, with a maroon down comforter for a cover and a shit-load of pillows at the head. She'd turned a small bedside lamp on and the room had a warm, seductive glow.

With her gaze locked on his, she reached under one arm and unzipped her corset. So that was how the damn thing worked. His dick swelled and pressed against his zipper in a painful way. When she dropped it on the floor and reached back to undo her skirt, Kane reached for the snap of his jeans.

Her skirt dropped to the floor and she stood before him in nothing but high heels. "Make love to me, Kane. Give me this one night."

Kane stripped his clothes off in record time and stepped forward. When he gazed into her eyes his heart swelled and he knew that, no matter what happened, he wanted more than this one night with her.

Cupping her dear face in his hands, he lowered his head and touched his lips to hers. "Your wish is my command."

He wrapped his arms around her, taking her down to the bed and covering her body with his. For the first time they were skin against skin, completely.

Emotion flooded him, and his hands trembled as he stroked her sides, her hips. She was soft, warm, and all things womanly. And his control was weak.

Vanessa shifted beneath him, spreading her legs so that he was cradled between her thighs, her hands roaming over his back and ass, trailing heat in their path as she writhed beneath him.

"Vanessa?" His breath caught in his throat.

A small hand wrapped around his cock and pulled a groan from low in his belly. Her thumb ran over the sensitive head and he reared back, but she wrapped her legs around his waist and guided him to her entrance.

"Now, Kane," she whispered. "I don't want to wait any longer. Love me now."

Kane's growl vibrated through the room as he thrust forward and slid home. A gasp escaped her and a small orgasm rippled through her insides.

"Oh, God," he moaned, his muscles trembling as he held himself frozen above her.

Vanessa laughed as joy filled her. She might only get one night with this man in her bed, but it was worth it. He was so passionate and caring. So loving.

She wrapped her arms around his neck and pulled him down for a passionate kiss. When he pulled away enough to rest his forehead against hers, they were both panting. She tightened her inner muscles and he groaned again. "You're going to kill me, woman."

"No." Her tongue darted out and licked at his bottom lip. "I'm going to love you."

Eyes locked with his, she let all her secrets show as she braced her feet on the bed and undulated beneath him. "Love me back, Kane."

His head dropped and he kissed her as he withdrew, then thrust deeply again. At first he was slow and steady, the sensual rub of their tongues matching the slow seduction of their bodies, but their breathing got heavier, their bodies more demanding. Soon they were slick with sweat, his moans and her sighs of pleasure creating a music that only they would ever hear.

Her sighs turned to mewls and her insides tightened around him. "Kane, now, come with me."

She looked into his eyes and fell over the edge into the

swirling light that waited, knowing that he was right there with her.

She must've fallen asleep. She didn't remember climbing beneath the covers, but she was snuggled deep, with Kane's body at her back and his arms around her. She closed her eyes in the dim room and listened for what had woken her up.

There it was, a faint beeping.

She pulled away from Kane, pleased when he tried to fight letting go of her in his sleep. "Kane, wake up. I think that's your beeper."

His body jerked awake. "My beeper?"

"Yeah, listen."

They were still for a minute and it sounded again. "Shit." He crawled over her and snatched his pants up from the floor by the end of the bed. He read the glowing screen and cursed again.

Vanessa admired the view as he climbed from the bed and started to dress. When he bent down to kiss her good-bye the look in his eyes made her heart stutter. "What? Kane what is it?"

"Something new in the Risqué Robber case." He pressed his lips to hers fast and hard. "I'll be back as soon as I can," he said as he walked out the door.

16

The sun was shining bright and Vanessa was quietly going stir-crazy when she heard the warning rumble of Kane's car pull into her driveway.

Shit, was he back to arrest her? What had happened? Was it possible they'd found her backpack? No way. She'd driven all the way out to the dump to get rid of it. Why would they even look there?

Footsteps marched up her steps and the door swung open. He hadn't even knocked. At least he was alone. He kicked the door shut behind him and strode into the room.

"What!?" She yelped when he bent low and swung her up into his arms. He strode down the short hallway to her bedroom, grinning from ear to ear the whole time.

"We arrested the Risqué Robber last night."

He stood over her bed and dropped her onto the mattress. She immediately scrambled off the bed and stood next to him, hands planted firmly on her hips. "What? Who? If you've arrested JJ I'm going—"

"Not JJ," he interrupted her with a shake of his head. "Your favorite person, Marissa DeVartan."

"What? How?" She was starting to feel like a parrot, but none of it made sense.

"She was caught in the act. She dressed up, put on a wig and tried to seduce her way into her own ex-husband's house. He blamed it on the drinks that he didn't recognize her right off the bat, but as soon as she suggested tying him up he knew who, and what she was. He sounded the alarm and kept her there until the cops arrived."

She was stunned. Marissa. What had that woman been thinking? "Did she confess to all of the robberies?"

"She doesn't need to. We have her cold on one robbery, and the MO is close enough that I can close the case. We figure she was approached by her friends that had been stiffed in their divorces and did it for them. When her own ex's new trophy wife was out of town, she decided to get a bit of her own back." He stepped back and gave her a solemn look. "Or are you going to tell me different?"

God forgive her, but Marissa was an evil woman. *And stupid enough to get caught.*

She met Kane's gaze and left the final choice up to him. Did he want to keep her around? Or did he want to send to her jail?

"Ask me no secrets, I'll tell you no lies."

Her pulse raced and her breath stuck in her throat as she watched the meaning of what she'd said sink in. He had her life . . . her heart, in his hands, and it was time to decide what he wanted.

He pushed her down on the bed and stretched out on top of her, whispering one word before covering her lips with his. "Deal."

ARRESTED

Alyssa Brooks

1

"Come on, move already!" Kirsten pounded the steering wheel. Her angry fist struck smack in the middle. The unintentional horn blast made her jump out of the leather seat.

How could the longest stretch of nowhere be so backed up? *Damn it.* Kirsten stretched her neck to look for a break, but all her gaze found was car after car of backed-up traffic for miles on end. After sitting at nearly a dead stop for three hours in the miserable dry Texas heat, she'd had enough.

The sun's sweltering rays had burned away the last of her patience, and her skin along with it. Not to mention cramped legs, a dry mouth and sharp hunger pains.

She needed relief. Now. Patience had met its blowing point.

She should have flown. Kurt wasn't worth all the trouble he'd cost her. Hell, she'd put enough miles between them today to sleep safely tonight. She saw an opportunity, having finally inched her way to yet another rural, going-nowhere exit and this time she'd best take it.

Kirsten gritted her teeth and veered her Corvette off the shoulder, around the stilled vehicles toward the nearest exit.

A whine reminded her she wasn't alone. She reached out and ruffled the fluffy white fur of the Samoyed moping in the passenger's seat. The poor pup. He had to be thirsty. They'd run out of bottled water an hour ago. "It's okay, Snowball. I know you're tired. I'm bushed too. We'll take a little break. I'm sure there must be a gas station and a diner out here in no man's land somewhere. How about a steak?"

Snowball perked up and yapped in response. The sparkle in his beautiful blue eyes showed she had his complete attention.

"You'll like Alabama so much better, Snowball, you'll see. There's a big yard with plenty of room to run, and the country air is fresh and crisp. No more inhaling smoke and pollution for us. Best of all, Kurt won't be there." She swore she could see the distaste in Snowball's eyes at the mention of the scoundrel's name. "Yeah, you never did like him, did you? I should have listened to your instincts."

Snowball gave her one more bark then dived to the floorboards to curl up in the shade of the dash. "You got the right idea, boy."

Thoughts of Kurt brought on a frown, wrinkling Kirsten's brows. Sharp discomfort followed. Another quick glance in the mirror revealed her newly attained sunburn. Though her face maintained an even tan, redness tainted her scalp under her pale blond tresses. Kirsten reached up and touched her head. The tender skin stung like the devil.

After living in Malibu for five years you'd think she'd have adjusted to the sun. But no, her fair skin burned on even the cloudiest of days, even with the protection of sunblock.

It would have been best to have the top up, but she'd have baked. As it was, she'd resorted to turning off the air to save gas nearly an hour ago.

And now the little red light in the dash blinked an annoying threat anyway.

Damn it.

Though its lack of signs gave her an eerie feeling, what real choice did she have but to take the exit? Man, she hoped she wasn't headed deeper into nowhere rural Texas. "At least in the bayou, we'll have plenty of shade trees. Hotter than hell down there, but we're used to that, huh Snowball? We'll finally have a normal life—if we ever get there. And at this rate, I'm beginning to wonder."

Kirsten doubted Kurt would follow her. No, he didn't seem to give *that* much of a damn about her.

Nevertheless, she wanted to be as far away from him as she could get, and as fast as possible. Better safe than sorry. From what she'd learned, her ex could be a dangerous man. Too bad it had taken her five years to figure it out.

The exit dumped Kirsten on a tar and chip country road. On either side she saw nothing but endless stretches of Texas fields of green. "What do you think, Snowball—north or south?"

Snowball raised his head and barked.

"Then south it is. You know best. From now on, you make all the calls. You see where mine got us."

Every second along the rough road felt like nail-biting torture. She kept the gas pedal pressed to the floor, sure the car would putt out at any moment and leave her stranded.

Finally, a sign appeared along the road. She squinted, sure she'd misread it. The worn paint flaked away from the yellowing white sign, but she couldn't mistake the town's name.

Paradise, she read with a slight grimace.

It figured. There were probably a thousand dead little towns in Texas, and she had to land in the one with that name.

Paradise Club. Its image rushed back to her mind, a memory she'd wished a million times she could erase. The night she'd met Kurt, and the months following, the naïve way she'd partied and played there with him. Under the glitter. The lies.

Oh, their days were spent at the pool, their evenings sipping martinis with friends, their nights chock-full of dancing and wild sex. They'd been like two peas in a pod.

Until she woke up, thank God.

Kirsten shook her head. Her purse had been full, but not her life. She knew now she'd never loved him. Idolized him, yes. Loved, not ever. Even the sex had gone cold after the first year.

How could she not have seen the signs? Kurt could never have made such money off of one club and a mediocre line of coffee shops. Worse, he'd shut her out of everything, dangling the profits in front of her like candy to a hungry kid. And she'd eaten it up.

She just hadn't taken Kurt for the type.

Kirsten pressed down harder on the gas pedal as she flew into the small town. It all made so much sense now.

"Shit!" Panic snapped her attention back to the road. Out of nowhere, a dog jumped alongside her car.

Her heart leapt in her throat as she swerved. Panicked, she slammed the brakes too hard and the tires screeched as she fought to keep the sports car on the road. Terror seized her. Alarm and fright tensed her body. Instinctively, she grasped the steering wheel so hard her knuckles turned white.

Snowball jumped up and leaned over the side to give the strange dog a piece of his mind. Kirsten imagined his growls and barks to be a thorough tongue-lashing. The annoying shepherd mix continued to chase her as he yapped his threats.

Livid, she held back the fire burning her tongue, said her prayers and straightened out her car. The idea of turning back tempted her to no end, but the irate notion fled as she spotted a gas station next to a diner.

A sigh of relief escaped Kirsten. "Thank God."

She pulled over, parking her car in front of the lone gas pump. Out front, a wrinkled old man dozed in a rocking chair.

His gnarled fingers wrapped around a rolled up newspaper, and every couple of seconds, he'd jump to swat away a fly.

Kirsten laughed to herself as she got out of the car and yanked the nozzle free. She grabbed a card out of her purse and swiped it. After several moments passed with no response, Kirsten's panic grew. Then the screen blinked back. She'd been denied. *Kurt*, she grimaced. He'd cut off her credit cards.

Anxious, she sifted through her wallet in a search for some cash, fished out a twenty, and headed in to pay.

Looks like my instincts proved right, Reid thought as he replaced the radio on the dash. With a shake of his head, he refocused on the red Corvette parked at ole Henry's pump. The little blonde had just sped into the wrong town.

He narrowed his eyes and rested his jaw in his hand, flicking stubbly growth against his fingers. The stranger drove the sports car like the typical spoiled rich girl, without an ounce of respect for the law—or other's lives. Just the type he didn't want in his town.

Three minutes ago, he'd have been content to write her out a hefty ticket and send her on her way. Yet, as he'd watched the look of anger, not fluster, cross her face when the pump denied her credit card, he'd known something had to be wrong. Women who owned Corvettes didn't typically fly into his town wearing sweats and frantically searching for cash.

The nation-wide search on the tags had revealed the car as stolen, just as expected. What bewildered him was why the pinched car had been driven into a tiny town like Paradise.

Reid leaned back in his seat, keeping one eye on the Vette as he decided his approach. The aroma of tonight's special, Edna's slow-cooked roast beef, floated through the air. His empty stomach growled, so he lit a smoke to cover the mouth-watering smell of it.

Like a fool, he'd skipped lunch today, up to his elbows in drywall mud. Redoing his office and the single cell in the town jail had turned out to be quite the task. More mess than he ever expected, or wanted.

He'd just set aside the half-finished job for the day and been on his way to the diner, when she came squealing wheels into Paradise to interrupt his plans.

Reid didn't like that. Not one bit.

Dinner would have to wait. Right now, he had a car thief on his hands. Under-construction jail cell or not, the law said he had to take her in. Reid started the engine of his Blazer and pulled into the station parking in front of the stolen car. He flashed his lights, leaving them on as he got out to walk around the vehicle, and inspect it as he waited for her return.

The radio had been left blaring. Annoyed, he reached in to flick off the noisy rock tunes, but the sight of the white dog curled under the front seat stopped him. Ice blue eyes followed his every movement with a cold glare.

"Howdy, boy." Reid reached in his pocket and pulled out the jerky strips he liked to keep handy for snacks. He tore back the plastic wrappers of two and offered them to the dog. The fluff ball yapped and accepted the peace offering, choking it down in one gulp. The pup sniffed for more, then disappeared back to his spot on the floor. "Hot, ain't it? You're a smart one."

Reid shut off the radio, leaned against the car, and waited. After several moments, the flaxen-haired beauty exited the store holding a twenty-ounce soda and a bottle of spring water.

Reid's breath caught in his chest as he watched her. Her luscious curves swayed under the baby-blue cotton of her sweats, and bounced to the beat of her feet. A tight top that read "flirt" stretched across the deep curves of her chest, and nipples the size of quarters hardened against the pull of the fabric.

Her perky breasts jiggled up and down as she increased her

brisk pace, her shake more and more tantalizing the closer she drew.

No way could she be wearing a bra. Not a chance. And the fabric of her shirt was entirely too thin.

The gall of some people, Reid gulped.

When his breathtaking perp rounded the pump and caught sight of him, she stopped dead in her tracks. For a moment she just stood there, a deer in the headlights look. Her huge jade eyes flew to the flashing red lights on his Blazer, then returned to him. Reid stared back at her heart shaped face with a hard glare.

"Can I help you?" Her sugary voice sounded smooth and calm, like syrup being poured over pancakes.

"Yes, ma'am. You most certainly can." Reid told her in a flat voice. Her eyes widened, big, green and devastating as he approached her. "What brings you to Paradise?"

"Just passing through."

"Where to?"

"That, sir, is absolutely none of your business." Curtness laced her reply.

"I disagree. Sheriff Reid, ma'am." He held out his hand and she shook it, but not without obvious reservation. "And since I'm about to place you under arrest, you might make it my business."

"Arrest?" She took a step back as she squeaked the question. Ruby red lips, full and lush, hung open at the question. "You must be mistaken."

Man, she played the innocent act well. Hell, she probably thought she could get away with murder with only a flash of those wide emerald eyes.

Reid had to admit: the little blonde tempted him. He hadn't felt such interest in a woman in years, not since Lisa left. Not even the porn channel or Suzy May had managed to awaken his cock since his ex-wife's cold betrayal. And every bachelor in town had fallen for Suzy's wanton ways.

But he had to uphold the law.

"Not at all. Now, we can talk here or at the station. Your choice."

"Look, *Sheriff*. I'm only passing through."

Reid raised his eyebrows in question but was met with silence and a cold look.

"To?"

"Bay Crest, Alabama. Home to live with my folks." Her hard voice softened a notch, then she looked at him as if for understanding. "So if you'll just let me be on my way, I can get back to a simpler life—a normal life. You can appreciate that, of course."

Reid nodded. "So you're coming from the city then?" She took a wide step back, and he matched her movement. "What city?"

"Malibu."

"And this car, whose is it?"

"Mine," she asserted. "Kirsten Montgomery."

"Yours? And where did you acquire it?"

A sudden look flashed across her face. Her eyes widened and her jaw dropped a notch, then they both snapped shut. "It's a gift, from my ex-boyfriend. Kurt Black."

A chortle of disbelief escaped from his throat. If the convertible was a gift, then he was Mister Rogers.

From the blank look of disbelief on Kirsten's face, he expected she'd try to run. He needed to get the cuffs on her.

As predicted, when he advanced, she stumbled backward, taking off in a sprint toward the diner. Reid pursued her, amazed by her speed. Like a flash, she darted from his grasp, and he actually had to put forth some effort to catch her.

Before Kirsten could round his Blazer, he caught her arm

and stopped her in her tracks. With a forceful yank, Reid threw her against his truck and pinned himself against her.

Feisty as a wildcat, Kirsten continued to try to break away from him with desperate yanks and tugs. Sharp nails began to dig into his skin as he pulled her hand behind her. Pain pinched into his wrists, and Reid rushed to slam shut the cuff and grab for her other flailing arm. A slight cry escaped her, a hint of desperate pain traced in it, and he softened his touch just a notch.

He didn't want to hurt her, but Reid couldn't help but think a sound spanking was exactly what the hellcat needed as she started to struggle against him once again.

His grasp tight on her arm, he detained her against the Blazer as he tried to grab her other wrist. The vixen wriggled and twisted to keep away from him, and the movement caused her bottom to rub against his hips.

For the first time in years, Reid's cock twitched and started to harden.

"Stop it," he commanded as he grabbed her thrashing hand. "Stop resisting."

"Let me go," she begged. Like a worm, she twisted around and gazed up at him with a pleading expression.

Reid whirled her right back into place. The sprite might be bewitching, but he didn't plan to let a pair of beguiling green eyes fool him. When he managed to catch her other hand, he wasted no time locking the cuff around it.

No way would she be getting away from him.

He didn't take kindly to outsiders in his town, especially not reckless drivers in stolen cars. One tragic accident had been enough. No family in Paradise would lose their loved ones as he'd lost his parents, not on his time.

"This vehicle has been reported stolen, and I'm placing you in custody. You have the right to remain silent . . ."

2

"Please, this must be a mistake," Kirsten growled through gritted teeth. "This is my car. It's not stolen."

"Hold still."

Right, like she could even if she wanted to. Adrenaline rushed her body as panic raced through her, spinning her in a million directions. Wild beats thumped her heart against her ribs, and her breath came in heavy gulps. She yanked at the cuffs trapping her hands. "This is ridiculous. Release me at once, you overgrown hillbilly."

"Can't do that, Ma'am." The sheriff pushed her against the muddy side of the Blazer. His hands fell on her hips, their touch searing right through the soft cotton of her sweat pants. The intimate feel of his hands upon her coursed a strange tingle through her. Shocked by her body's betrayal, she reared back. Her head slammed into his shoulder, yet he didn't even wince. With a firm grasp, he encircled her waist and pinned her once again. "You're going to hurt yourself if you don't stop. Stay still a minute, then we'll talk. I'm going to pat you down for weapons."

The sheriff's large hands assailed her once again, their touch like tortuous fire as they slowly searched her body. Kirsten squeezed her eyes shut as he patted her down, sure his determined fingers grazing across her hips and legs would drive her insane. Jolts of desire flashed to her breasts and groin, dampening her with desire. Kirsten bit her lip a little harder as embarrassment rushed to her cheeks.

For Christ's sake, she'd recently left the biggest jerk of all time. What was wrong with her? She'd just met this man, yet her body felt more alive than it had in years. How could she be responding to a stranger like this?

Her mind willed her body to turn off, but it continued to fill with need as he moved his fingers around her ankles, running his calloused fingers inside the hem of her anklet socks. Delicate skin collided against his coarse touch, setting off a burst of tiny fireworks. Everything in Kirsten prickled, angry at the invasion. It took all her willpower not to kick him in the face right then and there.

Finally, he stopped and stepped back. Relief hit her, laced with a traitorous disappointment. In spite of her fear, she actually *enjoyed* his touch. She wanted more of it, though she loathed the very thought. Disgusted, Kirsten directed her anger right where it belonged—on him.

He had no right to touch her like that, so . . . so . . . deliberately.

Kirsten whirled around, prepared to give the sheriff a piece of her mind. Her face collided with the expanse of his solid chest. For a moment she stared, her breath caught in her throat. Muscles pulled at the tight white T-shirt. Through its thin fabric, tiny black hairs curled against built pecs. A hint of its dark trail across his flat, tight stomach teased her with the notion of where it led. The urge to reach up and tear away the cloth barrier pulsed through her and blinded her with the image of what she would find. With a gulp, she stepped back, her retreat halted by the Blazer.

There was no escaping him. Kirsten slowly pulled her gaze up his length, unconsciously drinking in every detail of his height. At first, she'd seen nothing but her fear, but now she saw the man.

Paralyzed, she continued to savor the sight of the dark and dangerous sheriff who towered over her. Whiskers shadowed his steel jaw like black sandpaper against his leathery-bronzed skin. Deep chocolate eyes, framed by thick black lashes, met hers, his hard gaze an obvious challenge.

No doubt, his rough and tough looks were tantalizing. The Sheriff was one hot cowboy.

And she embarrassed herself. She snapped her jaw shut, then reopened it to make her demand. "Listen, *sir*, I'm not sure what kind of redneck bullshit this is, but I did not steal this car. It's mine. All mine. Uncuff me now, and I won't press charges."

With a cold look he ignored her, bending down to pick up his cowboy hat, which must have fallen during their scuffle. Kirsten swallowed at the sight of his tight rear against form-fitting Levi's, firm and sculpted, as if it had been chiseled from stone. Everything in her told her to reach out and take a squeeze, to feel him, as he'd felt her. The only thing stopping her was the cuffs around her hands.

He stood, and she forced herself to shake away the naughty thoughts. She needed to get herself out of these handcuffs, not into his bed. "My lawyer won't be pleased. He could tear a tiny town like this in two."

His full lips carved into a sarcastic smile that hardly budged his cheeks. "Lady, I'm doing my job. Sorry, can't let you go, won't let you go, and not a one of your nasty comments or threats will make the darnedest difference. We might be a small town, but we follow the law. You city folk should try it."

"Oh, come on. How do I even know you're a real cop?"

He flicked a silver badge pinned to the pocket of his white T-shirt. "Sheriff Reid Walker, ma'am. Pleased to meet you."

"You've got to be kidding." Kirsten rolled her eyes. Christ, it was like something out of an old western movie. Next he'd pull out his six shooters and whistle for his sidekick.

"Nope."

"Come on, damn it, it's my car. My boyfriend, *ex-boyfriend*, gave it to me for my birthday this June."

"Would that be a Mister Kurt Black?"

"Yes! Yes, exactly. Look in my purse, you'll see. Why else would I have everything from credit cards to health insurance identification in his name? It's my car, that's why. He gave it to me."

The sheriff shook his head and strode over to her car with a fast stride. Tightly muscled legs pulled against his jeans as he moved and Kirsten found herself imagining the knotted strength in them, their rippled mass covered in tiny black hairs, thicker high on his thighs, dark and manly. Then her gaze darted up to a bulge of power between his legs.

Stop it! She inwardly chastised herself, unable to tear her eyes away from him. Had she gone insane? For heaven's sake, the man had her in handcuffs and all she could do was check him out and drip with desire.

As much as she wanted to turn her back right now and blind herself from the sight of him, she wouldn't have him rooting through her car unsupervised. Eyes narrowed, she watched his movements. The sheriff reached into her car and Snowball chose that moment to finally show himself. Why he hadn't jumped out of the car long ago amazed Kirsten. Usually he leapt to protect her.

Snowball bounded from the floorboard where her purse lay to pounce right on the sheriff. Her heart skipped a beat at the sight of him attacking before she realized he wasn't defending her at all. Quite the contrary. Snowball covered the cop's face with licks while he yapped a greeting.

"Snowball, stop it!" she yelled at her traitorous pet. She'd never seen Snowball so friendly with any man. "Get down, Snowball. Right now."

"It's okay. Nice dog." The sheriff held up her purse and waved the thin black bag. "Got your permission, ma'am?"

"Yes," she gritted through her teeth, hating the thought of anyone rummaging through her belongings. Especially him.

And wouldn't you know it, the very first thing he pulled out: her emergency tampon. She winced as he held it up in wonderment, his cocoa eyes analytical and narrowed. A wide smile broadened on his face and she could have died. "You don't need to pilfer my whole purse, you know. Just get out my damned wallet, and then you can release these ridiculous cuffs."

He pulled out her leather wallet and unsnapped the clasp. One by one he sorted through the cards, reading each as he laid them out on the roof of her car. "You're absolutely right, Ma'am. Looking in your purse has proven something. You must be quite the skilled thief."

"What? No, look, you just call Kurt. He'll tell you."

"Yeah, I'll bet, being as he's the one to report this stolen. Why, I'd wager these are all reported stolen as well. You haven't proved anything to me, except maybe that I need to hold tight to my wallet and keys." She stood shocked as he swiped the cards all up, and stuffed everything back into her purse. In three wide steps, he returned to her side and had the Blazer's door swung wide open. He motioned her to get in. "Let's go."

"No. You've got to understand. Kurt, he—"

"Lady, we'll finish sorting this all out at the station. Let's go. Get in or I'll put you in."

Kirsten shook her head, slow at first, then furiously. Oh God, if Kurt had gone as far as to report the car stolen, and cancel her cards, maybe he hadn't taken her leaving so well.

Like a sudden shadow cast over a once bright and cheery land, the dark truth crept in. Reality sunk into her mind and wrapped its claws around her psyche. Kurt wasn't going to let her go. Not ever.

No, she knew entirely too much.

And since she'd left like she did, no doubt he suspected that. He wouldn't let her go. Oh gawd, what had she gotten herself into? "No, I can't. I have to get out of here."

"Fine, have it your way." Before she could even open her mouth again he had her by the waist. She kicked as he lifted her, twisting in his hold. Cursing in pain, his grip relinquished. Rather than ending up over his shoulders, she half landed on her feet, half in his arms, still tight in his grasp.

She glanced up at him, shocked by his gaze. She'd expected anger. Instead, he looked like a hungry animal, one ready to ravish her mouth with a hot kiss. Her insides trembled, but she did not move away. She was too damn attracted to him. The sight of his lips paralyzed her.

Thank God he did not hesitate.

His mouth claimed hers into a hard, demanding kiss. Hot desire shot down her spine at the touch, shooting straight to her lower regions. Need possessed her body. She kissed him back, swooping her tongue into his mouth. She grazed it along his, enticing a battle.

The sheriff devoured her, flicks and swirls of his tongue matching hers. Their tongues fought each other with fury.

Every inch of her body tingled, her clit pulsating as she dampened. She wanted him to touch her, explore her, all while the cuffs still restrained her from resisting him.

He increased the demand of his lips, his grip around her lessening. He ran his hand up her back, the touch lighting her spine with electric heat. Cupping her left breast, he rubbed his thumb across her hardened nipple. Her areola burst with sensation.

She moaned in his mouth, and leaned into his touch. Damn, she wanted him to kiss her there. To . . .

Sudden awareness shot through her. He'd freed his hold on her. She fought between her lust for him and harsh reality.

Now was her chance to get away. The sensible side of her demanded she run.

All at once, she broke away and leapt for freedom. She gained a few feet on him before his hand caught her arm. Halting her escape, he pulled her back, and tossed her over his shoulder. Her ribs slammed into him, momentarily stealing her breath.

Kirsten gasped, then screamed. Overwrought with the sudden need to flee, she banged her head into his back. It bounced back like a pebble thrown against a rock wall. Dizzy, she fell limp. He tossed her in the seat, and glared down at her. His dark, narrowed eyes looked cold. A chill ran down her spine, followed by the strangest feeling in the pit of her stomach.

He pointed at her, freezing her with the fierceness in his stare. "I'm giving you one last warning. Do that again, and you can add assaulting an officer to your list of charges."

She scrambled up just in time for him to slam the door in her face.

3

"Oh, come on," Kirsten pleaded in almost a whine. "For the hundredth time, if you would just listen to me."

He slammed down the phone and glared at her. "I know, I know. A drug dealer is going to murder you if I turn you in. I got it already." Thick sarcasm laced his tone and dripped from his voice.

"But you don't believe me," she hissed, though her story seemed distinctly unbelievable, even to herself. She didn't know how she could have been so blind for so very long.

Kurt's money and charm had made her a fool, that's how. In one full sweep he'd knocked her right off her feet with gifts and fast cars. She'd forgotten all about her dreams of becoming a star as he'd filled her wallet with credit cards and put her up in her own condo. It had been a new life for a small town nobody young enough to fall for its glitter.

Since then she'd changed.

Now she saw Kurt's true colors. This morning when she'd overheard where all it really came from, she'd lit out of there.

She'd just grabbed her purse and got in her Corvette, still in her sweats from her morning run with Snowball.

If only she'd gotten a clue years ago. Perhaps Kurt would've let her go more easily back then and she wouldn't now be handcuffed and jailed by Sheriff Bighead.

She stared into his handsome eyes; their almond shape narrowed into a dark stare serving to make him look all the more attractive. Like the dark, silent type—brooding, mysterious.

Sexy.

With a gulp, she tried to force herself out of the trance. Visions of his mouth trailing up and down her body, just as his hands had, overtook her mind. Poisoned with want once again, Kirsten tore her gaze away from him. No doubt he could see her hardened nipples right through her shirt.

His words came in a slow growl to remind her of his distrust. "No, Ma'am. I don't believe you."

Kirsten's anger increased. "I'm not freaking lying. Isn't your duty to serve and protect? Well, you're not doing a very good job. In fact—"

"Just be quiet already. Like a damned chatter box. My office has never been so noisy."

"Well, if you'd listen to me—"

"Enough. I have to make another phone call." He waved her away with the flick of his hand and picked up the phone. Kirsten stood and wandered around the sheet-covered desk in his office. Drywall dust covered everything, and buckets of mud and tools lay scattered everywhere. She swore she'd end up with cancer from the particles he had her inhaling.

The cuffs were still fastened tightly to her wrists, and though it hurt, she couldn't stop from pulling and tugging at them.

Jerk. Mr. Know-It-All, I'm So Damned Fine—Jerk. Everything about him disgusted her. He wouldn't even try to listen to her, and understand her dilemma. Worse, at the time when she had so much to worry over, all she could think of was what it would feel like to have him.

On the desk, the chair, the floor. Handcuffed.

She shook her head. She hadn't had such impure thoughts since the accident. After that, she'd gone to Alcoholics Anonymous, put aside drinking and the behavior that went with it. It had been as if her thoughts were dry-cleaned.

One look at Sheriff Reid Walker mucked up her mind with dirty ideas.

She went to the window and leaned against the cool glass. Snowball sat out front, politely awaiting his owner. *Traitor*, she thought as she recalled how her pet had taken to her new worst enemy.

Reid's escalating voice grabbed her attention. "No, damn it. We've been beating this around the bush for two hours now. *Listen* to me."

Kirsten wanted to tell him if he wanted people to pay him attention, perhaps he should try extending the same courtesy.

"Is that a fact?" he growled to the person on the other end of the phone. "No, no. Wait a minute. Whispering Branch is over three hours away. It's Friday evening. For one, you'd have me driving until the early morning hours. Two, it would be closed by the time I got there"

His face had turned beet red, and he looked ready to explode. "No. I told you I can't keep her here. We're into some remodeling right now."

"Then let me go," she whispered to him in a hiss.

Sheriff Reid shot her another mean look and went on with his call. His face contorted in twelve different expressions of disgust, then he shouted, "Fine. But you damned well better be here for her first thing Monday morning."

He slammed down the phone and looked at her with sorry

brown eyes. In contrast, a sexy little muscle in his jaw twitched in anger. "They cannot extradite you back to California until Monday."

"Oh no." Shaking, she stepped back. She looked around at the construction mess and held back the scream that threatened to explode. "No. I am not staying here until Monday. No way."

He glared around the room and nodded his head. His dark eyes met hers, and a cold chill ran down her spine. "You are absolutely right. You cannot stay here. You'll stay with me."

Reid winced as Kirsten's big eyes flashed in surprise. Golden flecks sparked from their green depths, and lit her face with disbelief, which quickly flashed into full-blown anger. Burned by her fiery glare, he averted his gaze.

He couldn't believe it either. But there it was, all the same. He had no other choice but to take her home.

With a clenched jaw, Reid put on his hard shell and turned back to her. All he needed to do was stay professional from here on out. No more losing it and kissing her. He'd gone six years without sex. Surely he could resist a weekend with the most annoyingly attractive woman he'd ever met. "Let's go."

He placed a hand on her shoulder and directed her outside. She yanked and jerked from his touch, but he kept his hand placed where he could guide her. With his luck, she'd run the second he turned his back.

Gripping her arm, he swung open the truck door and motioned for her to get in. As soon as he did, Snowball flew past them and leapt into the seat, finding his place on the floorboard. He curled into a huge white fluff ball and tucked his nose into his paws.

Kirsten stood firm, her eyes narrowed. "You know, this must be illegal."

The look on her face bothered him even more. He didn't like the way her eyes slanted into a feline glare when she didn't get her way. No, he much preferred them wide and open, big and endearing. Sweet.

Not that he cared how she looked at him. It didn't matter. Not one bit.

"Nope, ma'am. Don't believe it is."

"You could at least undo these cuffs. You can't keep me in them all weekend. That's mean and inhuman and I know it's illegal. What's it called? Cruel and unusual punishment. Punishment, hah! I didn't even do anything wrong, you know. You—"

"Enough!" he growled. His ears rang from her complaints. Never had he met a woman with such a mouth. "Okay. Get in and I'll take them off. And don't bother with any escape ideas. Trust me, where we're headed, you'd be a fool to even try."

"And where is that?" she snapped.

"My ranch," he answered as she climbed in and he unclasped the cuffs. As soon as he did, she started to try and shove past him. He held her back with one hand as his body blocked the door. "Where there's nothing but endless fields filled with cattle. Then you can run all you want. You'll only get tired."

As they topped the only hill for probably miles on end, Reid's ranch came into view. Red barns and white fencing corralling cattle surrounded an expansive single-story home. A huge porch wrapped around it, and chickens pecked in the front yard.

"We're home," Reid announced as he shut off the engine.

Kirsten frowned. What about those words felt so good? So comfy? "No, *you're* home."

She waited, quite impatiently, for him to open the door and let her out. Reid came around, and released her.

The smell of country filled the air, sweet and fresh as a breeze, and tickled her nose. On the porch, a swing blew back and forth, causing a tap-tap like the back rhythm against the music of a clucking and mewing orchestra.

Snowball hopped out after her, brushing along her legs to settle at her sides. Kirsten smiled. No doubt he'd like it here.

So would she, under any other circumstances, with anyone else.

"Let's go." Reid led her up the front stairs and swung open the door. Snowball breezed past them and disappeared in a flash, more than likely off for a drink from the toilet. *Yuck.*

A low chuckle emitted from Reid, deep and sexy. Amusement gleamed in his eyes, alluring with the shine in their deep, dark depths. She could have shaken him for it, but she was too afraid of what would happen if she touched him.

Or he touched her. All over. Like he had when he'd searched her. His hands roaming up and down her legs, her waist, then her rear. Touching. Feeling. Driving her crazy.

She automatically tightened at the memory, muscles in her lower regions contracting with desire. She started to drip with longing as she stared at him, her lower regions wetting to have him.

Reid slammed the door shut with a bang and knocked her out of her treacherous thoughts. Needing to distract herself, she wandered from the foyer into the living room.

Its emptiness hit her. He had nothing, nada, save for a large-screen television, a couch and a lazy boy. Not a thing for decoration, no wall hangings, no knick-knacks, nothing but bare white walls.

"It's clean, at least," she murmured, more to herself than him.

"Yeah." He just shook his head, and stared at her.

"The fireplace is beautiful." She nodded toward the huge stone focal point of the room.

"Yeah."

"It would look great if there were some pictures or something, you know, on the mantle," she hinted.

"Yeah."

Okay, apparently he wasn't much for decorating. Typical man. But still, you'd think he'd have something. It all seemed kind of weird to her. "Is the whole house like this?"

"Yeah," he answered again, his voice hollow. "Pretty much."

"Oh."

"Hey, listen. I'm gonna fix us something to eat. You want to take a shower, get cleaned up or something? I can lend you some clothes."

Yeah, she thought as her eyes ran over his brawny body once more, *like they'd fit me*.

Still, she'd welcome a bath. Especially since she felt grimy as hell, not having cleaned up after her jog.

Who knew when she'd next get somewhere safe enough to have one? When she escaped, she'd now be running not only from Kurt, but also Reid, and the law.

Besides, it'd look good to Reid. He'd figure she was done trying to escape. Yeah, right.

With a falsely planted smile, Kirsten nodded her head. "Sure, if you don't mind. I know I must smell by now. I left in such a rush."

"Right," he grunted. "Follow me."

He took her down a hall, and swung open a door. Kirsten took in the surroundings, a plain room with a king size bed, and nothing else. "What's the deal?"

"This is my room. I figured I'll sleep on the couch, and you can have the bed. Private bathroom is through that door. I'll lay some clothes out for you."

"What about the other rooms? Surely there must be other rooms in a house this big."

"Yeah, I've got five bedrooms. They're all empty."

"Did you just move in or something?"

"No." He moved to the closet and began to rummage through a shelf full of clothes. He pulled out a humongous

Cowboys tee shirt and a pair of gray sweats. He tossed them on the bed and shrugged. "The pants have a drawstring so you can tighten them up."

"What about underwear?"

"Go without. Best I can do on short notice," he snapped and looked away.

Kirsten brushed past him into the bathroom.

"The—" He started after her.

She slammed the door right in his face.

Beyond tears, Kirsten leaned against it and fought the flood of emotions. Now was not the time to cry. She had to think. Keep her head straight. Keep Reid Walker out of it.

A shower would help. Cool her down a bit. Reid seemed to have a talent for heating her up. She stripped off her clothes and started the shower. When steam rolled out from above the curtain she adjusted the cold nozzle and stepped in.

After a day of driving and a three-hour traffic jam while stuck in sweaty workout clothes, the water rolling over her skin felt like heaven. She reached for the soap, but as she lifted the green bar she realized it was men's soap. The smell of cologne, of Reid, filled the air. She slipped her hand down her belly, to her folds. Her finger found her clit, rubbing it in a slow motion. Pleasure rippled through her body as she thought of Reid and his kiss. Of how glorious his skilled mouth would be on her sex . . .

She dropped the soap like it was poison. She needed to banish the man from her mind. She sucked in a deep breath and blew out, trying to collect herself. She would not masturbate to the scent and thought of Reid Walker.

She grabbed the bottle of innocent shampoo and used that like an all-over body wash.

She finished washing and glanced around. *Great*, she realized. *No conditioner*. Now her hair would be in a million knots. She wondered if the empty house even sported a comb. What was with this guy anyway? Eccentric, she supposed, or alone. Very alone.

She slung back the curtain and reached for a towel. Instead she found an empty rack. *Shit.*

A door by the sink looked like a linen closet. She'd just grab a towel and wipe up the mess on the floor when she was done.

Kirsten raced across the bathroom, creating puddles on the floor with every step. She flung open the closet, only to find it nearly empty. Except for a comb and a brand new bottle of conditioner.

Figures. She slammed the linen door shut.

What else could she do? Maybe snitch some clothes from the closet in the bedroom and dry off with them. She certainly wouldn't be calling Reid for help. No way. She squeezed her hair out into the sink, as best she could, and then tiptoed out into the bedroom, only to come face to face with the Sheriff, his hands full of crisp white towels.

He stared down at her dripping wet naked body, obviously not the least bit shy about getting his eyes full. His jaw dropped. His gaze swept up and down, and his eyes filled with clear desire.

His acute appraisal churned her. Heart racing, Kirsten did the only thing she could do. With a slap of her hand, she knocked his gaping mouth shut, grabbed a towel and made a mad dash for the bathroom. Once inside it, she whirled to slam the door. Instead, she slipped on the wet flooring and went down with a shriek.

"Are you all right?" Reid dashed into the bathroom, terrified by Kirsten's blood-curdling shriek. The sight of her sprawled on the floor, limbs spread, made his heart do flip-flops.

He hurried to her and dropped on one knee beside her. She struggled to get up, her efforts useless as he forced her back down.

"Hold on. Did you hit your head or anything?" Dang it, she'd really let loose a scream. She had to be hurt.

"No. I'm fine. Please, get off me." Her voice sounded soft and sweet, helpless.

It agonized him with worry. An urge to gather Kirsten in his arms flooded him, and he battled against it. If she were hurt, it wouldn't do to move her.

When he moved his hands toward her, she started to wiggle away. "Hold up. Let me check you out."

"No."

Despite her weak protest, he continued to check her head, searching it for bumps until she shoved him away.

"A gentleman would realize I had no clothes on and leave me be." Her sharp tone damn near knocked him flat.

Hell, if she could snap like that, then she couldn't be too injured. Just loud, which made sense, considering her big mouth.

How could such torrents of deafening noise come from such beautiful, lush lips? So soft, and full—the sweet color of strawberries. Damned kissable. He could just imagine them wrapped around his cock . . .

"Yeah, sorry, um . . ." He should back away, leave the bathroom, and do it now.

Except he couldn't.

He just kept staring down at her, drinking up the sight of her exposed body like a thirsty man stared at a glass of cool lemonade.

But Kirsten was hot, very hot. On fire, in fact, and he just couldn't stop looking any more than he could help bending down to kiss her.

He claimed her lips with his own as he pulled her close and wrapped his arms around her naked body. Every one of her exposed curves pressed against him, soft and supple.

Ah, to touch them, to taste them. To savor her like the sweet treat she was.

Desperate need raked through Reid, and his appraisal of her grew hotter, more demanding. Kirsten responded with fervor to his kissing, matching his nibbling and tongue flicking with her own. Surprised by her eagerness, his mouth melted into hers, more and more desperate to possess all of her.

She tasted so sweet, like rich fresh honey. Overcome, distantly his mind wondered what other parts of her might taste like.

He had to find out.

4

Sandpaper against silk, Reid's calloused fingers roamed the length of her body and then returned to her breasts. He massaged them in his hands, gently pulling at her nipples, then bent down to suckle on them. His tongue flicked against their hardness, his teeth lightly nipping at them before he suctioned them so hard it made her hips arch.

Kirsten cried out. She needed Reid like nothing she'd ever known before.

Damn it, she'd have him too.

Frenzied, she reached out and began to tear at his shirt, yanking at the fabric furiously. She ripped at the cotton, wanting to remove the clothing barrier he still wore between them. She jerked it over his head, impatient to discover the dark trail she'd been ogling for hours.

Rewarded at last, Kirsten cast aside his shirt and roamed his chest with both her eyes and her hands. The muscles under her fingertips, hard and sculpted, tickled her fingers with the tiny ebony curls. The black path only grew thicker farther down, and she followed its shadow, impatient for more. She wanted the prize at the end of it, the trophy. So excited she'd turned all thumbs, she fumbled the buttons and pulled at the pants, frantic to get into them. Reid's hands closed in around hers, moving them away to aid her in her efforts. He rose onto his knees, allowing her better access.

Tingles thundered between her thighs, anticipation heating in her lower body. She clenched her dampening sex, overcome by desire, and licked her lips, ready when his long thick cock popped out from his jeans. Rubbing her hands up and down its shaft, she wrapped her lips around him. She swallowed all of him. With her tongue and teeth, she grazed his cock's soft skin, relishing the feel of him deep in her throat. He began to thrust back and forth, slowly, as if he savored the very feel of her mouth.

It was everything she'd pictured all afternoon. No, better. Such length and bulk were not imaginable. More like incredulous.

She needed every succulent inch of it deep inside of her. Large. Filling. Now.

When he made his move under her, pulling her around on her knees so her pussy leaned in his face, Kirsten nearly cried out in eagerness. His light breath blew against her, torturing her pussy with the gentle caress. What would come, just the simple thought alone, drove her mad.

Still, when his tongue attacked her with sumptuous lapping, she cried out in delightful surprise.

Kirsten could hardly bear it. Back and forth, up and down, little circles and deep probing, his lavish attentions stunned her. Electric shocks coursed through her body. Every last lick was sheer torment, and absolute bliss. Rapture.

The bulk of him remained in her mouth and she continued to love it, moaning on it every time he hit the right spot.

On and on it went, them trading praises with their tongues, their mouths. Reid, hard and filled with need, moaned against her pussy. Soon he would loose it, and fill her mouth, but not before she.

Intense pleasure boiled in her, ready to run over. To hold back proved impossible. She needed the release. The gratification.

With a scream, she exploded. A million little convulsions pulsed through her, as if heaven and earth shook with her as her body released itself.

Simultaneously, Reid overflowed her mouth.

Kirsten collapsed on top of Reid, curling into his arms. Exhausted, she let him pick her up, completely oblivious until he plopped her on the bed. Then she saw the look in his determined dark eyes, and knew he wasn't done with her.

Reid couldn't be sure if he'd ever get enough, but he'd damned well try. Kirsten was the hottest little thing he'd ever tasted. The second he'd come, he'd hardened all over again.

He climbed overtop of her, and stretched her legs out before him. The sight of her spread pussy begged for his attentions. Rigid with his hunger for her, his shaft beat as if it had its own heart.

And mind.

Wetness glistened on her slit, juicy and ready. Kirsten didn't need any more coaxing. No, she needed him inside her.

He pulled her hips upward and drove into her with one full thrust. Heaven wrapped around him, like he floated in a million rose petals, their delicate and soft texture tightly woven around him.

Never had he known anything sweeter.

She moaned, and the sounds of her cries made him mad. He took her like an animal, hard and desperate, thrusting as fast as he could.

Rhythmic beats to match his own powered Kirsten's hips.

Again and again she arched to meet him. They clashed together in a fury, violent as a summer storm.

"More. Give me more." Her nails dug into his back and he raced to please her.

How could he not? Every time he looked at her, under him, all hot and sweaty, her smooth skin glistening and her body arched, he went crazy.

The bed rocked under them. Kirsten grabbed hold of the headboard. Braced, she lifted her body and plowed herself against him.

He wanted to come again so bad it hurt, but he'd wait. Nothing could satisfy him more than to see Kirsten shake and quiver under him. Only then could his pleasures be complete.

Determined, he grasped her firm little rear in his hands, cupping each cheek. Kneading them, he slowed his movements to tease her unmercifully. His pelvis rotated in small circles, diving in and out of her.

"Reid," she groaned.

Anticipation gripped him as he watched and waited for mercy.

Finally the time came. Licking his lips, he increased his pace again, and Kirsten screamed out in pleasure. Her body thrashed beneath him, her womanhood tightening around him. Everything around Reid went black as he finished inside of her, so fulfilled he collapsed.

5

Kirsten snuggled deeper inside the strength of Reid's arms, and nuzzled against his chest. Faint scents of musky cologne and sweat intermingled with unadulterated country crispness, the smell of a man—the smell of natural. She inhaled deeply, then rolled over. His body curled against hers, fitted to her curves like painted-on jeans.

Her mind wrestled to free itself from its exhausted state, consciousness dawning as the setting sun disappeared in the darkening sky.

Like the snap of a whip, reality hit Kirsten. *Oh Lord.*

She bolted upright, clutching the blankets to her naked body as she tore away from the sheriff's embrace. Oh God, she'd slept with him. Her enemy. The man who'd arrested her . . . and who turned her on like no other. The past hour with him had been the most tantalizing, delicious, explosive experience of her whole life.

My God, what could she have been thinking?

Reid moaned and sat on the edge of the bed. His thick fingers ran through his dark hair and he shook his head. "Shit."

Her eyes followed the sight of his firm rear as he stood up, and walked into the bathroom. The hiss of the shower slashed through the silence.

Shit? What in the hell did that mean? What in the hell should she do? *Damn. Damn. Damn.* She'd never slept with a stranger before. Especially not one who so openly admitted he disliked her.

What Reid Walker thought shouldn't matter a speck to her. But at that very moment it did, and a whole hell of a lot.

He already thought her a thief and a liar. Could she add slut to the list? Had she just added a nail into the coffin of contempt he felt toward her?

If she had a choice, if she were anywhere else, and under any other circumstance, she would bolt from his room and his house so fast she'd have left a smoke trail. But this time flying off the handle wasn't a choice.

With a few deep breaths Kirsten reminded herself to stay calm. *Shit* could mean lots of things. Anything. And she shouldn't give a damn. It had just been sex. Nothing more.

The shirt he'd given her to wear lay amidst the rumpled blankets. She plucked it out and tossed it over her head. It reached almost to her knees, so thankfully she didn't need to bother with the jogging pants.

Stickiness dripped down her legs from both their passions, a distinct reminder of what they'd just done. She needed to wash again, and she needed to know what to make of the situation. Barefoot, Kirsten padded her way to the bathroom and leaned in the open doorway.

"Kirsten?" His voice sounded gruff and bothered.

"Yeah."

"Hey."

"Hey," she mumbled in reply, quite unsure of what else to say.

The water stopped and he flung aside the curtain. Water

dripped down his naked body and trailed across rippled muscles, glistening on his deep tan skin. Little droplets fell from his nose, and he shook his head.

The effect shook Kirsten with desire, and she swore she'd have to wipe away the drool soon if he didn't dry off and get dressed.

"Listen, I—" His deep eyes studied her for a moment as he ran his hand through his wet hair. "Kirsten. Are you okay? With this, I mean?"

"Are you?"

He tossed a towel down on the floor and crossed the distance between them as he spoke. "You're the most beautiful creature I've ever set eyes on. I want you like hell, even now after I've had you. But I don't want to overstep my bounds."

The space between them closed, Reid looked down at her for an answer. Desire choked her from him standing naked in front of her.

In her mind, she replayed his question a million times in two seconds. But all along she knew the answer. She wanted Reid, and she didn't feel the least bit sorry for it.

Truth be told, if it weren't for her crazy situation, she'd be letting herself fall head over heels for the man. He was nothing short of perfect. Exactly what she wanted in a man.

But her circumstances were something she could not deny. She couldn't love Reid. It just wasn't probable.

She could enjoy him though, and in the process she'd be making her escape a little easier. Surely he'd trust her as a lover, and his watch wouldn't be so careful. Maybe he'd even decide to let her go.

A fling with Reid Walker could only stand to benefit her, so long as she remembered to keep her heart out of the deal. Her top priority was getting on the road and home to Alabama, where Kurt couldn't find her. If she had to steal and cheat to get there, then so be it. At least she'd be alive.

"Okay with it? Reid, I'm great with it, so long as you are," she purred.

"Really?" Momentary confusion crossed his face, his eyebrows slightly raised, his forehead wrinkled. But when she dazzled him with a deliberate smile, the questions vanished into acceptance.

"Yeah, let's face it. We've been ogling each other since the moment we met. If we're stuck together all weekend, why not have a little fun?" She reached up and wrapped her arms around his neck. "And if you're going to see me off to prison, this is my last chance to have a man. Might as well take it."

"Vixen," he growled and lifted her into his arms. Demanding lips crushed her mouth as he carried her into the shower and peeled away her tee shirt. Hot water poured over them as they kissed, daring and teasing each other with their tongues. Reid grabbed the soap and slid it to her body, washing every inch of her with meticulous movements. Bubbles formed over her hardened nipples as he pampered her breasts.

He slid the trail of suds lower, slipping the soap between her private regions, washing away the sticky remains of their last encounter. Then he ran the bar of soap slowly down her backside, slipping between her cheeks as he kneaded them in his hands.

Kirsten gasped, and he chuckled. "What's the matter, sugar? Shocking?"

"Yes."

"You don't know the half of it yet," he whispered in her ear. "But you'll learn, naughty girl."

He grabbed the removable showerhead, using the massage-spray setting to wash her clean. Merciless, Reid held the high-pressure water current to power away the lather in her most tender of spots, and she clenched against the force of it.

Heat burned her lower regions, desire heating from her very core. Even her thighs quivered as passion seized her, turning her nipples hard and her breasts heavy.

Unable to stand it any longer, she pushed the nozzle away. "My turn."

"No." The snap couldn't be mistaken for anything but a command. "I'm already clean. I want you. Now."

He grabbed her mouth with his, shutting up her protests with his own tongue-lashing. Her lips melted into his.

"Bend over." Unwavering hands guided her around, and she bowed to his wishes. His hardened cock slipped into her, and she moaned, bracing herself against the tile walls. He lifted her up by her hips as he moved to and fro, slowly pulling himself all the way out before diving deep into her again.

She propped her leg on the tub's ledge and spread her legs farther apart for him, desperate for more. She wanted him deeper. Faster. Harder.

His left hand reached around and pinched her nipples. Powerful fingertips rubbed back and forth against the sensitive buds until even they felt ready to explode.

Forces built in Kirsten with each of his savored, slow movements, knotting in her stomach, ready to be released. Reid reached down, found her clit, and gave it the same treatment as her nipples. A wave crashed over Kirsten and she gave herself up to the orgasm vibrating through her with a scream of pleasure.

Reid's own body hardened and shook deep inside her.

With a gentle kiss to her back, he let her go. "Damn, that was great. You hungry?"

Kirsten broke out in a laugh. Leave it to a man to concern himself with his stomach two seconds after a world-shattering orgasm. "Starved. You cooking?"

"Yup," he winked and scooped her up in a towel, carrying her into the bedroom as he made her crazy with more kisses. He deposited her on the bed with a flop. "Get dressed and meet me in the kitchen."

* * *

Reid popped the second Hungry Man in the microwave and pushed the automatic frozen entrée button. A yellow glow lit up the shadowy kitchen as he went about fixing their places at the breakfast nook. Just on a whim, he pulled out some candles and two wine glasses. Kirsten was right—why not have a little fun?

Hell, maybe she wasn't the best of people. A little annoying, and a lot dishonest, but she was fun. And hot. Fact of the matter was, he'd been alone so long he just plain didn't care.

He wanted her. Monday he'd worry about the rest.

He flicked a match and lit the candles. A beep from the microwave alerted him to the finished dinner and he turned to grab it. Kirsten stood in the doorway, her tiny frame swallowed up by his baggy shirt and jogging pants. *Cute*, he thought. Man, did she look sweet and innocent.

Boy was it an act.

"Dinner is served, madam." He seated her on a barstool and held out a bottle of wine. "Wine?"

"Oh, no thank you. I don't drink."

He sat aside the bottle and served the dinner. "Why? Any reason?"

"I had an accident, drinking and driving. The courts made me go to Alcoholics Anonymous." She pushed tiny bits of salisbury steak around with her fork, her eyes downcast. "But I'd have gone even if the judge hadn't made me. I hit a mother and an innocent child. I could have killed them. I didn't, but I could have. Since then, I've sworn I'd never touch the stuff, and I haven't."

Reid nodded, suddenly able to appreciate a side of her he'd never seen. Since his Ma and Pa were killed, he'd blamed their death on every reckless driver he came across. But maybe the other driver wasn't always as cold and heartless as Tommy Burkins. Maybe some were as sorry and vulnerable as Kirsten looked right now.

Reid narrowed his eyes at the sudden possibility. "You really weren't driving reckless when you came into town today, were you?"

"No. I told you, the dog ran out in front of me." She took a spoonful of mashed potatoes, then directed the silverware at him. "And—"

"Don't push it, sugar."

She rolled her eyes at him, and smacked her lips. "Okay then. Great food."

"Nothing beats a TV dinner."

Reid lifted his fork, the whole steak dangling from it. For a moment he prepared to bite off a hearty chunk, then he realized his manners. Had it really been that long since he'd eaten with a woman?

He slapped the meat back onto his plate and proceeded to cut it up into little bits.

"You know, I've never had one before." Wonderment traced the naïve tone to Kirsten's voice.

Reid raised his eyebrows. "Never?"

Hell, he'd eaten them nonstop since his Ma had died. Before then, he'd never had anything but home cooked. Then he'd made the mistake of marrying Lisa. She'd never cooked, just ran around on him, before she took everything he had. He'd have been better off alone all along.

But being alone could get lonely. Very lonely.

"Nope. Mama didn't believe in anything that came from a box and a wrapper." Kirsten smiled, her face lit with the fondness of a memory. The candle flames danced around her, casting shadows on her smooth skin. He reached out and stroked her cheek, sandpaper against silk.

Who knew little Miss California had a little country in her? He'd have sworn she was a city slicker to the bone. What a nice surprise. Never in a million years would he have guessed he'd be able to relate to her on anything.

Reid chuckled lightly at the thought of it. "So did my Ma. She's rolling over in her grave seeing me eat all these microwave meals."

"I miss home cooking, you know." Kirsten shook her head. "With Kurt, it was one fancy restaurant after the next. But believe you me—their prices are highway robbery. This steak beats any of them, hands down."

"I have an idea. How about tomorrow you cook and we can have a real candlelight dinner?"

"You mean, how about *we* cook?"

"Deal." He winked at her. "You cook and I'll set the table."

"Brat," she snapped in a playful tone. "Speaking of which, where's Snowball?"

"I fed him and put him out before I started dinner. I do believe he's made a new friend. I've got a border collie named Sissy that stays outside and sleeps in the barn. She was my Pa's. Snowball will be fine out there with her, I'm sure."

"Oh, great. He'll enjoy the fresh air . . . probably the chickens too." Kirsten joked.

"Better not." False seriousness coated his voice, but then they both broke into a smile.

Reid finished the last of his dinner, and so did Kirsten. He was surprised to see she ate it all. For a woman of her small size, she had a healthy appetite.

In more ways than one, he thought with a wicked grin. She caught his gaze and returned his attention with a look of appraisal. Desire veiled her green eyes, her lush lower lip curled in a promise of ecstasy.

For a moment they sat and ogled each other. The need between them hung heavy in the air like thick clouds. He couldn't breathe he wanted her so much, so bad, all the time.

Reid cleared his throat. "Let's step outside. I want to have a smoke."

"Sure." She wrinkled her brows and her eyes shot to a glass ashtray on the counter. "You don't smoke in here?"

He did, but right now he wouldn't. Apparently, from the curious look on her face, she'd never been around anyone with manners. "I do, but not when there's a lady around. Just as rude as wearing your hat inside, or your boots in the bedroom."

She nodded as she stood. "I like that. Your Mama raised you right."

"We can sit on the porch and look at the stars. Come on." He grabbed a throw blanket from the closet in case Kirsten got cold. In such wide-open land a gentle breeze could tickle the skin with chills in the dead of night, even though the air itself was dry and hot. No doubt it was still plenty warm, but she might find it a touch cool.

He folded the blanket over his arm. This way, if she did, they'd have something to lie on while he heated her up.

He latched his arm in Kirsten's, the closeness jolting him with a craving to pull her closer against his body, so tight they meshed together as one. With a hard swallow, he did his best to force away the idea for now and led Kirsten out through the sliding glass doors of his empty dining room.

"So . . ." Curiosity laced Kirsten's voice. "The whole house is pretty much the same, huh? Five bedrooms, this big dining room, a country kitchen, a living room the size of a house, all empty. Any particular reason why, or do you just have a strong aversion to decorating?"

Reid stepped onto the wooden decking, and tossed aside the blanket onto a chair. He pulled out a cigarette, lit it, and pulled a long draw before he answered her. "I came home one day, and everything was gone. Every speck of it. Ex-wife took it and ran off with some city slicker."

He expected talking about Lisa to bother him, as it once had. But it didn't. It was just something that happened, done and over with now, a piece of his history. Nothing more.

"And you didn't try to get it back?"

"I didn't want it back any more than I wanted her back."

Reid grunted the truth. "Ahhh, I made Lisa's life hell, moving her back out here. She always hated this town. Should've never married her in the first place."

"So why did you?"

"High school sweetheart." Reid drew another draw of his smoke and turned to lean his back against the porch rail. "We both went away to college, and right after I graduated, my parents were killed. I came home for a little while and I just couldn't go back. My Dad had been sheriff here, and the town offered me the job. I took it and asked Lisa to marry me. I guess I missed having family and figured I could just make one. We moved out here to the ranch and realized real quick just how *not* meant to be we were."

Kirsten nodded in understanding. She'd found the rocking chair and curled up in it. The blanket wrapped around her feet, she looked right at home. Like she belonged there.

He wished she did. If he woke up with someone like her the rest of his life, he'd be one happy man.

6

"Some things are never meant to be. I guess I knew that with Kurt as well, but a little part of me always refused to believe it. It's like when you buy something new, you're so sure you'll love it. But when you get it home, you don't. It turns out to be nothing but a big mistake, but damned if you can admit it." Kirsten sighed and looked to him for understanding. Instead she found hard eyes, devoid of even an ounce of sympathy. "Reid, can't you at least try? Hear me out, please. This business with Kurt could ruin my life—or end it. I should have opened my eyes a little sooner . . . but I didn't. So I'm a fool, but you must see—"

"Enough," Reid growled, flicking aside his cigarette. He straightened, and devoured the distance between them. "Don't you ever know when to shut up? I told you I don't want to hear it."

Before she could protest, he snatched the arms of her chair and ceased her gentle rocking with an abrupt halt. Anger contorted his features as he leaned over her. So close his breath tickled her nose, like a whisper of warning.

A shiver coursed through her, not from fear, but want. The ruggedness of his demeanor radiated fury and passion and heated her with desire. Uncontrollable ragged breaths escaped her, and her nipples hardened into two sensitive buds.

His calloused fingers caressed her jaw then gripped it firmly. Dark eyes, unforgiving and resolute, imprisoned her gaze. "You're ruining a perfectly good night with lies. And I'm just not up for them."

"Well, too bad. You have to hear this. I'm not shutting up until you do." Kirsten gulped, unable to choke back the need clenching her. Her lower lip shook with irritation, both at him and herself. She would not let him win like this. If he didn't hear her out now, he never would. "I will keep you up all night if I have to—" Her attempt at coolness failed, and a thick husky tone dripped from her words. All too aware of the fact that her threat sounded much more like an invitation, she snapped her mouth shut.

But Reid had already accepted. Primal hunger hung between them, so thick a knife could cut it. One quick look at the fire in his eyes, and she knew he intended to ravish her, like the dominant man he was.

She waited, ready for the taking. A million tiny pinpricks enflamed her, and her skin prickled. Her body clenched and creamed with need. A thousand seconds passed within one, every moment seeming like forever.

Just as she decided to take matters into her own hands, he pounced on her. His mouth crushed hers, hard and demanding. Devouring her with his lips, he tangled his hands in her hair and pulled her head back.

She challenged him with her own tongue, each flick a dare for him to take her. Deft hands tore away her clothes in a flash, stripping her bare.

Grabbing the blanket, he spread it on the deck, then lifted her within the strength of his arms and deposited her.

A million stars twinkled in the black sky, and crickets chirped a symphony. Heaven floated around them and teased them with the notion of an ecstasy so pure, so primal it almost couldn't be real.

Reid cast aside his shirt, revealing his sculpted chest. She reached up and ran her fingers through the tiny hairs, relishing in the feel of his tight muscles. With a snap of his Levi's, his long cock thrust out, hard and ready. He pulled apart her legs, and nudged himself against her. Positioned to enter, he paused, and Kirsten grabbed at his rear to drive him into her.

He resisted, driving her mad. The tip of his manhood rested against her pussy, and she longed to feel it inside of her. The need tormented her. She could hardly bear it. "Please, Reid."

"No. I want to have some fun."

"This is torture, "she panted.

"Exactly." Amusement laced the growl of his voice as he spread apart her legs and rested them on his shoulders. With his thumb, he massaged her clit in tiny circles. She stiffened, jolts of acute pleasure shocking through her as he alternated between hard and light pressure.

Just when she thought she'd nearly lose it, he began to use his fingers as well. He explored her folds, traced the length of her slit then dived deep inside her. She arched her back as his thick finger caressed her inner depths.

"Reid, I cannot take any more of this exploration." She scooted back, surprised when he allowed her to escape him. No sooner than she freed herself of his roving hands, she regretted it.

Eyes narrowed, Reid shook his head. "Don't think you'll get away that easily."

With a devilish smile, he reached behind him and pulled out his cuffs.

"Don't you dare," she stared in disbelief, but didn't move an inch. The thought of it was too naughty, too wicked—and oh, ever so thrilling. On all fours, he crept over her. She choked on her protests, too enthralled with the prospect to pretend to be shy about it.

The handcuffs locked around her wrists, the cold metal bolting her to a slat in the deck railings. There would be no more fleeing.

"Now, back to work." Reid grasped her legs, and returned them to his shoulders.

Her arms stretched above her head, her pussy spread out before him, Kirsten had never felt more on fire. Two fingers plunged into her, then three. With a cry, her body bowed to his wishes, falling in sync with the torturous playfulness.

"Tell me you're mine," Reid demanded, and pressed deeper inside her.

"Reid, please," she gasped. Intense pleasure choked away any ability to think rationally, much less protest. Her body was burning, her mind mush. With every passing second, she grew wetter, her nipples harder, to the point where she could hardly bear it. She needed him, now, inside of her. She could wait no longer for satisfaction. "Please."

He withdrew his fingers, and swatted her rear. The sharp sting of it branded her, creating an electric shock through her. Her pussy clenched against the abandonment, needing to be filled with him.

"I'm yours, Reid, I'm yours. Please."

"I'm not so sure you mean that." He yanked off his jeans and crawled over top of her. "But I'm going to make sure you do."

With both hands, he gathered her breasts and pushed them together. He buried his face in them, and grabbed her nipples with his teeth. Lightly, he nipped and pulled at them, then formed a vacuum over them, as if to suck them dry. Appraising them, even as he dropped away his hands, he reached down to grab her rear. His fingers slipped between her cheeks and held her round curves in a tight grasp.

Through his mouthful of breast, Reid made sure Kirsten knew what he wanted. "Say it again. Over and over again, until I'm sure of it."

He might explode any minute, but there wouldn't be a speck of enjoyment to it. Not if he didn't get what he truly wanted. Using Kirsten's body wasn't enough. She was more than legs and tits, and he wanted all of her.

"I'm yours, Reid. I've been yours since the moment I set eyes on you. Only your body can own mine like this." The sweet and husky tone to her voice sounded believable, but he wasn't sure.

Lies. Kirsten was full of them and he didn't want to hear it, save that she would be his. That she could lie about all she wanted. At least then he could make believe the nasty truth didn't lie in wait, ready to strike.

Kirsten was his prisoner, a car thief, and nothing but trouble. Not a love prospect. The thought alone was preposterous. But oh, how he wanted to pretend just that, and tonight he would. He'd worry about tomorrow, tomorrow.

He swatted her rear again, determined to drive her so crazy she had to give him her all. She moaned, her body stiff with need in his arms. "Reid, I'm yours. I'm yours."

In a fury, he trailed his mouth down across her belly. His tongue and lips devoured her, as if he could consume her. Fulfill himself from just the taste of her. He was a hungry man, starved in fact. Kirsten Montgomery resembled a sweet morsel of chocolate, and he could eat her a million times and never grow sick of her deliciousness.

Making his way to her lower regions, he spread her open and dived in. With every lick and stroke of his tongue, his cock grew harder and more needy. He could wait no more. It was time to make Kirsten his.

He thrust inside her, enveloped by the bittersweet softness of her tight hole. He could have come right then, but he hung on, determined to savor her. With slow strokes, he built the pleasure between them, making sure Kirsten got every inch of what he had to give. She writhed and whimpered beneath him, the ecstasy written clear on her face.

If she didn't come soon, he would surely explode. He could hold back no longer. With stealthy movements inside of her, he explored her limits and tested his own. He circled hard and fast, and she screamed out. Her nails dug into his back, and tore through his skin as she arched and shook.

When her cries ceased, he buried himself deep inside her, and gave himself up to the rapture.

7

Brilliant streaks of yellow cut through the pure blue sky as the sun awoke and reached out its arms to greet the world to a new day. Crisp morning air, laced with fresh dew, tickled at Reid's nose and wrestled him from his slumber.

Kirsten lay entangled in his arms, her flaxen hair sprawled in his face and her every curve pressed against him. The swell of her bare breasts squashed against his own rock-hard chest tormented him. Everything about her was so soft, lush, tantalizing. In immediate response, his cock grew stiff as a steel rod, ready to take her.

As tempting as that was, he couldn't. Not right now. The animals needed feed, and he had to have some space. He needed to think, and he couldn't do that here—not around her. Gently he lifted her arms from him and wiggled away, careful not to wake her.

Reid threw on his dirty jeans and headed out to the barn. Snowball and Sissy greeted him with happy yaps. They danced around his legs, almost causing him to trip twice.

They were like two peas in a pod, strangers become best

friends overnight. It should be the same for him and Kirsten. With the way they made love . . .

Wait.

Love? With the way they fucked like rabbits—

Damn it, that wasn't it at all and it didn't take a genius to figure it out. Being around her was eating him alive. God, he was such a fool! How could he be falling for a liar, a thief?

It bugged him like hell to think of the kind of person she was—everything he stood against, she stood for. He upheld the law, and she'd broken it. He despised reckless drivers, and she'd stolen a car. He had no business feeling so . . . well . . . *much*. Not about someone like her.

He smashed into the barn. The bang of the door echoed in his ears, and made him jump.

He slammed his eyes shut, and gritted his jaw as he made himself stop in his tracks before he lost it. How he wanted to kick something. The urge pulsed through him hard, like thunder in his heart, and he barely held back. She was trouble; nothing but an absolute nuisance, and the very last thing he needed.

She'd cut right into his peaceful life, and tossed everything upside down. Damn it, he liked his house empty. His life was good—quiet, serene, calm. All Kirsten did was muck it up with senseless noise.

Desperate for composure, he squared his shoulders and steeled himself against thoughts of her. The horses and cattle needed his attention.

He shoved the lid off a barrel and began scooping the grain into a bucket, enjoying the repetition. Weekends were usually his favorite time, when Skip had time off and he handled the ranch himself. Sometimes he even thought he'd quit his job as sheriff and concentrate on building up the ranch. Right now, the few studs he raised kept the ranch going, and nothing more. With a little extra input the place could really prosper.

What did he need extra money for though? He had no family to care for, no kids or wife to support. No. Better he spent his time protecting others from the kind of loss that had ruined his life.

He dumped the feed into the trowels and ran his hand through his hair. Nothing felt the same with Kirsten on his mind. Everything suddenly seemed so very empty, meaningless.

But it wasn't. No. He wasn't missing anything in his life. Things had been fine before she came, and they would be great when she was gone.

He couldn't wait til Monday.

The sweet melody of birds chirped through the air, their song the sweetest of alarm clocks. Groggy, Kirsten tossed over and moaned. She tried to snuggle deeper, and her nose met wooden planks.

This wasn't her bed. She snapped upright, flooded by memories of the previous night. Visions of ecstasy danced in her head, and her body responded immediately. Desire tickled at her, and she looked around for Reid.

Disappointment followed. Where had he gone? She ran a hand through her hair and encountered snarls. Lord, she'd probably scared him away. Another shower definitely couldn't hurt. This time she'd use the conditioner and maybe, if she were lucky, Reid might meet her in there.

She stood, stretched her naked body and reached to gather the blanket. The handcuffs fell out as she lifted it, and she snatched them up. The cold metal burned reality into her. Last night had been her perfect chance. She could have easily handcuffed him in his sleep, stolen the Blazer and run. Instead, she'd cuddled in his arms and slept like a baby. What had she been thinking? Monday she'd be in jail, or worse, if Kurt found her.

Well, tonight she wouldn't make the same mistake. This time she'd be ready. And Reid wouldn't be getting these handcuffs back. She balled them up into her clothes and strode inside.

The telephone caught her eye as she passed through the kitchen. Did she dare? Maybe, just maybe, it wasn't too late to reason with Kurt. If she handled it right, perhaps he'd opt to leave her alone and forget the whole thing.

Somehow she doubted it, but anything was worth a shot at this point. Worse come to worse, she'd be in no stickier of a situation.

On the other hand, if she could get him to drop the charges and leave her be, then she'd be free—in more ways than one. Reid would have to believe her. Then maybe . . .

No.

Before she could change her mind, she stomped from the room, off to the shower.

Every time she caught a whiff of the soap—its smell of a man, of Reid, of yesterday—it conjured memories of their shower together. Of the way he'd washed her down, paying special attention to all those special areas. The shower sprayer he'd all but tortured her with. Then the way she'd come, so glorious, so explosive.

She cranked the cold nozzle, but not even the icy water could cool her down from thoughts of Reid. Never had anyone heated her as he did.

Or invaded her mind so furiously.

Even after they stayed up past midnight last night, talking and cuddling, she hadn't been able to sleep. Thoughts of him had kept her from drifting off, and awakened her through the night.

Reid was a feeling she couldn't shake—and truthfully, didn't want to. The conditioner massaged through her hair; Kirsten turned the warm water back up and rinsed off.

She knew what she needed to do. Determined, she all but jumped from the shower, and dried off. Towel wrapped around her and tucked in, she made her way to the phone and dialed Kurt's cell number before she could stop herself.

"Hello?"

"Hello." Saccharine sweet sarcasm traced her voice. "We need to talk, Kurt."

"Kirsten, baby. What a pleasant surprise."

"Don't baby me, Kurt. Why are you doing this to me?"

"Doing what, baby?" Cool and calm, his voice ate at her nerves. She could just imagine the cocky smile on his face, the confidence in his icy eyes. How she wished it were possible to reach through the phone and give him the slap he deserved.

"You know what! I don't want to be with you any more, Kurt. I'm sorry, but you have to let me go."

"You know I can't do that, baby."

"You can, Kurt. Please. Just leave me be, and I'll leave you be. We can forget each other ever existed. It's just that easy."

She hated begging. It made her feel like mouse droppings on the floor. But she had no choice. If it took her on her knees to get him to quit, then she'd do it. She just wanted her life back.

"Kirsten, Kirsten. You just don't understand. I'm not letting you go. Not ever." A hard edge coated his voice, and sliced right through her.

"Kurt, I swear to you, I won't tell anyone what I know. I'll just disappear. After all those years, you owe me this."

"Kirsten, you were paid quite well, I believe. But a pimp never lets his whore go, you know that. I'm on my way right now. Sit tight, and I'll be there in no time."

Try as she might, there wasn't any holding her rage back. Her calm snapped in two, and twisted her in knots. "How dare you? You . . . you . . ."

"Cat got your tongue?"

"You lousy bastard! If you think I'm coming back home with you, I'm not. I hate you. I have for years. You'll never get me back, despite your money and your connections. No amount of trickery is going to get me back to California."

A sinister chuckle echoed through the phone. "Now *that* you are absolutely right about. I never said I wanted you back. Once you leave me, you're gone forever."

Eyes narrowed, Reid stood in the doorway of the kitchen watching Kirsten. The one-sided conversation he'd just overheard rang in his ears and beat through his mind.

Kirsten dropped the phone as if it were on fire. Her towel fell along with it, exposing her beautiful curves, still wet and glistening. Wincing, he stood paralyzed as she buried her face in her hands and crumpled to the floor.

The painful sound of sobs filled the room, her heartache reverberating off the walls to punch him in the chest.

My God. Could she have been telling the truth all this time? Was it even possible? He no longer knew what to believe, to think. But he knew seeing her like this cut him into pieces. The unbearable sight of it tore into him, yet he didn't have a clue what to do.

The phone still dangled, the cord hung over the counter, straining to remain plugged into the jack. He crossed the room, and stepped over Kirsten to grab it. "Hello?"

Silence answered him, but someone remained on the line. He could hear the resonance from their phone. Even the best cell still had an echo.

"Hello? Damn it, answer me! Hello?"

Click.

The line went dead, and he banged it back on the hook. "Shit. Kirsten?"

What should he do? Damn it, she looked so tiny and helpless. He knelt down at her side, unsure as hell how to handle a crying woman. "Hey, hon."

Cradled in his arms, her tears soaked his chest. He held her tight, desperately trying to think of something smart to say, but his tongue tied up. So he just cuddled her until her sobs slowed.

"Oh, God." She pushed away from him, and lunged for her towel. He let her go, almost thankful to be freed. Comforting a woman wasn't his thing. Holding her just made him feel downright helpless. He didn't know how to fix the problem, but he should, and damn it, he wanted to.

"What was that all about?" He needed to know whatever had her so upset. Strong doubts began to overfill him as he thought of the story she'd told him at least a hundred times.

She stashed away a few remaining tears as she covered up. "How much did you hear?"

"Not enough."

"Hah, you mean not enough to believe anything I say, still?" Jade green eyes narrowed at him, golden flecks lighting them afire. "Please, I see the doubt written all over your face." He started to reach for her, but she jerked away. "No, Reid."

She smacked his hand away, and he let it fall. What had he done? For once, he'd been trying to listen to her. He wanted to hear her side of things. Yet she looked madder than hell.

Her eyes burned into his, and her wet hair hung in mats around her face. Dampness still coated her reddened cheeks, which tensed and distorted in a furious slant. Almost the look of a madwoman: flamed with passion. Wild. Untamed.

Primal urges pulsed into him, and he found himself conjuring up more than one way he could savor such feral spirit.

If he wanted, he could take her right now.

But he couldn't. Not like this. Somehow, it didn't feel the same. Not after he'd seen her cry.

Her tears attested to the truth. He was the biggest, most stubborn jerk in existence. "I—"

"Don't bother, Reid." She swung her back to him, a crack in the towel baring just a hint of her creamy white skin. The uncontrollable urge to pull her close and feel her soft body against his pulsed through him. Immediately, he hardened.

Reid bit down hard on his lip, determined. It would be so easy to coax her out of her anger, and put the heat in her to good use. It would also be wrong.

Before it had just been about sex. She'd been his prisoner, a liar and a thief. Someone he could never like.

A lot had changed.

8

Kirsten could stand Reid's presence no longer. Head hung, she started to back away. Embarrassment burned her cheeks as tears slipped down them, scalding wet trails against the heat of her anger.

She glared at Reid's concerned face. His deep brows frowned down, furrowing creases across his forehead. The shadowy look, hard and sketched with worry, just plain pissed her off.

She didn't need his pity.

Or him.

Not if he didn't believe her. With a whirl she fled the kitchen, holding a tight grip to her towel as she ran. The sound of Reid's boots pursued her, and she picked up the pace.

"Kirsten, wait! You have to talk to me, please."

Her wet feet slipped and skidded across the wooden floor, and she fought to keep herself upright. If she were to fall, there wasn't any doubt as to what would happen.

Her towel would drop. Reid would rush to her side. And they'd be going at it like animals again.

All else would be forgotten, except the searing passion between them. The way he commanded her body to follow his lead was an infuriating magic.

If she were to stop, she simply wouldn't be able to resist. "No" meant nothing; not to her. Not to him. It was naught but a damned word, an empty one, as meaningless to their bodies as where they did it.

Even now she could just imagine him slamming her against the hall's paneled wall, her buttocks cupped in his hands as he took her away to a place so sweet . . .

This time she couldn't let that happen.

There was entirely too much at risk. Her pride. Her life.

"Kirsten, damn it. Wait a sec, hon," the soft plead to Reid's voice beseeched her to stop; so gentle, yet gruff, needy. False.

Kirsten moved faster. "Leave me alone, Reid."

All she wanted was to be free of his presence, yet with every step, he got closer instead of farther. The never-ending hall just went on and on, as if it had suddenly grown longer in an effort to stall her.

"Not until you talk to me."

Reid was ready to hear out her story? Hah! *Hah!* It took crying to get him to decide to listen up?

Well, it was too little, too late. Kurt—he'd been dead serious. She had no doubt of that. Soon he'd show—when they were sleeping, when they least expected it—and he'd kill her dead.

Damned if she'd sit around and patiently wait for it.

Before he could make another protest she slammed the bedroom door in Reid's face. Its crash reverberated off the walls as she quickly snapped the lock.

She dropped the towel to the floor and set about digging through his closet for clean clothes.

"Kirsten!" Bellows shook the room, and his fists banged at the door. But she didn't care. Reid could go to hell.

Eventually, his protests dwindled, then disappeared altogether. The quiet expanded around her, it echoed from the walls, it reverberated off her very soul. She slipped on some sweatpants, then a baggy tee shirt, all the while sure Reid would come to the door again.

But he didn't.

Pacing, Kirsten prowled the room like a caged animal. What had she been thinking anyway? Calling Kurt like that! As if he would care. As if it would make some sort of difference to Reid.

Oh, but it had. He'd quite come around, all ready to hear her out. Until she told him, and then he'd simply accuse her of lying again. Why should what he thought even matter?

She halted in her tracks, her feet nearly skidding to a stop on the oak floor.

It didn't. No way.

Her fingers ran through her damp, knotted hair, and she sat down on the edge of the bed to work them out.

She'd enjoyed his body and the passion between them. But now it was done.

Right?

A huge snarl caught in her fingers, and try as she might, it wouldn't tug out. It remained stuck, just like Reid did in her mind.

My God. Could it be? Could she really be falling in love with him? After two days? No. But she did like him. Too much.

All the more reason for her to leave right away, before it was too late. Reid had stolen a little piece of her that she might never get back. A part of her heart would always remember him.

But she was alive, and planned to stay that way. If she didn't go soon, the chance might never come.

The first second she could, she would take to those fields. Even if she wandered through them for days, at least Kurt wouldn't find her.

Hungry or tired, thirsty or petrified, she didn't care. At least she'd still be breathing.

* * *

Damn it. Reid stared at the shut door in disbelief and leaned back against the paneled wall.

The little wildcat had slammed the door in his face. Just run away from him and banged a heavy oak door right in his face, nearly smashing his nose.

What had he done so terrible to deserve that? He'd never known anyone to shut him out like that.

Not true. With a pang, he remembered Lisa, and the way she'd turned her back on him. A million times.

Everything in him fought against the urge to bust through the barrier between them. Just kick it flat, and make Kirsten continue the conversation she'd cut all too short. Instead, he crashed into the kitchen and prowled its expanse.

What could he do? What did it even matter?

He didn't know Kirsten, not at all. Hell, they'd only met yesterday. So they'd had some hot sex together. So what?

It doesn't matter, he swore to himself. *You're just imagining it.* What he needed was a distraction.

Food.

He ceased his pacing and opened the freezer. A mist of icy air gusted out and faded away, revealing row after row of Hungry Man frozen meals.

Silent, he stood, unconsciously counting them. Two. Four. Seven. Twenty-three? Nineteen Salisbury steaks? Four fried chickens?

My God. What was wrong with him? Years of loneliness sank in around him as he traced his fingers through the frost on the boxes that had stapled his life for all too long. With a whirl, he shut the door and turned to the rest of his house. For the first time, he truly saw its emptiness. It hit him like a hard punch to the chest. Dumbfounded, he wandered from room to room, and in each one the realization struck him a little harder. They were too bare.

Before Kirsten, it had never even occurred to him much. He'd slept here, ate here, functioned. But not *lived* here.

He hadn't done in years. *Live*. The thought of it was too scary—to become attached to something, to love only to have it ripped away. All he had was the house, the ranch, and his job. Nothing could take them away from him.

Kirsten could, his mind echoed. What he'd done with her could ruin everything he had left in the world.

But why even have them if they were going to feel so very empty?

Kirsten could fill them. She can fill your whole life, his mind answered as his heart constricted.

Where had that come from?

With a thump, he fell against the couch and rested his hands on his head. He liked Kirsten. A lot. And he simply could no longer believe she was the monster he'd originally thought her.

To the contrary, he wanted her in his life, at least for a little while. He wanted a chance to get to know the real Kirsten, to enjoy the sound of her chatter filling his house, his heart.

Could he really just turn her in Monday, aware there was something more to her story? Knowing she could be in some sort of danger if she went back? If he did, she would never come back. He'd never hear from her again.

He needed to hear out her story completely. Whatever had happened between her and Kurt, he had to find out. Not let outlandish jealousy deafen him. Not resist the truth because it scared him. Not shut out possibilities when lives depended on them.

Decided, he stood and headed out to his Blazer. He'd give Kirsten a little time to cool it, and meanwhile he'd go pick up some real food. Maybe he'd even grab a cheesecake. Tonight they could cook dinner together as planned. And talk. Really talk.

* * *

Kirsten listened to the *vroom* of the Blazer's engine turning over and ceased her pacing. The sound of pebbles churned under the vehicle's tires, the smacks and spatters ricocheting against the wheel well.

A quick look out the window revealed the truck's tail end as it disappeared down the drive.

Where could Reid be going? And why?

You think he'd at least have told her. Disappointment bubbled around her for two seconds, before reality smacked into her. Now was her chance. If she left immediately, she'd have plenty of time to put some distance between her and Reid, even if he were gone only a short while.

Finally, she could escape.

Excited, she raced around the room, and tried to decide exactly what to do. Her arms flung up and down as she jumped around, her mind anxious for a complete plan.

The handcuffs. She should take them in case he did catch up with her. Reid wouldn't expect her to have them, so it would be easy to snap them around his wrists. That would prevent him from stopping her.

If he didn't find her, at least she'd always have something to remember these past two days. A spicy reminder of something so sweet, so perfect, yet impossible.

She plunged into the bathroom and snatched them up from where she left them on the floor in her pile of dirty clothes.

Her only defense stuffed in her oversized pocket, Kirsten fled the room. In the kitchen, she searched the cabinets and refrigerator, swinging open doors like a madwoman in search of necessities to take along.

Nothing. How could Reid have no food? The only thing edible was a ton of microwave meals. They wouldn't do her any good.

She grabbed a water bottle and filled it, then slipped on her shoes and dashed out the back door.

"Snowball! Snowball, come here boy!" The sound of her call sliced through the air but went unanswered. "Snowball!"

Nothing.

Just to be sure, she gave the yard another once over. Chickens pecked at the ground out front, bluebirds tweeted and flew through the air. Calm surrounded her, even in the air, in its serene smell. A hauntingly tranquil breeze tickled at her skin, and goose bumps rose on her flesh.

Never had she called Snowball and he not answered. Where could he be?

Oh, God. She whirled around, a rush of sudden panic flooding her body. Oh, God. Could Kurt be here already? What if he had Snowball?

"Snowball, this isn't funny. Snowball, come." Frantic, she raced to the barn, her heart pounding. Fear tightened her throat, and constricted it with sick bile. Kurt could be anywhere.

He could pounce on her any time. From behind any bush, any wall, any door. If she went into the fields to run, he could follow her.

No one would even find her body.

She was on her own. No one could protect her but herself, and she needed a better weapon. The handcuffs weren't any kind of match against a large man. Not one like Kurt.

She required something sharp and deadly, something like a pitchfork. Then she would find Snowball, if he were even still alive. Oh, how she prayed for that.

"Snowball." Continuing to call for him, she kept her eyes all over the yard as she made her way to the large red barn. "Snowball."

With a fling, she swung open the door.

9

The creak cracked through the air as the door swung open, followed by dead silence. Kirsten crept inside, then immediately whirled around to check behind the opened entrance.

Frantic, she fought to keep her breath steady as her eyes chased across the wide span of the barn. They landed on several stacks of hay at the back of the barn, hidden under the shadows of the loft above. There, nestled in the crisp yellow straw, Snowball lay curled beside a fluffy Border collie.

Sissy.

The collie rested her head against Snowball's chest, cuddled up so close to him it seemed as if Snowball's fluffy white coat was one with her brown and tan fur.

Relieved, Kirsten forgot everything but her gratitude in finding him and cried out, "Snowball!"

She knelt, patted her thighs and beckoned to him to come. For a moment Snowball just eyed her with his cool gaze, their ice blue depths twinkling with certain warmth. The ornery pup inched forward on his paws just a bit before he snapped up and bounded into her arms full force. She squeezed him tight as he planted sloppy licks all over her face.

"You bad dog. Bad. Bad. Bad." Her tone contrasted with her stern words, affection overriding her reprimand.

Snowball's nose nuzzled under her chin and she rested her forehead against his. She gazed hard into his sapphire stare. One could almost swim in his eyes. Never had she known anything more perfectly blue. They were so incredibly beautiful.

To think she'd feared she might never look into them again.

"You scared me to death, Snowball." She ruffled his thick coat in her hands. "What would I do without you, huh? Don't you know you're my best friend? Why didn't you come?"

But Snowball didn't have to answer that question, Sissy did. Guarded, she approached Kirsten, rubbed against her side once, and then sat dutifully by Snowball's side.

"You're kidding!" A laugh escaped Kirsten, despite the worry still pulsing in her heart. "You've found yourself a lover haven't you, baby?" Amused, she pulled them both into a light embrace. "Well, I do hope you're using protection."

Snowball yapped, and she cracked up. For a few minutes all three of them rolled through the hay together and played. Both dogs covered her with kisses as she ruffled their fur and wrestled with them.

Then reality sank back in. What was she doing? If she didn't get out of here soon, Reid would get back and it'd be too late. "Come on, Snowball. We've got to go."

Head in his paws, Snowball whined. The other pup followed his lead.

"No. We have to go. Come." She stood and began to walk from the barn, but Snowball didn't budge. "Snowball."

Still he didn't move.

"Snowball?" Impatience slashed out from her cry. When he still didn't come, she nearly lost it. "Snowball, Kurt is coming for us. We have to go. We *have* to. Now come on. Right now."

A cold feeling sank into her. Snowball didn't want to come, and she couldn't blame him. He had a beautiful ranch with endless room to run and play here, instead of a top floor condo overlooking unrelenting concrete sidewalks filled with noisy bustle. Grass to roll around in, not hard cement. Fresh air. Not thick smog smelling of chemicals and too many people.

Moreover, he had a true friend. A lover. A real home.

Deep down, she wanted to stay as much as Snowball. Yeah, she could go home to Alabama and still have the yard and clean atmosphere. But there were things here she could never find anywhere else.

Reid.

But she couldn't stay. Her life depended upon it.

Tears brimming in her eyes, she raced from the barn, not even bothering to grab her water bottle back up. As fast as she could, Kirsten took to the fields, and ran through the grasses, past the cattle, over the manure. On and on she raced, until a pain in her side ceased her rapid pace. Only then did she slow to a brisk walk, her attention focused entirely on the opposite direction to the little town of Paradise.

Not once did she let herself look back. But she thought about it at least a million times.

As soon as Reid swung open the door to his Blazer it hit him. A sixth sense struck him, freezing his heart and tightening his chest. He gulped back pangs of worry fluttering up from his stomach and prayed he was mistaken.

Something was wrong. Terribly wrong.

He left the groceries in the back seat and raced into the house. But all along, the answer rang clear in his mind. Kirsten wouldn't be there. She'd taken off.

Still, he checked the bedroom, and then all the other rooms in the house. Each and every one echoed with their emptiness.

Suspicion confirmed, he dashed to the barn as anxiety bubbled over in him. *Damn it*. What had he been thinking? He should have never left her alone. Kirsten couldn't be trusted.

Kirsten had made a foolish decision running off in the fields. A city slicker like her didn't belong out there. There were snakes, holes to step in. No food, no fresh water. Damn it, she could get hurt out there.

Exactly why he'd warned her against it. Figures she wouldn't listen.

His feet pounded the ground like hurled rocks, his walk that of a soldier on a mission. Anger raged into his blood as he thought of her possibly hurt. Damn it. Why couldn't she have heeded his warnings just once? The hellcat needed nothing but a good lesson taught to her—a swift, sound spanking to knock a little common sense into her stubborn butt.

Sissy and Snowball greeted him at the barn door, the howls and yaps frantic. Snowball bounced back and forth under his feet and grabbed at his jeans legs as if desperate for his attention.

"Stop it." Eyes narrowed, annoyance pulsing through him, Reid fought the urge to kick them away. Violence was never the answer. But damn it, he needed a break from all this nonsense. The darned mutts just wouldn't let up their constant pestering. "Would you—Snowball!"

One dog took a nip from his leg, and he winced in pain. "Owww."

Damn, what could be up with them? Never had Sissy acted like this, and Snowball had seemed like a real nice pup.

Whatever their problem, he certainly didn't time have to fool with them. He had to find Kirsten.

Or . . .

Could it be? Were they trying to tell him something? No way. Real dogs didn't do that, did they?

It sure seemed that way.

What the hell, why not give it a shot? It could take him a

long time to find Kirsten with so much room for her to run and hide. Maybe they were smart enough to lead him to her. At any rate, it couldn't hurt to try.

With determined strides, he broke free of their pestering, and went into the barn. Still they followed him with barks and yowls.

Fast as he could, he threw a saddle over his black stallion, Raven, and mounted. Using the mane as a bridle, he guided his horse from the corral. "Okay, guys. Show me the way."

Both dogs took off into the fields, and he followed at a light gallop. The canter increased as the dogs ran as fast as their little legs could take them, erasing any doubt that they knew exactly where Kirsten was.

The distance they covered amazed Reid. He would have never guessed she'd have gotten that far, but then he remembered the way her long legs had darted from his grasp the day before. No doubt, Kirsten was accustomed to running regularly. No wonder her body was in such great shape.

Finally he spotted her on the horizon. Her figure glowed under the bright sun rays. He kicked the horse into a sprint and left the dogs behind.

In no time, he caught up with her, but he didn't stop. Instead he swept down upon her, leaning low over Raven's side.

With his grip locked under her arms, he snatched her up as he rode, and tossed her over, belly down, in front of him. Not a single word emitted from her, and he could only guess she was too stunned. Bent over the horse, her tight little rear strained against the cotton of his jogging pants.

So round. Perfect.

Tempted, he reached out and ran his hand across the sweet cheeks. With a squeeze, he slowly slid his finger down along the groove in the fabric, and the silent Kirsten came to life. With a screech she fought against him, hurling herself every which way.

"Stop, you bastard, let me go." Sharp teeth gnashed into his thigh, and cut into him, even through his jeans.

Blinded by pain, he raised his hand and delivered a sharp, well-deserved swat to her bottom. Then two. Then three. He didn't hit her so hard that he'd actually hurt her, but only enough to give her plenty of warning. Still, she continued to bite him. Well, he'd been chewed on enough for one afternoon.

Thigh burning, he reined Raven to a halt. Desperate to be free of her infliction, he tugged to dislodge her teeth off him. With a tight squeeze, he gripped her head and yanked it back, finally pulling her teeth free.

Mouth now empty, she began to screech again. "Let me go!"

Release her? Never. Her body remained tight, unyielding in his grasp. He pulled her up farther in his knees, and held her down tight with one arm.

His little hellcat was about to learn a lesson.

Kirsten gritted her teeth as her body clenched. Not in fear, not in pain, but in want. Already her intimate places had begun to ready themselves, her aching nether lips starting to drip as her nipples hardened.

She struggled against him, determined not to let him have his way with her. From the way he'd pulled her closer, up over his knees and held her down so tight, there wasn't any doubt he intended to continue his spanking. Her bottom already stung from his attentions, but even worse, her pride smarted. Dear God, she actually wanted more.

The strangest of feelings bubbled in the pit of her stomach, a strange concoction of discomfort, fear, and anticipation. Another slap bit into her bum, and she gritted her teeth. A maddening wash of heat overcame her and lit her body with desire.

No one had ever spanked her before. And she liked it so much she couldn't stand it. But her words contradicted her urges. "Stop it, right now. Let me go, you insufferable pig."

Useless against his strength, she twisted and fought anyway. The more she thrashed about, the harder her captor held her down. His punishment refused to cease, and her body refused to deny him. Slowly, her protests ceased as his deliberate strikes patted and teased her body. His palms kneaded and gripped the muscles of her rear in between slaps. Sometimes his fingers enticingly began to explore before he would yank back to bite into her with more chastisement.

She could not resist the white-hot desire boiling in her. Her body overtook her mind, and insisted on raging her with dirty needs. Wicked thoughts.

The position she lay in, folded over his knees, so deliciously close to his cock that she could feel it rubbing against her belly, nearly drove her mad. How she wanted to reach for his thick, hard rod and swallow him. To push forward the lovemaking she was all but nearly dying for. To feel him inside of her, *right now*. To have him take her from behind like an animal and continue his lesson.

Wild. Uninhibited. Naughty. But not the least bit nice.

Caught up in her thoughts, she hardly realized that his spanking had ceased. For a moment everything ceased, even her breath, as she waited for his hand to come down once again.

But instead of a biting slap, his hand slipped under her jogging pants and roamed the curve of her buttocks, once again slipping between her cheeks. He prodded, explored, and then grasped her throbbing bum into a tight grasp.

"Have you learned your lesson yet, hellcat?" The growl to his words wasn't a threat, but a naughty promise.

"Never," Kirsten hissed. Although she had no doubt her refusal would bring more punishment, she would not let him win like that.

Deep down, a large piece of her wanted his stiff penalty, hard and deep inside of her. Now.

"Fine, have it your way." Fast as lightning, Reid dropped

down off the horse and grabbed her all in one movement. As he held her tight, he smacked the horse's rear and sent the black stallion trotting off.

Reid crushed her mouth with his, his bruising kiss not the least bit sweet or endearing. His lips set her on fire, as his tongue fought against hers. With stealthy movements Reid disposed of her shirt, then her bra. His mouth came down upon her breasts, suckled at their hardened nipples, and then bit at them lightly with his teeth. The nips didn't hurt, but shocked though her with heightened intensity. A deep, throaty moan escaped her. She started to push down her jogging pants, but was stopped by his large hands.

"Reid . . ." she panted.

"No." Unrelenting in his control over her, Reid's hands yanked away hers, and swatted her rear once again. His tongue roamed over her stomach, and dove into her belly button. He suckled on it, flicking his tongue in and out. "Today I want to explore every inch of you. Don't you dare move."

Did he really expect her to obey him? No way. Kirsten wanted what she wanted. She started to struggle out of her pants again, and he caught her. "Now you've done it."

With a tight grasp, he swept her off her feet and laid her down on her in front of him. He pinned her arms up above her head with one hand and continued to suckle on her breasts, his grip on her wrists unrelenting.

Hips arched forward, Kirsten tried to steel herself against the waves of burning heat. Finally he released her and tore down her jogging pants. Impatient, Kirsten waited for him to take her, her pelvis vaulted toward him.

In a light caress his callused hands brushed over her fanny, and tingles coursed her spine. One of his thick fingers slipped into her slit, while the other pierced her anus. Shocked, Kirsten cried out at his invading touch. The slight pinch of pain only served to heighten the shocks electrifying her body, tensing it with want so badly that she hurt for him.

"Stop," she moaned, but she didn't really mean it.

"What's the matter, Kirsten? Are you enjoying it? Is that the problem?"

"You bastard." She squirmed as he massaged inside of her, overwrought with the intense shock of his raid on her body.

"I think you're a bad girl, Kirsten. And I think you like being bad. But don't you know, naughty gals must be disciplined." His fingers flicked deeper inside both holes, and she pushed against him.

With his other hand, he spread her lips wide apart and took a long deep lick. His hard suction found her clit, and Kirsten shook as if an earthquake had hit her.

"No, Reid . . ."

"And I think this bad girl enjoys getting taught a lesson, don't you?" Withdrawing his fingers, he delivered another whack to her bottom. "I want you on your knees."

With a gulp, Kirsten choked on the idea of it. What would he do to her if she listened? If she didn't?

This had gone quite far enough. Reid didn't have the right . . . her body didn't have the right . . .

But how could she escape him? If she jumped up, he'd catch her.

The handcuffs!

Another one of his threatening slaps hit her bottom, but his hands freed her body so that she could obey him. Instead she jumped from him, pulled up her pants and ran, barely escaping his grasp. Her hands dove into her pockets for the cuffs.

Within three seconds Reid had caught her, and when he did, she whirled in his arms and snapped a cuff around one hand. The other she had to struggle and fight against him for, but somehow, by a miracle above all miracles, she seized his wrist and snapped it shut.

Hands locked, Reid looked at her shocked, his jaw dropped, and his deep brown eyes widened. The world around them ceased to spin as she stared back at him, passion thick in the air.

Kirsten could run right now. She could. She should.

But she wouldn't. Not until she gave Reid Walker a hearty taste of his damned medicine.

With a sinister half smile, she giggled. "Looks like it's my turn now."

10

"Don't you dare." Reid's dark words and equally dark stare only served as more threats, ones she did not heed.

Kirsten laughed, enjoying the prospect of having him at her command. No way she would give it up. Not for the world. "Oh, no, *Sir*. It's your turn." With a playful shove she pushed the shocked Reid back. He wavered, then stumbled to his knees. The level of his head met right with her lower abdomen, and she grasped his hair, thrusting his lips to her. He obeyed her lead, planting a trail of wet kisses across her belly.

How Kirsten loved the feel of his tongue and mouth all over her. Everywhere. Desire danced inside her, its flames burning her with ultimate need. How she wanted to bury his thick cock into her dripping wet slit and satisfy her body.

But she couldn't. Not yet.

The power Reid held over her body was unbelievable, and she wanted the same control of him. She wanted to see him squirm under her and groan in ecstasy, so pleasured he could never forget her.

Methodically she went about stripping him of all his clothes then pushed him back, shoving his hands above his head.

When Reid lay spread out before her, bare, exposed, and hard as the rocky ground he lay on, Kirsten licked her lips. Oh what fun he would be. Just the sight of him naked drove her crazy. His rippled muscles glistened with a deep tan covered in black curling hairs, the lower the darker. Slowly, Kirsten ran her fingers across the coal trail that had tortured her with notions the first day they'd met. She let her long nails run down its length, their touch ever so light. Soon she reached the path's end, and there she found his cock, erect and ready for her. On its tip she placed a gentle kiss as she knelt down on all fours and wrapped her hands around the shaft.

Any other time Reid would have taken control, pressing her to swallow his cock right away. But not this time. Instead she teased him with her tongue, harassing him with gentle nibbling. Balls in hand, she massaged them until her lips made thier way to the succulent orbs. One at a time, she took turns engulfing them in her hot mouth.

"Oh God. Kirsten, stop." Reid's hips pushed upward as he moaned.

With a devilish little laugh, Kirsten suckled them just a bit harder. His back arched, and his body tensed against her attention.

"That's too much. Stop it now."

Kirsten let a sinister notion overtake her and became naughty. If he wanted to punish her for being bad, then that was what she would be—very wicked, very disobedient, just plain bad girl. She had a feeling he'd love every minute of it.

With a tighter grip, she moved her hands up and down his rod. It pulsated under her grasp, and she grabbed the head with her mouth. She suctioned its tip, loving it with her tongue as she explored his tenderest of spots.

Reid groaned.

Kirsten giggled.

Like concrete in her grasp, his hardened cock would no doubt explode any minute if she kept at it, and that she would not allow—at least not until she had hers, which she wanted badly, so badly her pussy actually hurt. It needed to be filled.

With her legs spread wide she knelt on the field's green grasses, and straddled his face. Her fingers interlocked tightly in his hair, she forced his head to her pussy and demanded pleasuring.

Reid had no choice but to obey.

With his tongue, he granted her wish. Anything to get her off his cock. Her torture had him ready to explode; so damned hard, so damned ready he ached with pulsating need.

The salty sweet taste of her made him desperate for more and he attacked her pussy with lavish laps. Her juices flowed into his mouth, and he drank it up, in heaven.

Right now, Kirsten might be in charge, but he'd be sure to show her he still had complete control. Even handcuffed, he could drive her body insane. Kirsten couldn't deny him—she was his.

All his.

With gentle nibbles he teased her clit, torturing her. He sucked and licked it, pulling gently with his teeth. Then he moved onto her slit, praising the whole length of it, diving in and out of her hole with his tongue. She rode his face like it was his cock, commanding him with her moans and groans.

The game did little to relieve his cock, and he grew harder, if that were possible. But still, he had to make it last. To take Kirsten places she'd never been.

But before he could even get really started, Kirsten tore away from him. The luscious taste of her pussy abandoned him, leaving only traces of her creamy juices on the tip of his tongue.

Still straddled across him on her knees, Kirsten moved down, each slow scoot backwards tantalizing as her wet sex grazed his chest, then his belly. When she finally reached his lower regions, she hovered inches above his ready cock, a wicked look in her laughing green eyes.

How he wanted to grab her and yank her down atop it. To drive into her full force and end the torment. But the handcuffs disabled him from any movement, imprisoned him to her will.

In only a second, a million lifetimes seemed to pass. He waited for her next move, and prayed for reprieve.

Instead, Kirsten wrapped her fingers around him and used the tip of his cock as a tool on her nether lips. The tease massaged herself, the pressure applied just enough to drive him nearly insane. The most sensitive spot on the engorged head of his shaft burned against her busy inflictions. Desperate. Thumping.

He needed a release. Now. To wait any longer simply wasn't possible. As if she sensed it, her wet slit engulfed him.

The very world shook.

Up and down she moved, slow and in control. Every inch of him moved inside of her.

Her sheath wrapped around him, silk and satin.

Heaven on earth was Kirsten Montgomery. And oh, how he loved her.

One hand at a time, Kirsten pushed herself up from atop Reid. Beneath her, he rested from their little siesta. He stretched, his perfect tan body supple with the tight bulges of muscle.

If she weren't so worried, she'd want him again. *In fact . . .* but no, she had no time for such things.

An empty silence hung in the air, the country smell thickly laced with grasses and wildflowers. Neither of them made a move for conversation. Relieved, Kirsten searched her mind, disappointed in herself. How long had she been passed out? Two minutes? Two hours?

She and Reid had played for so long, going places she'd never been. It had taken her to a point she didn't know existed, where worlds collided and shattered. After such a mind-blowing orgasm, the only option had been collapsing, much as she'd wanted to stand and run away.

And now she'd lost precious minutes, time in which Kurt could very well be closing in around her. Who knew how close he'd gotten by now? He could be at the ranch already, searching her out. Ready to end her life.

No. As fast as possible, she jumped up and gathered her scattered clothes. Pulling on each leg, each sleeve felt like a million years' worth of work. Her shoes lay half-laced and flung nearly ten feet away. *How did they get off?*

After she finished pulling herself back together, she didn't waste a moment's time.

His eyes followed her, burning holes in her back. Without turning she could envision his hard glare, cold and unrelenting. Disbelieving.

As she ran away, Reid remained silent, without a protest, without a care. His quiet ate at her. Each and every time her feet hit the ground, taking her farther from him, her nerves incensed.

How could he just lie there and watch her leave without a word? Didn't he even care that she was going? That she was abandoning him, handcuffed? He could at least say something. Anything.

Annoyed, she stopped in her tracks and swung back around. "Good-bye might be nice."

"Hey, you're the one leaving."

Flustered, Kirsten narrowed her eyes. "You know, you're absolutely right. Good-bye and good riddance."

Jerk. Reid Walker thought he knew it all. Well, he was the one in the handcuffs this time, not her. And he could stay in them.

The hell with it. She had better things to do than worry about him. Like getting the hell out of here.

"Kirsten wait." Reid's gruff voice commanded, as if he had the right.

"What?" Kirsten kept walking, her voice sure, her shoulders square. Pretending his call didn't matter. That *he* didn't matter.

"Take the keys, Kirsten. They're in the pocket of my jeans."

That stopped her. She whirled around. "What?"

"Take the keys, take the Blazer, and get the hell out of here." The low growl to his voice scared her.

He wanted her to go. Not stay.

Her eyes darted from the heap of blue jeans then back to Reid. Why would he do that to her . . . no, *for* her?

To let her go was to break the law. Something Reid obviously wasn't accustomed to, not with him being Sheriff.

No, a man like him always followed the rules.

So why would he bend them for her? She didn't want him in trouble over her. Hell, he could lose his job. "No, I can't do that, Reid. It . . ."

Reid shot up from the ground like a snap of a whip. His cuffed hands still above his head, he glared at her with deadly eyes and a snarl. "Go!"

His deafening holler answered her question, clear as the disgust in his eyes. Reid wanted rid of her. The truth had shown itself this afternoon, and he'd finally realized the trouble she could cause just being around.

"Fine," she shouted back. Wasting no time, she snatched the keys, and held the cold metal tight in her fists. It burned right through her. Well, at least Reid believed her. Finally. And now he was sending her away.

Just what she wanted . . . right? Right?

A piece of her broke in two as she ran off, her legs flying across the long stretch of field as fast as they could carry her. Her thighs burned, her chest ached, but she kept up the pace.

She couldn't stop. If she did, she'd never be able to start again.

God help her, for some reason she wanted to stay with Reid more than anything in the world. Even though he wanted her gone, even though she needed to go.

Like the same fool who'd run off to California with super-star dreams. Who'd been hoodwinked by a drug dealer, and naïvely stolen his car.

How many times her silly heart had cost her . . .

She wouldn't do it again. She couldn't. This time her mind was in charge, and good common sense told her go.

Go. Go. *Go.*

11

The sun's brilliant rays cast pink and yellow hues across the clear blue sky as it set into the horizon. Night threatened darkness, though light still ruled.

Another day lost to him. Just like Kirsten.

With brisk, determined strides, Reid crossed the field toward home, heading straight into the setting sun. At least hot rays no longer beat down on his chest, left bare by the impossibility of putting on his T-shirt.

His boots crashed into the ground, sending swirls of dust around the bottoms of his jeans. The cuffs locked around his dangling hands in front of him gave proof of a truth he wished he didn't have to believe.

Kirsten had left.

No. He'd *sent* her away because she'd needed to go. It was for the best, wasn't it? Of course. For Christ's sake, if what she'd said held even the slightest morsel of truth, then her life depended on it. She couldn't stick around, not if her ex had the slightest clue as to her whereabouts.

How Kurt could have found out baffled Reid. Could the system be so corrupted that a slime ball like Kurt could easily obtain such information?

Guilt gnawed and chewed at him. It ate him alive with every step he took. Maybe if he'd listened to Kirsten in the first place he could have done something from the start. But even now he didn't know the whole truth. No, sending her away was best for the both of them.

He didn't give a hoot that he'd broken his oath to the town and the law. To hell with being sheriff. What mattered more than anything was that she was in danger. And she was gone. Forever.

The ranch emerged, at first a dot on the horizon, growing with his every passing step. Brush from a sage bush tripped him and he stumbled, the cuffs making him fight to stay upright.

"Damn it."

Once again he cursed himself for a fool. Why did he have to give her all the keys, including the master? Now he'd either have to wait for Skip to come out to the ranch Monday and saw him out, or he'd have to go into town like this.

"That'd go over real well," he muttered to no one in particular.

Eventually he'd have to call the state authorities and tell them she'd bested him. Maybe they'd send someone out and the story wouldn't have to go too far.

Hell, it had been a fun game they'd played together. Never had his blood boiled so furiously for any woman. Kirsten had taken him to an altogether different world, one where pleasure and ecstasy ruled.

Just as expected, the Blazer no longer sat in the drive. Tracks in the dust marked where she'd sped out. Kirsten couldn't have but a half an hour on him. He supposed it would be best if he waited an hour or two before he made the call, and let her get a good jump-start. He didn't want anyone catching up with her. She belonged home in Alabama, safe and happy. Not with Kurt, not in jail, and not with him.

With heavy feet he treaded up the stairs to the back door. He started to turn the knob, but a snapping sound stopped him short. Coldness washed over him and sent a shiver down his back.

"What the hell!"

Under his feet shards of glass cracked. He stepped back, realizing the side panel had been shattered out.

Ready for anything, Reid shoved open the door. Shit, someone had broken in all right. And ransacked the entire house. What little he owned had been tossed upside down and inside out. From room to room he wandered, his heart in his throat. Slashes ripped through his furniture. The drawers, cabinets, and closets had all been rummaged. The refrigerator hung open, obviously searched. Even the carpet had been pulled in places.

What a mess.

No doubt, Kurt was responsible. What could he have been looking for? Kirsten? No, she couldn't have been hidden in a kitchen drawer or under a rug.

No, Kurt desired something else. Something of value, and he obviously wanted it bad.

And he'd be after Kirsten for it.

It hit him like a punch to the gut. His insides twisted in realization. It had taken time to tear the house up like this. More then it would have taken between Kirsten leaving and his arrival. No, Kurt had to have been here when Kirsten got back. The Blazer was gone, but only Kirsten had the keys.

What if he'd followed her out of town? What if Kurt had Kirsten even now?

Oh no. Oh no. Oh no.

Utterly panicked, Kirsten's foot automatically pounded

harder on the gas, and the Blazer choked to get up to speed. The engine roared, and sputtered in refusal, but Kirsten held down the pedal and prayed for a miracle.

With dread, she readjusted the rearview mirror once again. There wasn't any denying what she saw.

Shit.

In the distance, a little white spot continued to emerge, growing larger and more like Kurt's BMW with every second. Just to be sure, she whirled and looked out the back window.

The sports car sped right up to her tailgate, so close she now could make out the sinister glare on Kurt's face.

How could he have caught up with her? For over half an hour she had been driving along on the quiet country road, its long, empty stretch all to herself.

It didn't make any sense. None.

Once again she slammed down on the pedal. The speedometer reached seventy, then eighty. The truck shook, and the steering wheel vibrated in her tight grip. The Blazer couldn't take it. She let her speed drop just a bit, and tried to focus on the road.

Kurt drove up alongside of her. What could he be doing? It wasn't as if he could run her off the road with his little tin can car. If he attempted to broadside her in the Blazer, it would be like a pebble flinging off a rock wall.

So long as she kept driving, she should be safe.

Or maybe not. Kurt's ice blue eyes pierced right through her as he brandished a handgun and aimed at her. A wicked grin curled his lips, and the cold man under the Hawaiian print shirt shone through.

On the outside Kurt might look sunshiny and carefree, like a true Californian ready for "surf's up." But Kirsten had discovered the man he really was. A dangerous man who would no doubt pull the trigger without a second thought.

Horrified, she did the only thing she could. She pressed her foot down as far as it could go. Her heart beat faster than the Blazer sped. The sooner she found a town the better, because she could never outrun Kurt's car. Evening dimmed around her, and if she didn't get somewhere safe before dark, then she had no hope at all.

Sweat dripped down her face as she forced herself to look straight ahead. She couldn't look at him—her death. Her knuckles whitened under the pressure, but still she squeezed the steering wheel as if holding it tight brought her some measure of safety.

Just keep going. Don't stop. Don't look.

The roar of both vehicle's engines beat at her ears, a deafening noise. All of a sudden, the racket became unbearable. Without thinking, she started to reach out and turn on the radio, but before she could touch the switch, a loud pop blasted through the air.

The Blazer swerved, and she lost control, the flap of a flat tire the last thing to echo in her ears before the truck rolled.

For a moment everything went black.

Slowly she came to, fighting for consciousness against the void that wanted to consume her.

Blood trickled into her eyes, and the seatbelt cut into her waist. Pinned upside down, she tried to prop herself up for relief. But nothing could provide that. A large sob escaped her as salty tears blurred her already fuzzy vision. Searing pain pulsed through her body, but her ankle . . . oh shit. It felt as if a million nails were being driven into it, splitting it into pieces. Carefully she tried to move it, forcing her mind to concentrate on the task despite its throbbing. But no amount of willpower would budge it. Already she could feel it swelling.

A new panic swept through her and for a moment all she could think of was impossible escape. She reached down slowly and unsnapped herself. All dead weight, she fell hard against the roof. A moan caught in her throat, and she stifled it back as a new idea hit her.

If she ran now, no doubt Kurt would catch her. Maybe her best bet was to play dead. She let her body fall limp, but unfortunately her plan did, too.

Kurt's fist busted through the side window and she screamed. His hands grasped her by the hair and yanked, dragging her through the broken glass. It cut through her clothes and dug into her skin, but she didn't utter a peep.

Damned if she would beg.

He wrenched her up onto her feet. Agony shot through her ankle, and she stumbled backward, fighting to keep her balance in a world of spinning pain.

Kurt jerked her up again. "You look like hell, Kirsten."

"Fuck off."

The back of his hand rose up and hit her hard across the face. Dizzy, Kirsten could hardly acknowledge her stinging cheek as she stumbled right into his grasp.

"I want what's mine, Kirsten." The hiss of his words breathed down on her, his stale breath laced with cigars. It gagged her, the smell of his threats sickening. Bile rose up in her throat, and before she could help it, she spewed all over his feet.

"Awww. Bitch. You stupid bitch." With a hard thrust, he shoved her backwards and she tumbled to the ground with a thud.

The taste of vomit burned in her throat, and she propped herself up to spit its remaining vileness from her mouth. With a swipe of her sleeve, she wiped her mouth clean and tried to swallow. She wanted to face him, woman to man. Not wallow on the ground like a coward. She started to push up then stopped. The anger radiating from him froze her.

Whatever it took to stay alive, she had to do it. Even beg. "Please Kurt . . . I'm sorry. Be reasonable about this. You don't want to kill me."

"Reasonable? Hah! You should have thought of that before you stole from me."

Hard as she tried, her tongue couldn't be held. "You know damn good and well you gave me the convertible."

"I'm not talking about the Vette. I'm talking about what was in it, and you know it. Don't play the idiot with me." He reached down and grasped her by the chin. The painful grip yanked her up to face his venomous words. "I didn't pay all this money to track you down to go home empty handed. Info from the California State Police doesn't come cheap, you know. I want what is mine. Where is it? Tell me now and maybe I'll let you live. I'll just cut out your tongue."

Soft fingers caressed her jaw, their tenderness more terrifying than his hard gaze.

"I swear I don't know."

His fist rose in the air. "Then I'll just have to beat it out of you."

12

Reid pressed down hard on the gas and the car flew down the tar and chip road. Rocks spattered against the wheel wells as the speedometer reached eighty, then ninety, then a hundred.

Seven years had passed since he'd driven at such outrageous speeds, yet the thought of it didn't even faze him. The only thing that mattered was finding Kirsten. Fast.

Thank God he'd never sold the Camaro. Thank God.

It was a miracle he'd even been able to coax it into starting. For years dust had coated it as it sat buried in the very back of the barn, hidden even from him. He hadn't wanted to touch the fast car he'd driven as a young guy. After his parents died he hadn't dared to speed.

But now he damn well did. The stinking car couldn't go fast enough. If he didn't find Kirsten soon, he might never find her.

Like a runaway train, his heart pumped a million beats a minute. The thumps rang in his ears and pierced the air, even over the roar of the engine. His stomach knotted in worry as sweat trickled down the back of his neck.

The cuffs were still locked around his hands, the cold metal chafing his skin. Red welts circled his wrists. But he didn't care. Only one thing mattered. Getting Kirsten back, safe and sound.

Reid held tight to the wheel and pushed harder on the pedal.

Ready to strike, Kurt loomed over her and he meant business. She didn't know what to do besides tell a lie. Right now she'd do just about anything, *anything*, to get him off her back.

"Wait Kurt. I'll tell you." Her voice shook as much as she did. Her body shuddered at the thought of what he would do to her. This man wouldn't just beat her. He'd kill her, without a second thought or moment's remorse.

It couldn't happen. She couldn't let it.

Darts of ice spat from his eyes, their blueness clouded with gray thunder. A violent chill ran straight down her spine.

"Spit it out," he roared with the fury of a lion.

Oh God, how could she tell him where it was hidden when she didn't even know what it was?

Think fast, Kirsten.

A million plans raced through her mind, not one of them worthy. Then it hit her. Perhaps she could lead him back to Reid. Somehow she knew he'd protect her at all costs, and besides, wasn't he sheriff? Who better to run to than a man with his own gun, and a badge at that?

She prayed he'd gotten rid of those handcuffs by now. Wincing at the thought, she cursed herself a thousand times for leaving him like that.

Unconsciously, she shook her head. Kurt grasped her by the hair and yanked her onto her feet. His face contorted into a warning, a deadly threat.

"It's . . . it's in the Sheriff's barn . . . hidden under the hay." Kirsten stuttered out.

"Now why would you leave two pounds of cocaine in a sheriff's barn? Come on Kirsten, don't expect me to buy that."

Oh, God, she'd run off with his drugs? She'd left because of them, and instead she took them with her?

Damn. Damn. Damn.

Anger once again seethed within her, and she had to ask. "Why were drugs in *my* car?"

Kurt laughed at her like a little boy who's gotten away with a naughty trick. "You're just so naïve Kirsten. Do you think I really bought you those cars because I *loved* you? You're just some country bumpkin, one who has been running drugs for me for years now."

"No way," Kirsten whispered incredulously.

"Oh yes, way. I hid them in your car under the spare tire, and the dealers had the keys. All I had to do was call them and let them know where you'd be for them to make a pick up."

The bastard! If only she could punch him. Hard. Right in that damned perfect nose of his. Oh, it would make her feel so very much better.

How could he have done that to her? How could she have been such a fool? Well, never again.

Eyes narrowed, she looked at him intently. "Why are you telling me this now?"

When she heard her own question, she snapped her mouth shut. Oh God, that had been the wrong question to ask. There could only be one answer.

Kurt just laughed, his tone full and hearty and ever so dangerous.

Kirsten's mind raced. No wonder he'd gone to such trouble to find her. Damn it, he wouldn't be getting them back, any more than he'd get away with this. Those drugs were her proof, her freedom, and Kurt's biggest slipup. If she had anything to do with it, they'd put him away for a long, long time.

Kirsten drew a slight breath and willed her voice to be cool. "No, I did. I swear. The sheriff isn't exactly the sharpest. I even seduced him into letting me go. I planned to send someone back for it when things cooled, maybe sell them to start a new life. But they're still there, I promise. I can take you to them. They'll be hard to find."

His evil eyes slanted, a grin curling up the corners of his evil mouth. Kurt shoved her.

"Nope, but thanks anyway." Gun raised, Kurt aimed directly for her head. "Too bad I have to kill you. You could have had it good with me, Kristen."

A rush of adrenaline flooded her body. It erased her pain, and turned her fear into power. Damned if she'd go down without a fight. With a silent prayer she whirled and took off, her feet flying beneath her. Behind her the shot rang out, its loud echo booming around her like a fireworks exploding on the fourth.

A razor-like pain sliced into her and she fell. The world went black.

Reid dropped his aim as Kurt went down. The gun caught on his cuffs, and he slung it to the ground. The slime ball wouldn't be going anywhere with the bullet he'd just shot in his knee.

His heart thumped in his throat at the sight of Kirsten lying sprawled on the ground, lifeless. Panic swept him into a race to her side, but common sense stopped him short. First he needed to secure Kurt and disarm him. Then he'd find out how badly the scoundrel's shot had injured her.

On one knee he knelt beside the groaning half-unconscious man. A steady pulse beat in his neck. Just to be safe, Reid yanked off his belt, fumbling with the maddening cuffs locked around his own wrists. After a struggle, he managed to secure Kurt's wrists behind his back and then Reid grabbed up Kurt's handgun. In a fury, he tossed the weapon a good distance away, and sprinted to Kirsten. Facedown in the grass, she lay unmoving until he touched her. Then she stirred and started to struggle to get up, obviously in a panic.

"Don't move. Let me check you out." She stilled at his words. With careful fingers, he searched over her, careful not to move her. The only injury he found was a flesh wound on her shoulder, barely more than a scrape.

"Is it bad?" Kristen moaned.

Reid couldn't help a little chuckle. "Oh yeah. You might need a band aid."

With that, Kirsten flung around, eyes wide. "I'm okay?"

He pulled her tight. "Oh yeah, hon, you're fine."

Kirsten stared at Kurt who lay facedown in the field, a puddle of blood beginning to form around him.

"You must have shot him at the same time he was pulling the trigger and knocked him off." She snuggled into his arms, and tiny tears began to slide down her face. "He would have killed me."

"But he didn't." Reid rocked her in his arms, never more grateful in all his life. "He didn't."

She swiped away her tears and gazed up at him. "How did you know?"

"Kurt ransacked the house. Tore it all up."

"He must have been looking for his drugs . . . they're in the car, I think."

Drugs. Just like Kirsten had pleaded with him to believe in the first place. And all along, the proof had been there. Damn it. Why hadn't he searched the car?

This whole weekend could have been different.

Hell, maybe he couldn't go back. But he could go forward, and if she were willing, he could do it with her.

Almost losing Kirsten had taught him one very important thing. Empty couldn't even begin to describe his life with her gone.

Maybe he hardly knew her, but he needed her, in more ways than one.

"Good." Reid nodded. "This is all the proof I need. Kirsten Montgomery, you are cleared and freed as far as I am concerned. Now will you be mine?"

Kirsten chuckled, and sniffed. "Do you mean it?"

"The thing is, I could really use some help decorating. And you did seem awful interested in that." He tried to sound nonchalant—*tried*. "What do you think? Give me another chance? You never know, you might even come to like me."

An incredible smile lit her face, laced with a hint of orneriness. "Deal. But does this mean I get to go shopping?"

Contentment filled Reid. His little hellcat could have whatever she wanted, so long as he got his. Leaning down, he stole her lips and embraced them with his fire for her. After he tasted every corner of her mouth, he broke away and whispered. "You, sugar, can buy whatever you want, whenever you want."

Epilogue

"Shopping again?" With a slight chuckle, Reid crossed the kitchen, two little brown pups with icy blue eyes bumbling under his feet. With careful shifts to avoid them, he reached to help her with her bags.

Thankful, she let him take the three blue plastic bags of groceries. They were so heavy, they'd rubbed lines into her hands.

"Hey, you said whatever, whenever, I want." Kirsten shrugged her shoulders and tossed the mail down on the counter. A package lay on top, unmarked and wrapped in brown paper. Gingerly, she sorted through the pile, and let that one rest.

Reid began stacking formula into the cupboards. "That was four years ago."

"So?" She threw back. "Two little ones eat a lot, you know."

"They're with your mother this week."

"But they'll be back."

With a hearty laugh, he dropped the bags and grabbed her, wrapping his arms tight around her. With curious, narrowed eyes, Reid pointed to the package. "Hey, what's that?"

"You'll see."

Without another word, she strode from the kitchen, all too aware of him following. Before he could trail her into the bathroom, she slammed the door shut, and snapped the lock.

"Hey, what's the deal?"

"You'll see."

With a quick tear, she ripped open the package and pulled a new negligee from it. Black lace, and silk: it was a tantalizing combination of both naughty and nice.

Since the last baby three months ago, things between had been a little slow. It was time to spice them back up.

After a pair of fishnet stockings, she slipped on the negligee and then a pair of high heels. One look in the mirror revealed a woman ready for loving. In her head, she turned on the music, its beat high and thumping, then opened the door.

With one leg, she kicked out for a tease and then ran her body up and down the doorframe.

Jaw hanging, mesmerized by her every movement, Reid stared. Slowly he dropped to sit on the edge of the bed.

Kirsten danced, her body titillating, and swerving. Hips rocking to her imaginary beat, every move making her body hot, and his heat more visibly ready beneath the strain of his blue jeans.

She moved closer, until she stood right over his lap, where she shook and taunted him with her curves. With her teeth, she released the buttons on his Levi's, and grabbed his cock in her mouth. It sprang forward, ready for attention. Eagerly, she savored it, running her teeth and tongue up and down the stretched, heated skin.

Her pussy dripped with desire, her nipples hardened into two buds that strained against the lace of the negligee. The texture of the fabric against her soft skin tantalized her tender breasts, and made her ever so hot.

She stood and straddled him, his thick rod slipping into her slick slit, and she cried out in pure ecstasy. Riding him with hard thrusts, Kirsten took what she wanted, his cock her tool into heaven.

Together they exploded then collapsed. Reid pulled her close, and murmured, "Do you have any idea how much I love you?"

"Almost as much as I love you?"

Reid rolled over on top of her, attacking her with tickles. Laughing and gasping for air, she struggled against him to no avail.

"Okay, okay. I give. You love me the same as I love you, which is very, very much."

"Forever, hellcat," he growled as he captured her lips into a hungry embrace. "Forever."

DETROIT'S FINEST

Renée Alexis

It was a beautiful spring day in Detroit, nice and hot, a convertible day for those who had one. I wasn't one of those people, yet my 1995 Camry had all four windows down and I was flying with the wind—literally. I decided that since it was such a beautiful day, why not go to the mall for lunch? I was given an extended lunch, since my floor at the police department had to be evacuated due to a criminal at large. I took advantage of two hours and went shopping like any other red-blooded American female would have.

As I lingered over my martini at Dublin's Bistro, I noticed the time. Damn, just when I was getting started with my own personal party, it was time to get back to work. Surely, every cop in the building with their expert bloodhound abilities had captured whoever it was they were looking for. That didn't help my cause, however. I needed more time to find a nice miniskirt to try to entice this cop whose trail I was on. Another day maybe. Good thing I had already purchased my new Swiss Army watch. A good timepiece was what I really needed since I was prone to extended lunches—all at the expense of Detroit's finest.

The police department knew me, knew my tactics and expected me to be late to work. Not that day, what with reports to be filed for an audit. That was my job, filing—yeah, really big time, I know, but someone low on the totem pole had to do it, why not me for my $11.85 per hour? Yes, I can see it now, in about one hundred years, I'll have enough dough to get that Benz I've been drooling over since the tender age of five.

I flew down I-75 to make time, as did every car. The average speed for that freeway was Mach #1, and my Camry moved into warp speed as well as any other car out there. The bad thing, I passed my exit. I kept going, but no other exit was in the immediate vicinity. What was a late girl to do? You guessed it, drive across the median and come out looking and smelling like a rose.

Almost!

My rose wilted the minute the flashing red sirens attached to a navy blue and white Crown Victoria caught my eye in the rearview mirror. "Darn!" *I was late enough as it was. I didn't need Detroit's Finest on my ass—well, except for the one I had seen on the eight floor.* I looked down at my new watch, counting the minutes as he decided to get out of his car and write the damn eighty-thousand-dollar ticket! At that point, I really didn't care about the ticket. All I wanted was to get back to work before my boss, Daisha Miller, AKA Queen Bitch of the Universe, docked me.

Mr. Policeman decided to exit from his car. I didn't want to look at him because I knew my stunt was super stupid and that he'd drill me like crazy for even thinking of crossing a median in the middle of the day. My nerves got the better of me so I looked, and what do you know, the officer turned into Mr. Cop from the eighth floor. The very man I wanted to sport my new mini in front of, had Nordstrom's not run out of my size. How could they have run out of a size six? No one in Detroit, or anywhere else for that matter, wears a size six! Yet they were out of it, which left me high and dry—no skirt, late for work, Daisha Miller soon to be on my ass, and then the best of all, a hot-ass ticket from a hot-ass cop! The day was really shaping up.

I got it together so I could maybe talk my way out of a jam; help him to remember it was better to be kind to a coworker. The hell he was going to have that! Coming face to face with reality, *cute* reality, was a hard pill to swallow so I leaned against the seat and was ready for my punishment.

Mr. Cop leaned against my rolled-down window. "License and registration, please."

Isn't that just what you want to hear from a man you have been hot for? For five months? Sure it is. I smiled, reached into my glove compartment. "Here you go, officer. Is there a problem?" *Why would you say that stupid shit? You know what you did.* I looked into the face of a cop so fine that I was ready to give him every single thing he needed—and buff his pretty black boots if he required that. Certainly, I had seen him before, but not as close up as now. Normally I pass him in the halls, and look up with time enough to see him dropping files on my desk with a quick hello, but nothing like this. He was beautiful, dark caramel skin, tall, lean, built and with lips juicy enough to get arrested for trying to kiss. The dude was scrumptious, almost made me forget about the ticket—almost.

I could feel his eyes on me, searching me, sizing me up, then back to the license. He was probably trying to figure out what would make a person pull a stupid freeway move like that. Then came his voice, that awesome, so completely male voice that shook my world, but *without* irresistible words. "Ma'am, do you know what you did back there?"

I smiled politely. "I know it was stupid, officer, but I'm late getting back to work and—"

"No reason to speed down the freeway and risk killing someone, or even yourself."

"I understand, but—"

He backed away from the car and pulled a notepad from his back pocket. "You were going ninety in a seventy-mile zone."

"I'm sorry. I hadn't realized my speed." The hell I didn't. I had to get back to my job so I could perform something so entirely revolutionary—filing.

"There were flames behind you, Miss."

"I wasn't going that fast, officer."

His eyes narrowed in contempt, hardly believing that someone had the nerve to talk back to him. "As I said, you were twenty miles over the speed limit."

"So was everyone else!"

"But you're the one I caught, not them!"

"Sexist!"

"Step out of the vehicle, ma'am."

"What?" I knew my mouth had really done it this time.

"Step out of the vehicle."

"What for?"

"Just get out before I pull you out."

I cautiously did what he asked, then looked into his sexy face again. "Am I under arrest?"

"That depends. Have you been drinking, Ms. Shane? That would be the only logical reason I can figure for someone to do warp speed on I-75."

"I . . . uh . . ." *Damn! The martini. That, along with my smart-ass mouth could land me in jail, courtesy of a mouthwatering cop!* "I had a cocktail with lunch but only one."

"Walk a straight line for me."

Again, I did as asked. His eyes were on me the entire time, watching me do my best imitation of a straight-laced human being. That was the very last thing I was, but for those purposes solely, I had to pretend to be the sobriety queen, and keep my ass out of jail.

As I walked his line, poised as possible, I wondered why he

had not remembered me. Then again, he worked with a load of people. 1300 Beaubien is a huge police station with a lot of super hunks wearing metal and dark blue. Everyone looked alike, other than him.

He gave me the green light on passing the sobriety test, but something told me he wasn't nearly finished with his persecution. He moved in behind me, his delicious dark eyes scanning me. He grabbed both my wrists and slapped cuffs on them before I could object. I had always wanted to be in tight quarters with him, but damn, not like that. I tried looking behind to see him but he forced my head forward again. His tone had gathered triteness, arrogance, roughness. I liked it, loved it, wanted more of it.

"After what you did, don't even think about looking back at me, Ms. Shane."

I twitched within his clutch. "Let me go, damn it! I passed that stupid test of yours and you have no right to detain me." A good acting job if I must say so myself.

He tightened the cuffs. "The hell I don't! I don't like your attitude."

"What attitude? I did what you said without a fight, so what's the problem?"

"My problem—women who speed down freeways in little beige Toyotas. That's my problem."

"Would it have been better for you had it been a big, thick, dark SUV?"

"Close your mouth!" He pulled me behind the car and leaned me over the trunk. "I would take you to headquarters, but I think I can deliver a better punishment than my overworked and underpaid coworkers. I could at least spare them one trouble-maker."

"By doing what to me?"

"Don't worry about it!"

"I won't be the one worrying once my lawyer gets word of

this. He'll be all over you when I get out of this." *Work it, girl. Work it good!*

"Who says you'll be getting out of this?" He pressed my size 34C's against the trunk and reached for them, feeling them, squeezing them between his ever-so-masculine hands before searching the rest of me.

"Why are you searching me? I don't have anything."

"You look dangerous; beautiful and dangerous. God only knows what you might have up that thigh-high skirt."

I bucked him, but all along I was enjoying how he maneuvered his hands across my breasts, gently squeezing my nipples. He did the same on my thighs, searching between them, feeling silky smooth skin against his big, hot hands. It was nerve-wracking . . . nerve-wrackingly erotic. He searched my slippery folds with those thick, long fingers until it purred pathetically for him. That's right, he was digging for Montana gold, pressing me harder and harder against the car, between medians on the freeway, and in the middle of the damn day. He was fearless, and had the right job to be so.

Though I thought he was a maniac version of *Dirty Harry,* I was liking the attention in major ways and wanted to dare him not to stop. For that matter, had he stopped with that incredible friction, I would have used his own gun on him.

His warm breath lowered to my ear as his hands continued to assault my now stiff nipples. "You like your punishment, girl?"

I stiffened to make him think that receiving a good feel wasn't on my *to-do* list. "I think you're losing your mind!"

"I haven't begun to lose my mind yet."

He parted my legs further with his thick boot, speaking in a heated growl. His warm hand massaged my buttocks, squeezing it as his other hand continued assaulting my breasts. I could feel his erection pressing against his pants, practically drilling into me with rocket fuel. My God, it felt as good as a chocolate truffle tasted—and I love chocolate. I wanted it, wanted him, and the fact that we were in the middle of a crowded section of town became my last concern. His voice excited me as he continued to caress me. "You feel so good. Do you taste just as good?"

"Why not find out yourself, jerk!"

"Something with a saucy mouth like yours must have some good stuff. Maybe I will find out and unload my bullets straight into you, smart mouth!"

"Then get on with it and stop torturing me."

"Is that what I'm doing, torturing you?"

I gritted my teeth. "Yes, sir."

"Good, precisely the effect I was going for. Torture makes me hot, and I like it super hot, Ms. Shane. I like it hot, so hot and loose that I could get lost in it all day long."

I felt another finger slide into my sopping wet juncture. With his penetration came a release that I had wanted for five months, and his reaction was so well worth the wait. "Goodness, you're too incredible to be a speed demon."

He rocked those demanding fingers in and out of me so expertly that I came hard, shivering, wanting to call to him, but not wanting to give him the satisfaction of knowing he was totally punishing me in all the right ways. My muscles squeezed his fingers, adding to pressure, along with wicked words. "Why don't you really punish me? After all, I did cross a median. I could have caused one of those eighteen-wheelers to roll over and close the freeway. Don't I need to be beat down for that?"

"Damn straight you do."

I screamed at him. "Then do it, Mr. Big Strong Policeman."

I heard him pull his zipper down and I smiled as wickedly as possible. I was about to get what I *really* deserved.

He smoothed his feverish tip up and down my behind,

barely dipping into my quivering sex for a tease. I screamed at him again, "Do it, or are you too meek to be wearing that decadent uniform?"

"Screw you!"

"Let's hope."

I guess my mouth was just too much for my pretty cop, and my ultimate punishment was a long, stiff shove straight into me, making me howl like an American werewolf in Detroit! I had spied his erection every time I saw him and wondered what it was like—now I knew.

He slowly moved that talented cock in and out of me with such precision. I could feel him fumbling around my clit, making it hum, singing praise to him as he caressed it. Then his action really started. He leaned over me, gyrating his hips and nailing me like I had never been nailed before. I was getting the bang of a lifetime, and from the one cop I needed it from, without courtesy of a new miniskirt.

My wonderful cop with the mile-long baton clinched me tighter to him, making me feel exactly how hard his muscles were—especially one muscle. He jerked ferociously, spilling bubbly hot liquid onto my lower back and derriere, then massaged it in as he came to a low simmer. His breathing calmed my own heaving chest that had his hands melted into them. I was sure my hair was a mess, but again, I didn't care. The rest of me had gotten its punishment, and I *so* deserved it!

He fixed my clothing, released my cuffed hands and proceeded to his squad car.

"Hey," I called out, almost in a frenzy, "What about my ticket?"

"Call it time served." He winked at me, that amazingly hard cock still pressing against his pants, before driving off.

My officer tapped on the car door, getting my attention. "Ma'am, are you okay in there?"

What had I done? I'd completely zoned out right before his eyes. I knew I had it bad for the guy, but daydreaming about him taking me in broad daylight had taken me to a whole new level. I regrouped as best I could and smiled. "I'm fine. Is there a problem, officer?"

"Do you know what you just did?"

Other than live out a fantasy in the front seat of my car? Sure! I resigned and answered him. "Yes, I crossed a freeway median."

"What for? That was awfully dangerous."

I could barely breathe, barely speak without blurting out, *"Are we going to get it on or what?"* He was so gorgeous, more gorgeous than what I had remembered from catching glimpses at him on the sly. I managed a reasonably sane response. "I'm late for work. Sorry if that caused a problem."

"It did, but it could have been worse."

"A semi could have nailed me, right?"

He peered suspiciously into my eyes as if he had actually said those same words at one time or another. Do tell. Then I figured he had finally recognized me. It would have been about damn time. "Ma'am, have you been drinking?"

Wrong response. No, no recollection of me just yet. "All I had was a martini with lunch, officer."

"Step from the vehicle."

"It was just one drink, hardly enough to get me inebriated."

"I want you to take a sobriety test."

I did as told and walked a straight line in front of him, hoping for a hot session against my trunk. Then again, I wasn't one for exhibitionism. This man deserved to be made love to in the privacy of a bedroom built for two. Once my walk was finished, I stood barely inches from him, seeing beauty beyond reason—in a cop who was *by the books* to a fault. "Did I pass your test, Mr. Cop?"

"You're some lady, Miss Tracey Shane. You did just fine." He handed me my license back, but looked to me again. "Watch that speed and . . ." He paused, his eyes leering into mine. "I know I've seen you before, and I think it was at the police station."

Finally!

"Have I arrested you before?"

Still not quite there with the recollection part, are you? "I've never been arrested in my life—well, maybe once in college."

That seemed to intrigue him. "Really? What for?"

I looked close at his badge, "Would you really like to know, Officer Troy Davenport?"

I moved my hand up and down his baton. "A sorority pledge. I had to disconnect the siren from a squad car. Is there anything that I can disconnect for you?" My lashes batted in a fake flirt, but I was very serious.

"You can get back to work safe and sound. That's what you can do for me." He shook his head again. "I have seen you before."

"Indeed, you have."

He scanned me from head to toe again. I could see a smile wanting to happen as he scoped me, but he kept it professional. "But where? I know now that I haven't arrested you because I would have remembered."

"I work on the eighth floor of police headquarters."

"I remember now. How could I not?"

"Tough day for everyone, I guess. Filing stacks of forms that you and others toss on my desk almost every week wrecks my brain too."

He slowly shook his head. "You're that beauty—I mean the file clerk for Chief Daisha Miller."

"Exactly," I said, smiling in hopes that he would tear up that tree trunk of a ticket. His Freudian slip hadn't gone unnoticed, however. I liked his compliment—loved it, in fact. It was what I needed to take my mind from that slab of concrete he called a ticket! There were *other* things that had taken my mind temporarily from my dire straits, the thickness in his trousers. The guy had a boner that I couldn't take my eyes from. It looked hot, seething hot and ready to set me on fire. See, there was a token from my sinful daydream. With a whiff of his cologne adding to his appeal, I was so ready for him, ready for him to slide his nightstick into me that I was sizzling.

His voice stiffened, bringing me back to attention. "I'm so surprised that I didn't recognize you immediately since I see you all the time."

"You have a tough job, Officer Davenport. Something is liable to slip from your memory sometimes, right?"

"Right. But you should have known better than to pull a stunt like that since you work with officers." He ripped the ticket from his book and handed it to me. "You may either appear in court and contest this or pay on the fourth floor." He turned to leave but faced me again with less of a trite expression. "I do show up for my hearings. Just so you know." He tipped his hat. "Have a good day, Ms. Shane, and be careful returning to work."

"Did they catch the offender on my floor?"

"We nailed him over an hour ago."

He was slow to leave, probably feeling bad for talking to me as though I were a common criminal. That was okay with me because it gave me more of an opportunity to scope him, bear witness to that tight erection that played a starring roll in my fantasy.

He wanted to act as though he was the calmest, smoothest cop on earth, but I saw him tense as I slid back into my car. He was still checking me out as he did on occasions at the precinct. However, he never inquired about who I was until he had to hand over the ticket. I looked down at the disgusting thing— $140.00. I'd have to work a whole day to recover those damages. I was okay with that because it would give me an opportunity to see him again, close up and personal. One close look at Mr.

Gorgeous, and I knew I had to have him, loosen him up, strip him down and wax that screaming magic wand he had in those cute dark blue pants. Oh yeah, he was all that!

My pissed demeanor would have been easier to deal with after a good roll in the back of his squad car. It would have taken away *my* pent-up tension and anxiety of having to share my paycheck with the cashier instead of giving almost all of it to my mortgage company. No deal. He was as straight-laced as a tennis shoe.

Before my beautiful, expensive officer drove off, I checked out his plate and badge number—107353. I had a little investigating to do on my own, to see what was cooking and how I could cook him one night in front of a nice cozy fire. My daydream minutes ago had started something that it had to finish.

Once I pulled into the parking lot at headquarters, I scoped the squad car lot and saw his license plate, but not one time that day did he bring his delicious cock up to my floor to tease me into fitful rages again. I couldn't even look for him due to someone adding to Troy Davenport's pile of bull sitting on my desk. That crap had to be filed by five, and it was two. Didn't leave a girl a lot of time to check the premises for a cutie. He never made his appearance that day or the next. *Sheesh!*

Two days later, I was sitting in traffic court listening to the many sob story cases before mine, and the judge was relentless, slamming that gavel down and sending people left and right to the cashier. I was determined to fight the ticket whether cutie-pie had given it to me or not. I didn't have that kind of money to give away without a fight, even though I really did deserve it for crossing a freeway median.

I kept looking around for my cop, but he wasn't there. I figured him to be chasing other stupid people with infractions falling from their butts. Cool. I wouldn't have to pay the ticket. Saving money is always a good thing. That was part of my miniskirt money anyway.

Just as my case came up, the doors opened and in stepped Officer Troy Davenport looking as dapper as ever in those tight blue pants, neat, tight-fitting shirt and shoes shiny enough to see every cloud in the sky. He took his hat off and sat on the bench across from me. He looked different with his hat off, sexier. I didn't think that was possible. His soft, dark hair glistened, making me want to run my fingers through it and lick from there down. The boy was slamming in that suit. Muscles rippled from it, showing me how stacked he was. Though I had been watching him for five months, wishing I could eat frosting from him and get satisfied in my own little fantasy world with him. Then reality awakened.

The judge's loud, aggravating voice bellowed through the mindless chatter still cluttering the courtroom. "Ms. Shane, you crossed a freeway median on Friday, June fifteenth, at 1:43 in the afternoon. Is this correct?"

"It is, your honor, but traffic was clear and—"

"You crossed traffic lanes nonetheless and Officer Davenport pulled you over." The judge leaned over. "Do you know how many semis travel I-75, young lady? You could have caused a major collision."

I know this already, for God's sakes! "But your honor—"

"Officer Davenport, your account of the scene, please."

"Your honor, it was clear-cut. I was returning paperwork on a felon from headquarters to the Beverly Hills police department when I noticed Ms. Shane crossing the grass median. I pulled her over, tested her for intoxication, gave her the infraction and told her she could either pay or show up today. Plain and simple, your honor."

Troy looked over at me, and I noticed how he could barely look me in the face. However, that did not stop him from narrowing to the short hem of my *other* mini, the one that had to play for sympathy—which didn't work. I couldn't get mad at him, though. He was so damn fine. Straight-laced, but that's what added to his appeal. There was a sweet man hidden behind that hard hat and uniform with a revolver at his side. I could see it in his eyes as he tried not looking at me directly. I paid the one hundred forty dollars, and that was that. He went his way, and I went mine, to cry behind a stack of papers as tall as I was.

Well, that was the end of my days with him, so I thought. Later, I ended up passing him in the halls and he would speak; actually, he acted as though he were happy to see me. As the days went on, it seemed like Troy Davenport was around every corner. I would see him in the cafeteria having lunch with his crowd of blue-clad buddies. I would see him with Chief Daisha Miller as they chatted in the halls. Funny thing, he always looked gloomy within her company, but the chief herself, AKA Demon Bitch Straight From Hell Itself, who was always ready to chew someone out if the least little thing went wrong, had a constant look of euphoria going on. She liked him, and I knew it. What other reason would her cheeks spread apart to show the world a row full of capped silver teeth? After thinking about it, what woman wouldn't smile at Troy?

Each day Troy passed me, he had a smile for me. I wanted more than that pretty smile of his. I wanted him, but apparently so did Chief Miller. Yeah, like he would go for the farm animal type. Please, girl. Get a life with something other than that gun of yours!

I was really pressed for time the Thursday before the station audit. There were papers and case files to put away and there was barely any time to breathe, let alone go to the toilet. But when Troy walked in, all was right with the world once again. I peeked from behind my file cabinet and smiled. "Officer Davenport, how are you today?"

"I'm great. You?"

"Wonderful." *Now that you're here.* "Where's your stack of papers that you usually have for me at the end of each month?"

"I'm not here for that today. But you can help me with something else."

"Anything you need, just let me know."

He smiled and approached me with an infectious smile. "That's good to know. Actually, the real reason I'm here is because I need to apologize to you."

"What do you need to apologize for?"

"The ticket last week."

"No, I deserved that. It hurt a bit in the pocketbook, but that's what I get for being silly."

"You're not silly. Everyone makes moves like that at times. But I was very rude to you, talking to you like you were a hood instead of my coworker. You are a coworker, Tracey. Without you and the others filing this shit away, the place would be swamped."

That really brightened my day. "That's sweet, Officer Davenp—"

"Troy. Officer sounds too official."

"Troy it is then." I couldn't help but stare dreamy-eyed at the pretty thing. Disrobing for him would make my infatuation for him grow even stronger. For that matter, the way he was looking at me was making me ache for the many, many inches I knew he had stuffed into that uniform.

His words brought me back from copland. "I'm actually here to give you your money back."

"My money back! Why would you do that?"

"Because I want to." He moved in closer. "I haven't really had the nerve to say this to you until now, but I knew who you were the second I saw your pretty face when I pulled you over. What I told the judge was a lie. I followed you out of here, trailed you, hoping I would have the nerve to meet you for lunch and get to know you. Surprise you. I'm shy, though."

"Shy around little old me?"

"You're really beautiful, Tracey, and beautiful women make me nervous for some reason."

He should never be shy around Daisha then.

"I've noticed you since you made your arrival to this department . . . on February eleventh at nine in the morning." He saw the shock on my face. "Yeah, I remember the first day I saw you because you were so gorgeous. I love how you dress in those short skirts, ruffled blouses. Each day you would pass me in the hall, I would turn around and watch you for a minute, relishing how you smelled, how your hair danced around your neck and shoulders."

Is he talking to me? I turned around in case there was a beautiful woman behind me. No one there, just a little pawn facing a knight, a knight in shining armor—and badge. I could hardly speak from being overwhelmed. My voice oozed compassion. "You . . . you remember the day I started?"

"Sure. How many beautiful women do you think work in this building?"

As I thought about it, hardly any. To me, a woman just didn't look dainty strapping on a pistol and cuffs. My meek voice continued. "I just can't believe you think I'm pretty. But there's others around here prettier than me, Troy."

"Yeah, who?"

"Well, there is Officer Randal."

"Not really. She's too butch acting and she's in love with her revolver."

"How about Chief Miller?" Going out on a limb here. I knew she looked like a horse, but I had to say something nice about the person who signed my overtime checks.

His eyes shifted. "She's okay, but you take the cake. I just wish I could have told you before giving you the ticket." He held out a hand full of cash. "Go on, take it."

I slowly reached for the money. "Are you sure?"

"I'm positive, Tracey. I know you guys don't make a bunch of money here and that one hundred forty dollars was a lot."

"But I deserved it."

"Stop saying that. Put the money in that cute little red purse you tote around."

"You even know what color purse I have?"

"I notice everything about you."

"Aren't you just a sweetie? A big, sexy sweetie who totes a gun."

"Does it bother you? I can take it off and—"

"Actually, Troy, I like it. It's arousing."

He moved in a little closer, close enough to give me a whiff of that famous cologne of his that made my legs weak from erotic attraction. That coupled with how he was staring at me made my panties disintegrate. I wanted him bad. I could just see myself dropping to my knees, yanking his zipper down, pulling out an erection and pleasing him until he fainted. The idea of my hands on his bare chest, tickling rippled pecs and a hard stomach was making me crazier than I already was. I had to divert my attention before he knew my true feelings. I looked at the money in my hands. "At least let me treat you to a drink after work since you were so kind to give it back to me."

"I can't. My wife might get the wrong impression."

"Oh, I see. I should have known someone sweet like you was married."

"Separated. She is still very jealous, even though we don't live together."

"How would she know I took you out unless she works here?"

He hesitated. "She . . . uh, she does work here."

"You're making my lungs deflate, Troy. She works here? Who is she, an officer?"

"Yes and no. It's Daisha, your boss."

I wanted to jump up and down, screaming, *No, Troy, no! It's against the law to marry horses.* Instead, I acted as calmly as possible. "I, uh . . . didn't know that."

"I'm sorry to spring that on you, but we're pretty much finished."

"Pretty much?"

"We've been married seven years and quite frankly, I think she loves that gun more than she loves me. That's why I got the separation, but as you well know, she still packs, and I'm afraid she will be stupid enough to use it."

I had to find a chair before I hurled the salad I had just had for lunch. I sat there looking up at that pretty, built Adonis wondering how in fuck's name he could crawl into bed with the likes of Daisha Miller for seven years. She was a hog in chief's clothing, and it sported a gun. Wasn't that just nice? I could get killed for looking at him. I had to regroup before I showed him what I thought of him marrying something that grazed in pastures.

"Any children?"

"I wanted some, but she was too busy with her career. What about you?"

"I would love to have children, when the right man comes along."

"He could already be here."

"Perhaps, but he might need a little more than separation papers."

"You have a good point."

"What made you decide to get the separation, other than the 'in love with her gun' thing?"

"There was never time for me."

"That's a pity because I can tell you still think about her."

He sat down in the chair across from hers. "Really? What makes you think that?"

"There's a sparkle in your eyes when you mention her." *Though I have no idea why. You don't look like the animal fetish type.*

"How do you know that wasn't for you?"

"Because it can't be, Troy. Daisha would put a bullet between my eyes."

He straightened his tie. "Daisha would never do that, nor would I let her. She just has a temper, is all. You're right, however. She has ways at times, but everyone does." He moved in closer, taking my hand. "That shouldn't stop us from being friends, right? Maybe more than friends, if you're interested."

I was interested, but Annie Oakley would have a problem, and I knew it. My eyes teetered back to his, wanting the man more and more simply because of his words and kindness alone. I was beginning to see him as more than a powerful sex machine. He was a man with needs, yet he still cared for Daisha, but not in a romantic way anymore. Did she know that? Nonetheless, I admired how he wanted to spare her feelings. "I would love to, Troy. A girl can never have enough friends. But what about Daisha? She would be hurt if she saw you with someone else, especially me. She doesn't like me."

"The thing about it, we are still separated, and she knows why." He took my hand and gently kissed it. "Besides, Daisha doesn't dislike you."

"Then what would you call it?"

"Jealousy. Anyone who is beautiful is a threat to her. That's why she doesn't have friends around here. That's why she didn't know how to handle a marriage."

I smiled. "You really think I'm beautiful?"

"Sure. Haven't other men told you that?"

"It only counts when I think the man is worth it."

"How do I rate?"

"In perfect standing, Officer Davenport. And I'm not beautiful."

He rubbed my shoulder and smiled. "Don't underestimate yourself. I've gotta go. You know how it is with us cops. We're never satisfied unless we're chasing something. But, I'd love to chase you if I had the opportunity."

"It would be a short chase, Troy. I'd stop in the name of the law—your law." I gently yanked on his tie. "Go get the bad guys. Come in and talk to me again when you can."

"Count on it, now that I finally got the nerve to talk to you."

"Oh. What about me treating you to a drink?"

"I'll get back with you about that. I just don't want Daisha causing trouble. You understand, don't you?"

"I guess." I watched him walk out, and slouched back into my chair. *Why would he have to be hooked up, and to all people, Daisha?* In a way, I wished I had never laid eyes on him. Now that I actually had contact with him, I didn't want to be without him. But it was either him or my job because Daisha would certainly cause trouble. I had a mortgage and a habit of liking to eat, so I had to keep my job. Unfortunately, Troy was not to be hooked with me romantically. Friends though, and I was happy knowing he would be in my life somehow.

Since that day, I would see him in the halls, and elevators, and we would give one another big hugs. That was how we got to be really good friends. Still, I wanted more than that, but knew I couldn't get it because he still, somehow, belonged to Daisha. What did she have that any other slug didn't have? Marriage papers with Troy's name on it. Sure, he was separated, but until a divorce was achieved, we would be friends and only friends. My heart broke into pieces each time I saw him.

The day after the audit was a bad day for two reasons: one, the audit took all day and there were files all over that had to be replaced. The second reason, having to return them to central files. The day before, Rhonda had been polite enough to get the files for me, sparing me the sordid job of going into the belly of the building to get them. I was scared of dark basements. I think that came from watching too many stupid-ass hacker movies on Sci-Fi on boring Friday nights after dumping my ex. Police headquarters had *that kind* of a basement—dark, gloomy, damp and musty. There were rows and rows of file cabinets just deep enough for a raving maniac to hide behind. My luck that day, I had to go it alone, and have it all filed before attending the departmental meetings. Having to stare at Daisha Miller for an hour or two in a meeting, knowing all I wanted in life was her hopefully soon-to-be-ex-husband, made the pit of my stomach churn. Wasn't it bad enough watching her graze fields from 9 to 5? Doing it again after work would take me to my limit.

As I exited the elevator in central files, I looked down the long hall, dreading every step I took into spookville. How was I to know that some simpleton hadn't escaped from some misguided cop, and sneaked down here to wait for me? I didn't know, but what I did know was that if the records weren't returned, Daisha would be in trouble with her boss and my own head would be on the chopping block. I was, at any given moment, close to that with Daisha anyway. There was something about me that she didn't like despite what Troy said. Sure, I knew she was jealous, but her treachery went beyond that with me. I think it was the fact that I wasn't barn-bred, corn-fed and fattened up for the roasting, like *others.* Actually, it was the fact that all the men at headquarters smiled and spoke to me. Can I help it if I'm friendly, and speak to everyone whether I know them or not? Daisha hated that, but that was her problem. My problem, at the time, was not only dealing with her, but with that ridiculous basement. I took a deep breath and treaded on.

I made time, knocking files out of the way left and right so I could get out of there. With only a few stacks left, I walked over to the W's and got to work. A knock on the door behind me scared the holy crap out of me. My files dropped to the ground and I whipped around to see Troy smiling at me. With my hands covering my heart, I closed my eyes, saying, "Troy, you scared me to death!"

He picked up my files and laid them on the cabinet. "I didn't mean to scare you. I thought you saw me enter."

"I didn't, thank you. What are you doing down here?"

"Got something to do. Need some help with those files?"

I couldn't say no to him, it would have been against my religion not to want his company in any way I could get it. "Well, I do want to get outta here."

He saw me shivering and took my hand. "What's wrong?"

I couldn't talk rationally with Troy's soft hands covering mine. For that matter, I could barely think straight. "I . . . I hate this basement. It gives me the creeps."

"You don't have to be scared now. I'm here with you."

"Yeah, but for how long? I'll be down here another hour."

His perfect light brown eyes stared into my own nervous eyes. "How long do you want me . . . need me?"

How about forever. "Don't you have crooks to chase?"

"Not today. I have desk duty."

"You have filing to do as well?"

His sexy smile lit me, filtered me like a long, deep menthol. "I don't file, Tracey. I doubt that I could do it, at least not the way you do. I'm sure you do everything pretty damn well." He inched in closer with my hand still in his. When his lips were barely inches from my ear, he admitted to why he was down there. "I saw you come down and wanted to ask you something."

Heat emitted from him, and I could feel it almost pressing into me, wanting to take it in and relish in it, but I'm sure Daisha would be able to smell me on him for the next fifty years. That's how much I knew I would explode on him if he got one more inch closer.

I tried backing up but he followed me. "What did you want to ask me, Troy? I've got a lot to do down here."

"This won't take long." His fingers smoothed and caressed my hands, warming them, making them, and the rest of my body, tingle with just the very idea of him so close to me. I loved the feeling, had imagined it, craved it since the day I laid my eyes on him. Knowing that he had partnered up with Daisha rather took some of the thrill away—but not enough.

"What can I help you with?"

"You seem so distant today. What's wrong?"

"The meetings after work, this basement . . . Daisha."

"Daisha? What's she got to do with the price of tea in China?"

"Everything, Troy. You couldn't even have a drink with me because of her. And I think I just let myself get a little too wrapped up in you. I think about you all the time, yet I can't do anything about that."

"Tracey. Don't let Daisha scare you. She may be a little cracked, but she won't use that gun on you. Take my word for it."

I laid the file on the top drawer. "Troy, I know she isn't that stupid, but she can make sure I don't have a job here. I interviewed with her. She gave me this job."

"Wrong. The city or state gave you this job, and she would have to have some damn good proof as to why you wouldn't be performing your job. She doesn't have that. You're here all the time, you get your work done and you even stay over two nights a week."

"You know that, too?"

"I know almost everything about Miss Tracey Shane. But I don't know enough. That is why I'm really down here with you. I came down to ask if you wanted to go to Enrique's with a few of us tomorrow night."

"But I thought you didn't want to go anywhere with me because of Daisha."

"You're right. That was holding me back, but after thinking

about it, I realize that Daisha can't run my life. We're separated. Though I will still do all that I can do for her, she is not my keeper. She ruined that part two or more years ago."

"Are you sure about this, Troy? I don't want you doing anything you don't want to do."

He moved in closer to me. "Baby, I'm so sure about this that I can't think about anything but you. I was going to leave a note on your desk about Enrique's, but I saw you enter the elevator and I . . . well, wanted to follow."

Why would he say it that way? He must have known that my panties were becoming a creamsicle from the mere sound of his voice. It was deep and husky, yet so innocent sounding. He had the perfect mix of brawn and sensitivity, and I wanted to experience it first hand. His invitation was very, well . . . inviting whether Daisha was in the picture or not. "Enrique's? I've always wanted to go there."

"The food is really good, so is the liquor. Do you drink?"

"A little. I like champagne."

"I'm sure it tastes great on you. What I mean is—"

"It's okay, Troy. I like you, too, the same way I hope you like me."

"There should be no question of that."

God, he was making me so nervous. There I was flirting with my boss's man—a boss who was a cop at that! She could nail us both in a dark alley one night, and no one would know anything except her and the smoke coming from the barrel of her gun. What the hell, Daisha wasn't exactly the one I was having orgasmic fits over. The time was mine and we were alone in a dark basement that was seemingly becoming romantic by the minute. Troy had a way of making my fear of Daisha become water off a turtle's back—no big deal. Still, I had to ask. "Will Daisha be there?"

"Maybe. A bunch from the station is going."

"Can I think about it?"

"Yeah, think right here and now, with me standing here waiting."

"You don't give a girl a chance edge-wise, do you?"

"Not when I want her more than I want life itself."

"You should really think about that divorce, Troy."

"I know I should, but I want to do it right, not leave her hanging. The fact of the matter, I used to love her, but she's so power hungry that she wants to possess me. That's why if I break things off, I have to do it the right way. I don't want to break her."

"What about how you feel? Aren't your feelings important?"

"I care more about others for some reason." He pulled open a drawer and filed a few folders as I watched him. He was in misery, wanting one woman while trying not to hurt another. That was compassion; something few men I knew had conquered. That's what made him more attractive to me. He was real, but in need of something more real than himself—love. I didn't know whether Daisha loved him or not, but he was right about one thing when it came to her: she was power hungry. What she wanted, she went for and apparently, Troy was one of her tokens. I was scared of that, because no matter how he tried convincing me that she wouldn't hurt me in any way, I still wasn't one hundred percent convinced. I didn't want to be made an example of who not to be. Daisha had that power.

He looked over at me after several minutes of awkward silence. "So, you wanna go to Enrique's with us?"

"Sure?" I had to conquer the fear if I wanted Troy in my life. In his own way, he would see to me getting over it by pushing Daisha in my face until I was nervy enough to take her on. If I ever had to. So I teased him. "You'll be my protector in case the big, bad Daisha confronts me while dancing with you?"

"My gun's already loaded, girl."

"You'd shoot her over me."

"That's not the gun I'm talking about."

Naturally my eyes lowered to the weapon inside his pants, already cocked and ready for action—my action—and I was so ready to give it, despite Daisha looming over me like a giant rain cloud ready to soak a newly done hairdo. Restraint was my only salvation because it would save me, and my overtime checks. If Daisha got one good whiff of Troy all over me, which he would be, I could kiss overtime and mortgage notes paid on time good-bye. I would be bold and brave with Daisha, but today wasn't that day. I stayed my distance and continued my work. So did he. He knew and understood my dilemma, until the question that practically busted his seams was asked.

"You would dance with me?"

"In a heartbeat. That's why Daisha better not show up at Enrique's. She may get embarrassed."

Troy smiled and inched closer to me. "Really? What would you do to me that could be so embarrassing?"

"Never mind, Troy. Go back to work."

What both of us continued to do was enjoy that awkward silence again, with a brief word or two shared and nothing more. One good thing, he was taking away my fear of that basement.

Minutes later, Troy slammed a file on top of the cabinet. "Damn!"

I looked at him with wide eyes. "Are you okay?"

"No, I'm not okay."

His hand slowly massaged his temple, and I took his other hand. "Troy, what is it?"

"I can't lie to you, Tracey."

"What are you talking about?"

"You don't know how hard it is to be near you and not have you. I know I should wait and get a divorce before even touching another woman, but it's too hard with you. I want to do the right thing by Daisha because basically, she is a good person.

But I've been doing the very thing I have been telling you not to do."

"What is that?"

"To not worry about Daisha. Is she so big an entity that she can control two lives without even being in the room?"

"She shouldn't. But it seems we are still letting her."

"That's about to end. My separation is legal, Tracey, and damn it, I want you. I want to feel your body pressed against mine. I want to know what it's like to taste your lips. I want to know how good my body will feel while filling yours. I want all of that, Tracey." He took my face into his hands. "But most of all, I want to know what it's like to have a real loving relationship. I know you can give me that. I know you care about me simply because you care about Daisha."

"What? I don't care about her."

"You do, or you wouldn't have cared what you would have done to get me, married, separated or not."

I hadn't thought of it like that before. And I admitted to it. "I guess I do care about her. But what I care about most is how you feel. I want a relationship with you, Troy, but only if it's right for you."

I smiled into his tempered face with words so willing to be free. "You know, the first time I saw you I went hog wild, but I didn't know you. I just wanted to screw you and get satisfied in ways I knew only you could satisfy me. Then I actually met you. True, you were giving me a ticket, but I had you nonetheless in my grasps. When you gave me my money back, I knew I wouldn't be able to hide my feelings . . . like now."

He moved so close to me that I could feel the powerful tenting erupting in his pants, and wanted it throbbing deeply inside me. He was so eager for me, but not for sex alone. This was different, and something I had always wanted with a man. A true relationship.

I shrugged my shoulders. "I won't lie and say what you have in your pants isn't doing something for me because it is. The only thing I've ever wanted to do was hold you in my arms and claim you, but Daisha was in the way of that."

"She's not in the way down here."

"You wouldn't think badly of me kissing you? I know you're still technically married, but—"

"Tracey. I would think badly of you if that's all you did to me."

"What do you want?"

"All of it. Everything!"

Troy laid his hat on the top of the file cabinet, then reached to loosen his tie. All along my eyes widened, hungry for every inch he could deliver to me. As I watched him slowly unbutton his shirt and loosen his belt, something exploded inside me. I rode the wave and let those tiny electrons invade my body as he exposed his to me. My hands shook, and I almost dropped to my knees when he slid his hand up and down a phallus that was ready to be uncovered and pampered by a woman who truly wanted him in every sense of the word.

With his shirt gaping open and his hand rubbing his chest, he reached for me. "You take me the rest of the way because I can't wait to have your hands on me. The minute I saw you, I knew this day was going to happen. I made it happen by following you down here. I almost made it happen the day I followed you to the mall, but I chickened out."

"I imagined you making love to me as you gave me that sobriety test, but that's all it was, a daydream—until now."

"I know the feeling and I'm not running scared anymore, girl. I don't care who is upstairs waiting for me to return to her."

He pulled me into him, and my body sizzled from the contact. My fingers traced his lip line, barely able to fathom touching him. God, he was as soft as I'd imagined. I stared into his eyes while stroking his full lips and finished exposing his chest. My hands were so busy that I hadn't time to think of my actions, didn't really care about anything other than what I was about to do with Mr. Troy . . . man of the hour, man of the day.

His lips nipped at my fingers, soon sucking them slowly, pretending his lips were mine as they coveted a taut erection in slow, sucking movements. My other hand stroked pecs so strong and sinfully satin that my knees buckled. Was I really touching this man? The feel of his nipples as my nails tenderly raked against them proved that very potent point. My hand traced the muscles of his ribcage, then tapered to his stomach, circling his navel and toying the band of his underwear. I could feel the heat from his engorged erection pressing against my palm, getting hotter and hotter, needing its flames doused. Gladly. I was already clinically insane from want, why not take my gift and pamper it.

Our lips finally met and we drank from one another in fusion. Lips, tongues and desire just got us higher as we intertwined, mating, pulling, loving. His lips parted from mine and sucked my neck. His hands tightened around my behind, squeezing, rocking against me. His cock was so ready to plunge into me, crack my code, and I wanted him to so desperately.

Our lips met again as he raised my skirt, quickly finding the seat of my wet panties. He groaned as he slipped two fingers into my damp sex, rocking them into me the way his hips rocked against mine. He devoured me, slipping finger after finger around my clit, rubbing it, making it his slave. Those same very active fingers stroked my labia, tracing the delicate folds with the tips of his fingers, making my juices flow. We parted, and he stared at my flushed face, smiling. "This is so incredible, Tracey. I knew you had to feel like satin. I'm so juiced for you that I can barely stand it."

He kissed me again with lavish pulls and tugs, breathing against me as he screwed the daylights out of my sex with his fingers. I could barely hold back, and he felt that same sensation within my body. "You ready to come, baby? You ready to release that sweetness to me, tighten around me?"

"Troy! Please."

He worked his fingers into me harder, rougher, until I collapsed and spilled my cream onto his waiting fingers. The more I came, the more he rocked me, kissed me, tightened his grip on me.

I took his rod, stroked it through his pants material, and took him hard, cupping him. His tip moved within my grasp and I whispered, "Take it out, Troy, and let me have it."

"You want it, baby?"

"Since day one."

He loosened his belt and zipper while I played in his hair, feeling the loose curls wrap around my fingers. I trailed the delicate hair on his neck and sideburns while staring into a face that was so magnificent. How could he be so incredible and not truly be mine? No answers to that impossible question, but I took what I had at the moment, and played it well.

His exposed erection took me by storm, made me remember my vivid daydream. Compared to the real man who was before me, the dream was so infantile, so dull. I could really see him, all of him, inside and out. He was beautiful. It was beautiful and perfect for deep satisfaction. My mouth watered from the sight of it. It glistened from moisture, his tip sprinkled from need of release, and I dropped to my knees to give *it* what it had to have. I stared up at him. "She must have been crazy to not stop that separation. If you were mine, you would have been treated like a king from the day I met you."

"You are mine, Tracey, and I do feel like a king. Now, let me feel a true queen."

"You want it now?"

"Right now, baby. Give me everything you can possibly give me."

I had to take him, all of him, and right away. I looked up at him time enough to see his head rear back, eyes tighten from pleasure, jaws clinching as insane words erupted from him, "Take it, girl. Take all of me."

That was my clue. I wanted nothing but to satisfy him, giving him everything he had been missing. His thick veins tickled my tongue, making me salivate from his taste. He was wickedly delicious.

His hands played in my long strands, forcing my mouth deeper onto him as he readied himself for the ultimate release. His fingers strummed my cheeks. "I'm so ready, baby, so ready to give you what I have. Do you want it?"

"Every inch—deep and hard, Troy."

He pulled that fabulous member from me, and I watched it dangle and waiver in the air, so tight with liquid love that he could barely walk. He stood me to my feet and pointed to the rug a few feet away. "I wish this was a more comfortable place for us because you deserve better. But I can't wait."

I kissed his lips again. "I can't wait either." I lay on the rug and awaited his entrance. Troy mounted me, and my legs automatically surrounded him. My arms wrapped around his bare back as he unbuttoned my blouse and lowered my bra. His lips met with the first tender nipple and tugged on it, making it perkier with each caress. Inside, my body howled as he licked down my chest and stomach, and tugged at my skirt and panties. Immediately, his tongue circled the curls of my pubic hair. I wanted his tongue inside me, circling me, taking me— any way Troy wanted to take me.

He massaged me, making me wetter than I thought imaginable, making me long for his penetration. Once again, he kissed my lips then stood up, bringing my sex close to his tip. He massaged the garters holding my sheer stockings and smiled. "I've always wanted a woman who wore sexy things like this."

His entrance was so smooth and quick, forcing everything

inside me in one thrust. He trembled with contact of my dew, sliding so tightly inside me that he had to bite his own lip not to scream.

As he rocked my soaking sex, his lips on mine matched his motion, kissing and talking as he rocked me to my very core. "This is so incredible, Tracey, and I've wanted you for so long. Five months of aching for you, but it was so well worth the wait."

My nails raked across his back and sides, my body tightened around his, my core constricted to his size. I was getting what I wanted, plus so much more, and from the man I wanted it from. I didn't know sex could be that sensational, but with a man like Troy, sensational was playing him down. The more he rocked me, the tighter that feeling inside me became. I could barely hold on, needing to release that powerful tension so I called to him, "Rock it, Troy, and let me bring it."

"Bring it, baby, bring it all." He went deeper, lifting my buttocks from the ground with his force. "Explode on me." He stroked my mouth, my breasts, stretched my core with both his hands and his rod until that rush bubbled from me. He smiled at my release. "You're so beautiful, and I can't believe anything this succulent exists. I never knew life could be like this."

We soon released together, grinding, squirming, smiling. His fuel filled me completely, dripping from me, against me, inside me and it was so hot!

Troy rested against me briefly before I packed his goodies away and kissed his moist lips. We stared at one another in pleasant silence over the miraculous event. When we finally stood, we hugged desperately, not wanting to part.

We quickly filed the last of the folders then walked the stairs together. At the top, we parted, and Daisha was none the wiser of the joy he and I shared in central files. I rode the elevator back to my floor, now more determined to see Troy at Enrique's no matter if all of Detroit was there or not.

* * *

Friday night . . .

I looked past the crowd of people filling Enrique's dance floor and saw a table of blue awaiting me. Troy's hand waved frantically in the air to get my attention. As I looked at my table of blue, and at the man I made incredible love to, I noticed yet another thing . . . his other arm around Daisha Miller's shoulder.

What the hell was I supposed to do, stand there in the middle of a crowded dance floor and pray that Daisha would just go away? That had been my original plan, but from the look on Daisha's face, she was there to stay, and there to get wrapped up in as much of Troy Davenport as legally allowed in a public place. It sickened me watching her swirl her glass of DiSaronno as though it were a fine brandy. Everyone around the precinct knew that was her drink because she reeked of it. Everyone also knew DiSaronno meant "of Saronno, Italy," somewhere we all wished Daisha would take a hike to. God only knew how everyone at the table could stand an evening out with her. They did it for Troy's sake and so did I. I stiffened my jaw, flattened my skirt and slowly walked over to brave the cold chill Daisha would surely blow my way if Troy as much as looked at me once. And he surely would.

Every male at the table stood to greet me, Troy being the first. "Hey girl, glad you could make it. You know everyone around here, Dan Schultz, Arnold Jenkins, Robert and his wife Jean, Tangi, Albert, Ryan—"

"I know everyone, Troy, remember, I work on Beaubien Street as well." I looked over at Daisha, seeing the makings of a smug look ready and waiting to attack me, but I was cool, calm and ready to take on anything—as well as take on Troy and have a blast of an evening with a man I was falling hard for. My hand stretched in Daisha's direction. "Captain Miller, it's nice to see you again."

She tipped her glass and remained quiet, ignoring my hand, as was her style. Troy and I exchanged a quick glance, knowing from that point on the air would be thick with emotion, remembering what we talked about regarding her and also with what we did in the basement of headquarters. That's what had kept me going for the past day or two, remembering the feel of his tight, muscular body across mine; feeling his strength between my thighs, hearing him tell me that he would never let anything hurt me. I could still feel his power, the essence of it as he moved through me, riding me, overpowering me, making me feel like a real woman for the first time in my twenty-seven years on earth.

I had to keep it to myself before Daisha smelled him in my thoughts like the sonar I knew she had on her insect exterior. Yes, Daisha had sonar attached to the antennae on her forehead. That was a common joke around the department when I started, that she could smell the scent of a woman in the pores of her man. At the time, as I was laughing, assuming it was true, I hadn't any idea at the time that her man was Troy. Go figure. But I wanted Troy, wanted him enough to try and pull him away from her. I had a good start, and that was for damn sure! We had shared not only sex, but desire, tension, emotion, all the things that a new couple were supposed to share.

To break the ice, Troy broke into the chatter at the table. "Tracey, order anything you like. This round of drinks is on me."

"Watch it there. I've been known to get expensive stuff."

His eyes twinkled in such a seductive manner, one that told me he understood the connotations. "I can handle that, Miss Shane. Besides, the next round is on Robert—go crazy when ordering. He's used to abuse."

I ordered a Long Island iced tea—anything to make me dull, and null and void to the idea of Daisha Miller stroking Troy's inner thighs. I guess that was her way of trying to get in good with him again. I was hoping it wouldn't have worked.

Amongst the laughter, talking and all-around good times, Daisha sat there like a bump on a log taking drink after drink from Troy's wallet. Maybe it was his point to get her plastered so he could feel free with me. Maybe it was Daisha's plan as well. She hated the looks I was constantly getting from all the men at the table, even from Robert who was there with his wife. I couldn't help it, and I'm glad to admit that I don't look like a five-foot-three-inch version of Dracula. Though Daisha probably assumed I was drinking Troy's blood straight from the jugular. How wrong. His blood wasn't what I wanted. Men found me sexy and that was a plus in my life.

The only man I was really interested in, however, had his arm around the one woman too stubborn to give me a compliment about anything from the way I dress to the expert way I do my work. One compliment from her would blow down her house of cards. I was there to have a good time and not worry about Daisha Miller for once in my life.

As the evening wore on, I got my share of dances from the men at my table and even a couple of strangers who actually asked permission from everyone in my company. I noticed how Troy would inspect them, making sure they would return me safely to him, though I hadn't had one dance with him. That was the only thing that made Daisha smile halfway. He was still in her arms, but why was still a mystery to me. That was the only thing in life I could envy her for. I had a part of him, though, a part she would never know about until he left her, if he ever would.

There came a point in the evening when my dance card was empty and I was alone at the table, with the exception of Allister, who danced with no one. The ultimate dance song for lovers came on and there I was alone with Allister. Where were my strangers when I needed one? Even Troy took to the floor with Daisha once Aretha Franklin's "Until You Come Back to Me" lit up the sound system. I wanted so badly to be in his arms, to be the one his hands were caressing, feeling his huge erection parting my legs as he glided me across the floor. Nothing doing. I sipped my iced tea and kept my eyes glued to the table. No way in hell did I want to see the king of my domain touching another woman, even though he had been married to her for years.

When I finally looked up from my drink, Troy's eyes were on me. He had purposely turned Daisha's back so he could see me, smile and wink his dazzling eyes at me. It made me feel that I had won anyway, whether Daisha was dancing with him or not. His heart wasn't on the dance floor, but at the table with me. My heart soared.

As he danced with her, hugging her tightly in his arms I watched, remembering the basement of 1300 Beaubien fondly, for once. I wanted more of it, needed to feel Troy's body inside of me, his heart locking with mine. Instead of getting what I really wanted, I ordered another drink. Getting pissy drunk was my only salvation until I was back in central files on Monday morning with Troy Davenport on top of me.

As it turned out, I didn't have to wait for Monday. *Another* ultimate lover's song came on. Each time I heard that song on the radio, it gave me chills, sexual chills that made me want to get up and slow dance alone or with whoever it was next to me at the time. Thankfully, the person at my side was Troy. He had pulled me onto the floor the minute the DJ put it on. The look Daisha gave us as we walked off could have melted iron. I didn't care. Troy was soon to be back in my arms and that was all that mattered in my life at that time. Dealing with Daisha, if I had to, would be on Monday through Friday, nine to five and nothing more. The weekends were mine.

Not lowering the lights for a romantic song would have been sacrilege, so naturally, the lights lowered. It was so dark I couldn't see my own hand in front of my face. I liked it that way. What I liked even more was Troy whispering in my ear. "I requested this song for us."

"You did? That was sweet, but what about Daisha? She looked at us as if we had committed mass murder."

"Forget her for now. This song is ours."

I moved closer into his well-tuned body, feeling the heat of his badge pressing against my upper chest—metal to hot, boiling metal—and it excited me. Still, Daisha was in the back of my mind, waving her finger at me in a hood-rat manner. I spoke quietly into Troy's ear. "We may take some heat for this."

"We're cool. Don't worry about it."

"Why don't you tell her you want your divorce?"

"Tracey."

"Yes, Troy?"

"I don't want to talk about Daisha when this song is on. Listen to how smooth it is, how melodic, how sensual. This is not a Daisha song, it's a Tracey Shane song."

"You're right. I'm sorry."

"Don't be sorry. Just relax with me like you did the other day. Wasn't that incredible?"

"Yes, like now." I moved into him, swaying my hips to his, feeling his body so eager to press itself against me and work miracles. The hotter Troy got, the more my hands stroked his taut shoulders, feeling his muscles, relishing in them. His hair felt so good against my fingers, and his lips—smooth as silk as they secretly caressed my neck. It was nothing but love from that point on.

His hands stroked my tight derriere during the entire song, feeling every skin cell. I bet he knew exactly what size panties I wore. In the dark, you can do that and find out about anything;

you can live out an entire lifetime. When the lights come back on, reality quickly tells you who your lover *really* belongs to. That's why I love the night. You can be whoever you want to be.

The current song stopped serenading us, but the lights remained off, making way for the Platters' "Magic Touch." He had the magic touch, all right, and he showed it to me by granting me a tongue kiss so magnetic and irresistible that I melted into him. What the hell? It was dark anyway, and no one who mattered could see us. We took advantage of the time we had and made the moment last.

Troy finally broke the kiss, talking rather slowly as if mesmerized by my very touch. "We'd . . . we'd better get back to the table before—"

"Before Daisha gets suspicious?"

"Yes."

"I would sure love to be free with you one day, Troy. Will that ever be possible?"

He looked deeply into my eyes. "I think that day is almost here."

"Then does that mean we can go to your apartment and be alone instead of living out our fantasies at the station?"

"Right now my apartment is off limits."

That startled me, not expecting him to be so blunt. "Why, Troy?"

"Because Daisha just shows up whenever she can."

"Can't you stop that?"

"Give me time, baby. I promise I will make all of your dreams come true."

I released his hand, and we slowly walked back to a half-occupied table. Everyone was still strutting to the music other than Allister, and, oh yes, Daisha. She gave us yet another gut-wrenching glare before Troy ordered her another drink. It sure took a lot of Mr. Johnny Walker Red to get her under the influence.

I left soon after that because Daisha looked as if she wanted to clean her gun—with my brains—so I fled the possible scene of the crime before one actually took place. Troy walked me to the car and took my hand before I disarmed a car that even thieves were no longer interested in.

I stared into his handsome face. "Thanks for tonight."

"You're very welcome. So, I take it you like Enrique's?"

"It's beautiful, and that DJ really plays some golden hits."

"Yeah, Andrew is good at playing all of my favorites. Do you like the song I requested?"

"I have the Dells' greatest hits collection, and "Stay In My Corner" is my favorite song by them. My only wish was that I could have had more dances with you. I feel so comfortable and safe in your arms."

"You'll always be safe with me, Tracey. And I promise we will be together one day soon at my place."

"My place is always open for you. And I mean that. Maybe one night you can come over and listen to my collection, dance with me before a roaring fire, maybe even—"

"Make love again?"

A coy smile spread across my face like wildflowers. "If you like."

"Are you kidding? Girl, if I stepped foot into your house, Daisha would have to burn it down to get me out of it."

"Then let her burn it. I have homeowners' insurance."

"Is that an invitation?"

"A standing one, but you really should do something about Daisha if you don't love her anymore."

"That's the really sad part. I used to really love her. When we first met, she was a lot of fun. We did everything together, but she was always a little on the possessive side. That concerned me."

"I can tell she's that way about you even now. Have you ever given her cause not to trust you . . . other than meeting me?"

"I've never laid a hand on another woman while married to Daisha until I met you. The thing about it, she got that way after getting this promotion to captain three years ago. I thought it would only take a few weeks for her to get accustomed to her new status, but I was wrong, apparently. Later in the marriage, she preferred to stay at home and clean her gun than spend time with me. She wants her attention when *she* wants it. My feelings never really mattered."

"Power hungry maybe?"

"I think that's it."

"I can tell in your eyes that you really loved her. I'm sorry she changed on you."

He got that dreamy look in his eyes, his voice listless. "At least I think I loved her. Maybe it was the sex."

My stomach churned in major ways imagining her without clothes on. *Get real.* "Damn! Was it that good with her?"

"Not as good as yours. That was out of this world, Tracey, just like I knew it would be the minute I laid my eyes on you five months ago."

"But you didn't recognize me when you pulled me over."

"I told you I lied about that. It was a ploy, and it worked."

"Like a charm, Mr. Troy Davenport." I kissed his lips again before getting into my Camry. In the background, I could hear another Motown classic playing and wanted to stay and dance to it. Instead, I ushered Troy off before Pyromania, Queen of the Fire People, came looking for him. "You go back inside and have fun."

"Easy for you to say. I'll call you when I think you're home."

"You don't have my cell number."

"Wanna bet? I toyed with your cell phone one day when you made a run to another floor. You left it on your desk."

"I would have given you the number, Troy."

"I know, but I love to sneak around, do silly stuff."

"You can stop that by ditching Daisha."

"Soon, soon. I promise. I'll give you a half hour to get home, if that's okay with you?"

"Anything you do to me, Troy, is okay with me."

He tapped the roof of my car and sent me on my way to dreamland.

I lay in my bed awaiting his call, and within ten minutes, a mechanical voice singing "Tip-toe Through the Tulips" on my cellphone got my attention. "Troy?"

"You got it. I see you made it home safely."

"I'm safe and sound, just a little tired and ready to make love to this pillow."

"What about making love with me, in your own bed?"

"Aren't you still at the club trying to think of ways to ditch Daisha?"

"Already ditched her. She finally got drunk so I had one of the boys take her home. Robert owed me a favor anyway."

"Why does she like to get drunk?"

"Because she can. I don't really know, Tracey, it could be the pressure from her job, her family. She has a mother pulling on her for money all the time."

"That's tight. Sorry to hear that. So, where are you?"

"In front of your house."

I sat up quickly in bed. "You aren't serious!"

"Very serious. What are you wearing?"

"Why not come in and see. Bring your gun, you know, the really big one."

"It's awfully loaded. Are you sure you can handle it?"

"Get your ass in here, Troy."

Seconds later, I flung the door open, and fell into his arms. "What is it about you that makes you so irresistible, other than a slammin' body, good looks and stunning personality?"

"Is there anything else in life?"

"Not when it comes to you."

"Then take me to your bed and act out all your fantasies."

"What about your fantasy?"

He pulled me closer into him. "I'm looking at her."

He spread my robe apart, strummed his fingers from my collarbone to my pubic hair and smiled. "Now I can really see you."

"You like what you see?"

He didn't answer, but proceeded to kiss my naked shoulders and moved down. I held my breath in anticipation of what he was about to do to me. He stroked my slick folds, tenderly brushed against them then looked up at me with an infectious smile. "Where's the bed?"

I couldn't hold back on him. As soon as we entered my room, I started on his shirt, quickly unbuttoning it while he removed his tie. It slid so easily from his shoulders and down his long arms, dropping to the floor. His belt buckle and zipper moved effortlessly through my fidgety fingers. Once those restraints were diminished, I felt the oozing heat coming from his pants. Goodness, I couldn't wait to slide my hands inside and feel him—really feel him—and in the comfort of my own bedroom, not some cold, musty basement full of criminal files.

I helped him with his boots and slid the pants from his legs. When I looked at him, my face lit like it never had before. He was amazing, finely toned, light brown muscles, tall, slender and staring back at me wearing nothing but a smile and a big erection covered by Hanes.

Troy moved into me and slid off what was left of my robe from my anxious body. His mouth parted, but words seemed to be difficult for seconds. Finally, what I had longed to hear escape a man's mouth since I had left puberty finally graced me. "You're the most beautiful thing I've ever seen, Tracey; beautiful mind, body and soul. My heart pounds for you. So do other things, as you can tell."

My eyes followed as his looked down at an engorged covered penis aching to be free and warm inside of me, and I touched it. He was so hard, pumping without effort. I needed it. Sorry, Daisha. He was mine, at least for that night.

Troy whisked me into his arms and carried me to my queen-sized bed, tenderly laying me across it. I switched off the night-light by the bed, and let only the silvery light from the moon illuminate us. Troy stared down at me as moon cast a shimmering glow across me. "I . . . I can't believe how much I want you, Tracey. In the few weeks I have known you, I know you're the only woman for me. No woman has ever brought me lunch before, and you manage to do that at least three days a week with all my favorite things. You also manage to take care of all of my files before you do anyone else's, you write me sweet little notes that brighten my day. You're just so sweet and thoughtful about everything."

"That's because I'm crazy about you."

I thought he would immediately spread my waiting thighs and enter me, but no, he took it slowly, starting with my lips. His kisses were succulent and sweet, putting my mind in a daze. We encircled, intertwined, arms and legs twisted and turned, rolling from my back to his, getting our feel of such a perfect match. His squirming penis, so hot against the thin cotton underwear, pressed against me, begging entrance. He was so ready, percolating for me, making the underwear wet from sweat and sex. Mercy!

I cupped his swelled scrotum and massaged it, tickling it with the tips of my nails. I spoke softly against his neck. "Do you like it when I rub it through your underwear like this?"

His back stiffened. "Yeah, it feels great!"

Then I clutched his shaft, tugged on it through the fabric, causing friction. "What about that? You like it?"

He moaned against me. "Take it out, girl, before I explode."

In the middle of the darkness, the middle of my bed, wrapped around my precious Troy, I heard another jingle, but not from my cell this time. His head popped up and looked around. "Where are my pants?"

"Why? What's the matter?"

"That's my phone."

"Do you have to answer it? We were right in the middle of—"

"I'm a cop. This could be an emergency." He slid from the bed, grabbed the pants and pulled a small, black phone from it.

I tried not listening to him, but I could make out a few words. "What is it? Is it bad? How long ago did this happen? Couldn't you have called someone else, for Christ's sake?"

He seemed pissed at whoever it was trying to take him away from super hot sex on a deliciously warm bed with a woman who was crazy about him. For that matter, I was pissed myself. My core was aching for penetration, nipples tightening to get kissed and stroked, and arms waiting to embrace a hot, tight man as he made awesome love to me. Why would the damn phone have to ring? Why would he have to be a police officer on call?

Troy closed the phone and walked back to me with a look on his face. Before he could say a thing, I said it for him. "An emergency?"

"Maybe."

"What do you mean?"

He slid the phone into pants he was slowly getting back into. "That was Daisha."

"Daisha! What? Is she checking in on you?"

"She said she woke up, didn't see me and got scared."

"A big old strappin' thing like her, scared of something? Hell, the bullets in her gun are scared of her."

"She said she fell down the steps."

"And you believe that? Troy, she knows we're together and wants to break us up."

"I have to see about her. I don't want her to be there hurt and not get any help."

I quickly slid back into my robe and followed him into the living room. My hands reached for his. "Are you coming back?"

"If I can. This could take a while if she is hurt."

"Troy!"

"I'm really sorry about this and I'll make it up to you. I swear, baby. I'm really sorry. I'll call you as soon as I hear something."

"You do know that I want her to be okay, but I also want you here with me, now."

"I have to do this." He quickly kissed my lips, then left. I stood at the door watching his slick, navy blue squad car drive from my street and into heartbreak hotel, where Daisha Miller was the proprietor.

I fell asleep that night hugging myself, pretending it was Troy's soft hands caressing me. Was I ever to have him? Would Daisha continue to control him as if he were a puppet on a string? Would he let her? Those questions loomed large in my mind until I drifted to sleep, and the throbbing in my sex finally subsided.

One week later . . .

Troy knew when my day off was and he appeared at my door with a bouquet of tulips and a smile. "Hope you don't have anything planned."

"What are you doing here? I thought you were at work."

"I took the day off."

"To be with me?"

"No, to be with Wally and the Beaver. Of course to be with you, silly. Besides, don't I owe you for the other night?"

I smiled and moved into his arms. "You do owe me. We could finish what we started in my bedroom."

"That's for later, but I have a surprise for you." He put the bouquet in my hands. "First, put these in water, then let's go."

I smelled them. "Umm, tulips. Thank you."

"No sweat, baby. Get your jacket."

When we pulled into the police parking lot, I looked at him in surprise. "What are we doing back here? This *is* our day off, in case you don't remember."

"We're not going to work. We're doing something fun, I promise."

Troy walked me to the other side of the building where the mounted police were stationed. He kissed my cheek. "Ever been on a horse before?"

"When I was nine, but I was scared of them, and I'm still scared. What are you planning?"

"You'll love horses once I'm done with you. Come on, take a chance. Nothing will happen to you."

He paid the officer and a beautiful black horse was delivered to us. It was a gorgeous horse, nice and friendly—but huge. I looked at Troy skeptically. "It's awfully big."

"I picked a big one on purpose."

"Do you have any experience with horses?"

"I was a mounted police officer for five years. Horses and I are friends."

He climbed on, adjusted the belts and stirrups, then pulled me on. He tightened my harness and rubbed my shoulders. "Ready?"

"I guess, but take it slow with this thing. The last thing I need is to be on a horse doing Mach 5."

"On the streets of Detroit? Too many cars in the way. You'll love this. Trust me."

We rode the horse down Jefferson Avenue, and toured all the important spots, like Hart Plaza, Chene Park Ampitheatre, the Joe Lewis fist, everything that made Detroit Detroit. I loved the downtown area with all the festivities going on, but

never expected to see a guided tour of it with a sexy police officer as my tour guide.

As we moved farther down Jefferson to Belle Isle, the
horse's slow, rugged trot moved Troy into me. I could feel his
erection pressing against me, getting harder with each move the
horse made. His lips tickled my ear. "You like this?"

"Better than I thought."

"It gets better."

The more we rode, the hotter his erection became. When we
finally reached Belle Isle, Troy was almost ready to explode. He
had found my tight nipples, slipping his hands into my thin
jacket, stroking them on the sly in secluded parts of the island.

We trotted farther into the island where it was nice and secluded and pulled back on the horse's rings. The black beauty
stopped and Troy hopped off, latching the leather strap to a
tree.

"What are you doing?"

He unhooked me and helped me to my feet. "What *we* are
about to do is finish what we started the other night." He took
a bag from the other side of the horse, pulled out a blanket and
spread it on the grass. "What does it look like we're about to
do?"

"Have a picnic?"

"In a matter of speaking." He flattened the corners of the
blanket, pulled a bottle from his duffle bag along with plastic
champagne glasses and patted the blanket. "Are you going to
stand there, or do I make love to the horse?"

He was all the stallion I needed, and thus I moved directly
next to him. "Troy, you really are something."

"I told you I would make it up to you. Are you game for
this in the middle of the day in a public park?"

"We could get caught."

"Too secluded. Besides, I won't take as long as I would in
your bed. I just wanted to do something different with you."

I looked around casually. "Yep, this is different, all right!"

"You don't like it?"

"Are you kidding? I love it. It's just that I've never made love outside before. You?"

"Girl, I've done it practically everywhere, boats, cars, motorcycles."

"Motorcycles?"

He poured the contents of the bottle into the plastic goblets, practically making them overflow. "I was eighteen, and my dad let me try out his new bike. What did I do? I took it to my girlfriend's house and we made love on it in her backyard."

"I would fall for a wild dude, wouldn't I?"

He slowly sipped his drink. "Is that what you're doing, falling for me?"

"Does that scare you, since you still have Daisha—"

"Nothing about you scares me, and Daisha isn't exactly the topic of conversation I would like to engage in. Taste your drink."

I took a small swallow, then smiled. "This isn't champagne."

"I know. I didn't know exactly what to bring for an occasion like this, so I went for the light and airy type."

"I love sparkling cider."

"Good. So, back to our conversation. What is it that you love? What do you like for a man to do when he's making love to you?"

"Everything you did to me in the basement."

"That wasn't very romantic." He swallowed his drink in a gulp and laid the goblet down. "If you had the perfect evening to make any kind of love your heart desired, what would it be like? I would love to give you that."

"You're so incredibly sweet, Troy."

He watched as I pondered his question, looking like he was falling harder for me as the seconds ticked. His eyes glanced down at the vee of my spring sweater, wanting to lick between and taste my flesh more than ever before. My voice caught his attention again before he fell hard into no-man's-land.

"I'm a fancy girl with fancy tastes." I leaned back on the blanket and stared into the baby blue sky, resting my hands behind my head. "I love those hotels down the street, you know, those skyscrapers where you can look out and see the world . . . well, at least you can see Canada."

He lay next to me, tracing my jaw line with his finger. "What floor?"

"The top one—penthouse. I love looking out at a midnight sky and seeing the sparkling city lights."

"And after looking at that breathtaking view, what would be next on your agenda?"

"Pleasing my man in every possible way."

"Starting with?"

"A glass of champagne toasting a wonderful life he and I would have together. Next, I would do a slow striptease and oil myself down with scented oil, as my partner watched in heated anticipation."

"Scented with what aroma?"

"Opium perfume, known to drive a man off his freakin' rocker. Next, a slow massage of his tired, aching muscles as his naked body lies against satin sheets."

"A massage would be an incredible added feature."

"Yes, and with warm oil. That way, my hot little hands could slide across his body with the ease and grace of silk gloves."

His face moved closer to mine. "What would you massage first?"

I could feel the heat in his pants, that perfect, hot tip pressing against his zipper, so ready to spill for me right there at the park. At that point, I didn't care where we were. His words were seducing me, making me want to pretend that we were in that penthouse and that his body was clay, ready to be molded by my oiled hands.

I moved my palm up and down the protruding zipper, my lips now only inches from his. "I'd massage his most potent places first, like this one." I palmed him harder, watching his eyes react to the intense pleasure of getting his scrotum caressed. "Would you like to be massaged there first—if you were in that penthouse overlooking the Detroit River, with a woman wearing scented oils?"

"I'm a river right now. And if you don't close this dam soon, I'll overflow like crazy, Tracey—beautiful, perfect, Tracey."

My nose wiggled against his. "Well, we can't have any overflowing around here; not yet anyway. It would scare the horse."

Troy stroked my moist lips with his fingertips. "Let's make sure she stays nice and calm then."

Our lips met briefly, barely touching in a teasing manner. With each tender caress, our lips met in tighter fusion, taking all in and releasing nothing until it was time for the ultimate release. My hands continued to palm his thick, tight erection, pressing my hands against the jeans material until he grew to monumental heights. "Umm, Troy, even touching you with clothes on makes me hot. I used to watch you all the time walking those halls, reacting to and socializing with coworkers. That's what really attracted me to you, the easy and free way you make everyone around you happy. All along I wished I could have just five minutes with you."

"Then we were having the same dream, but I let my fear of beautiful women get in the way. Let's have that dream again, together."

We both looked at the horse that was standing there watching us, not totally understanding what was about to take place before his eyes, but watching nonetheless. I rolled Troy onto his back and sat on his upper thighs. "You ready to get fucked in the middle of the day in a public place?"

"I want you anywhere I can get you."

"That's just the answer I was looking for." My hands rigorously slid up and down his cotton-check shirt, feeling his tight muscles, his nipples poking through. I wanted so badly to taste them. My voice cracked with wild excitement. "I wish I could kiss your bare chest."

He immediately pulled the shirt up, exposing to me a glistening caramel chest that looked even sexier in the midday sun. The dimness of the basement lights the other day hid his true hue from me, but I saw it that day, and he sparkled. My lips went dry at the sight of his stomach muscles tightening to my touch. My tongue pressed gently between my parted lips as I narrowed in on his erect nipples. I couldn't take it anymore. I had to feel him between my lips.

His back arched to the feel of my tongue licking in circles around his nipples. The slightly cool air on his slick skin heightened his senses, pressing him farther into me. All along, I could feel his fingers raising the hem of my skirt, pushing it farther up my thighs. I liked it and needed it, and edged him on with pelvic thrusts. He got the idea and moved directly to my pantiless middle. "No panties?"

"I had a feeling about something when you invited me out for the day."

"What a smart girl you are." He lightly tapped my bare bottom then feathered my soft crotch, sliding two fingers deeply inside. His rugged finger strokes made me ignite. Sparks went off between my ears and I shivered in waves of demanding orgasms.

He smiled at my reaction. "You went there already?"

"Don't worry, there's plenty more where that came from."

"Yeah? Prove it."

Our lips met once again before really getting started on the *pleasure factor.* My jittery fingers slid his zipper down, seeing perks of bulging white pressing out from his pants. I rubbed his stiff tip. "About to pop, aren't you?"

"Like a balloon full of water."

"You want to release it, baby?"

His hands reached up and stroked my breasts, feeling the tight buds against his hot fingertips. "I want to drip inside of you so badly that I can already feel release. Don't make me make a fool of myself out here without a beautiful woman to accommodate me."

"I'll be glad to accommodate you, if that's what you desire."

"Give it to me until it hurts."

I peeled the underwear from around his shaft and pulled it out. He was so hot and throbbing against my hands that he brought on another flush of waves within me. I shuddered as I pumped his stiff, wet phallus, hardly able to believe that something that glorious existed. I thought all heavenly things were up there with God, but he left one down here, for me to love and cherish. The hue of his shaft was stunning and glistening, liquid honey. I was slick and ready for it.

I flared my skirt around us and prepared for my decadent impalement, because the sight of it was putting a killing on my sex, needing to feel it slide past my folds and shatter my clit. Yes, I knew I'd had sex with Troy in the basement at work but knew that was going to be child's play compared to what I was about to get. With my breath coming in shallow, quick heaves, I stood to my knees and spread my thighs. His hands tightened around my buttocks, calling to me, enticing me—as if I needed enticing. "Come on, girl, give it. Slide slowly onto it and ride me. Ride me as though we were on that horse, running him, jerking him."

That did it for me. Remembering how that fabulous animal rocked my clit in slow, rocky movements as it trotted along Woodward Avenue and Jefferson made my teeth chatter for Troy to be inside my body. I lowered onto his tip, then pulled back to tease. He jerked under me. "You're killing me, Tracey. Damn straight killing me!"

"You wanna die a little more?"

"Kill me with it! Now! Now, girl!"

"You want me to take you hard?"

"Nail me. At this point, I wouldn't care if you put a bullet between my eyes, so long as your delicious body is draped all over me."

I slid further down and watched his eyes roll. "Is that what you need, baby?"

"Oh, God, Tracey. Keep doing it!"

Again I slid farther, feeling my own insides quiver and vibrate to his thrusts. I worked it, worked him and gyrated all over his precious body. He moved in and out of me swiftly, then jammed himself back in with hard, quick thrusts. His hands held my hips in place as he rocked the living daylights out of me. I bounced against him, sweated onto him as his hands moved up my body, stroking my breasts, pinching my hardened, sensitive nipples. I almost howled as he lifted to me and sucked almost my entire breast into his mouth. He pulled at them, sucked them while inching his love deeper into me. I had no idea anything in the world could be that magnetic. I thought the first time with him was *the max!* This outranked it, and I knew it because tears were running down my cheeks.

He wiped them with the pad of this thumb. "Are you satisfied?"

I couldn't talk because my body was quaking, shivering, tensing, getting ready for an orgasm I knew could mentally destroy me. When it came, I jerked and screamed tiny screams that only my lover could hear.

The onslaught of my orgasm brought his on. He pumped wildly inside of me, streaming his fluid so deeply within my body that I could feel it. Seconds of intense spewing made him collapse back to the blanket. His mouth was dry and open. His eyes stared at me in wonder as my own eyes returned the favor to him. Soon, my head landed on his wet chest. His breathing lulled me as my body continued to spark because of him.

The horse shifted hooves and we looked up at him. He had been quiet during our romp, watching us get our fill probably wondering what the hell we were doing.

We finished the last of the cider and packed up slowly knowing we had a long walk ahead of us. Less than an hour later, we returned our wondrous black beauty to his rightful owner, then got behind the wheel of Troy's Hummer. Another rough, rugged ride, but I liked it. We ate at The London Broil, then ate again that night. We were both dessert for one another, and not a hint of Daisha Miller was in the air. With that in mind, we explored all there was to partake of. He looked good on my bed, naked and glistening while waiting for me to disrobe and let him eat of my garden.

What Troy and I did in the park and at work was magic, but nothing compared to doing it with him in my own bed. It reminded me of being in the penthouse, with champagne, silk sheets and plenty of scented oil. The only thing missing was the actual penthouse. My nice, roomy house on Boston Boulevard had to suffice, and we made it our personal love shack. Troy lived between my thighs the entire night, delivering inch after inch of raw, hard thrusts that drove me to the brink of sexual insanity. What made it more outstanding was looking into the face of a man who did more to me than satisfy my body. He satisfied my soul, and made my heart sing to lyrics that I didn't know existed.

Hours later, I awakened to brilliant sunshine forcing its way through my blinds. Troy was resting next to me, sleeping as soundly as a baby. I wore him out the night before, plain and simple. Besides, he needed his rest because Daisha was sweating him big time. I knew not to bring the subject up because apparently there was still something between him and Daisha. I was glad to have a part of him, but for how long? When would I get to the point where *just a little of him* would no longer be enough?

I put on my robe and headed to the kitchen for coffee. Only caffeine would temporarily cure the sudden hopelessness invading my soul. As I sipped the steaming French vanilla, I poked my head through my yellow daisy curtains in time to see a squad car pass. Nothing ever happened on my street, so why was there a squad car traipsing past at seven in the morning? It also had the nerve to drive by my house slowly before pressing the accelerator into warp mode. Maybe the block club had decided to kick in for extra protection. That was all I could think of. My next thought, waking Troy and getting my sex thrashed and put into submission by the biggest, baddest cop in the nation. Yeah, that took care of any thoughts of Daisha!

Two weeks later . . .

I was used to getting calls from Troy on a nightly basis, even though I continued seeing him at night and sneaking a roll in the cement hay in central files. When Thursday night came around, and I hadn't receive a call, I thought nothing of it. After all, he did have to reserve at least one night to talk over marriage-ending plans with Daisha. Friday evening, no call; that was odd for Troy not to contact me and wish me a great weekend if he couldn't get away. Again, I rolled with the punches. Sunday evening, nothing, and I worried, taking a chance on calling his cell number. Still nothing. Sunday night was a restless one for me, hardly getting any sleep. Seeing Troy bright and early the next morning would cure all my ills.

Monday morning Daisha greeted me with a very pleasant smile for some reason, then handed me a stack of files and criminal reports the height of my own body. Surely that would keep me busy until it was time for Troy to come in and make his appearance—with another stack of files. His were ones I awaited, however. Those files never came that day and neither did Troy.

Suddenly making dinner for one became so hard. For weeks I'd gotten used to making dinner for him at least once or twice a week. I had to go it alone, and for what reason? I had not heard from him in five days. Was he dead or alive? I sat down at my dining room table and stared at my cordless phone, wanting to call him again but fearing becoming a pest to him. *Troy, where the heck are you?* The display suddenly lit and his number flashed across the screen. I jerked it up, frantically pressing the button. "Troy?"

"I know you hate me for not calling you back."

"You know I don't hate you, but I was worried. What's going on?"

He paused, then blurted it out. "Daisha happened."

"What do you mean?"

"You really won't believe this, but she switched my hours. I've been over there getting things together, doing paperwork, everything you can think of, I've been doing it."

"All that for a switch of hours? Why did she do that anyway? Isn't your work record impeccable?

"Slow down, baby. You know why she did this. To put space between us, like that would work. One good thing, I'm no longer on call."

"Is Daisha responsible for that?"

"No, you are. I was going for the promotion anyway but after seeing you, I knew Daisha would make trouble. I wanted you in my life, Tracey, so I put in for a transfer. I'm just taking this nightshift crap until my transfer takes effect."

"You sure you'll get it?"

"My track record is excellent, and I got word from reliable sources that it's about to happen for me. Good thing it is, because Daisha is on to us."

Tracey slumped into a kitchen chair. "I'm really glad about the move, but you've got to get away from her, get your divorce. I know you don't want to hear that but it's true. If you love me and want to be with me, you'll do it. Do you love me enough?"

"You know I do."

"Then what's the problem?"

"There is no problem, not anymore. She and I are talking tonight."

"No dinner with me then?"

"I have to do this in order to be free. I'm tired of fooling around, dragging a non-working marriage around when it's you that I really want. She can be a hell of a person to break from, though. She loves to cause problems. Are you still willing to stick with me knowing your boss could make your life hell for a little while?"

"You're worth it."

"No matter what, you know that I'll take care of you, Tracey, you know that. Daisha won't hurt you. She only wants me."

My meek voice came through. "Yeah, so do I."

Next Monday morning . . .

Troy had done a disappearing act again. I hadn't heard from him since the night he was to dump Daisha. To make matters worse, Daisha specifically came in with Troy's paperwork and tossed a bunch of it on my desk, telling me to get it done before the end of the day. Why didn't Daisha just send Troy in himself? By that time it had to have sunk in that Troy and I were an item. Daisha proceeded to leave the loads of reports on my desk, along with a smirk. The smirk was different this time. It had more hate in it, more fire. Troy must have really set fire to her doghouse, and left her out high and dry. That's not what I wanted. My idea wasn't to take Troy from her, it just happened. He was unhappy and, simply put, Daisha Miller wasn't the one making his dreams come true.

By mid-afternoon, I hadn't heard a word from my boy wonder and was a little worried. He hadn't mentioned taking any more days off before working the other shift. He knew

Daisha would blow a rod if her department started taking off, even if it was time *they* had coming to them. Daisha's motto: by the books, do or die. Too bad she conducted her personal business the same way. It may very well have cost her a delicious young cop. And maybe sending him straight into my open arms.

It was almost four, and I wanted to get the hell out of there and check on Troy. It was really odd for him not to check on me. I had gotten to know him over the few months, and knew his personality. Something was wrong. Just as I was about to close shop and call his cell, Daisha came in with another stack of reports that had to be filed for Captain Jones by the end of the day.

Was I the only damn file clerk in that giant-ass building? God knew there were five on each floor. I wanted to chalk that up to me being good at my job, but knowing Daisha, she'd brought those files into me just to get my goat. To top everything off, she had only said a few words to me since knowing me, and they were always on the crude side. It just killed her to talk to me, especially since I knew for a fact that she and Troy were on the quits. Before she walked out, she turned to me, telling me to see her before I left for the day. *Showdown.* I could feel it in the pit of my stomach.

Not having seen hide or hair of Troy, being overworked and having to look at Daisha Miller instead of the luxurious interior of my car wasn't exactly the way I wanted my day to end. Wasn't my stomach sick enough? Good employee that I was, I dragged into her office and spoke as politely as possible without hurling. "Captain Miller, you wanted to see me?"

All she did was reach into her stack of papers on the desk and hand me an envelope. I skeptically took the envelope and looked at it. "What is this?"

Without as much as a response, Daisha left me in the middle of her office and traipsed off—probably back to the tar pits of hell. Yes, she definitely had a clue that her man was gone. For that matter, he was gone from me, too.

I got on the elevator with the unopened letter in my trembling little hands, afraid to open it, afraid that the contents of the letter would spell out my demise—the demise of my mortgage, bank account and credit cards.

Before leaving, I opened the letter. *Motherfuck! What is going on here?*

I drove home in tears, wanting Troy, needing Troy, but suddenly finding myself not within his reach again. My life was suddenly a shambles, and it all centered around that letter, and Troy.

By seven that evening, I was in the middle of every thinkable comfort food and drink that I could think of. Anything from donuts, cake, candy, popcorn and, oh yes, lots and lots of Jack Daniels—straight! I didn't know my own name by eight-thirty and couldn't have given a hoot what man-hating movie was on Lifetime. My world was shot, and all I wanted to do was dissolve into a puddle and wash away. No more Troy. I looked at the letter again and started crying.

I awakened at nine the next morning and saw my cat, Euphoria, staring at me as if I had finally lost it. I had. The letter was still sitting on my dining room table crumbled up in as tight a ball as my fists could make it. I needed coffee bad. Jack Daniels and the rest of the stuff I had consumed the night before had taken me farther away than Calgon ever could have.

Looking like a hag and feeling worse than one, I brewed a pot of coffee and didn't even care by that time that I was still at home instead of at work. As I sat staring at the balled note, my cell rang. I debated answering it in case it was Daisha dishing out more crap to me. Then I thought about it; she didn't have my cell number. I quickly reached for the phone. "Hello?"

"Tracey?"

I leaped from my chair. "Troy? Where are you?"

"Staring at your empty desk. Why aren't you here?"

"It's a long story."

"Long story? Baby, what's going on?"

I slumped back in my chair, my voice on the verge of tears. He asked again. "Tracey, what's going on with you?"

All I could do was burst into tears. And on the other side of the phone, a solid click. Troy had given up on me.

Fifteen minutes later, I managed to have enough self-control to stand and see Troy's squad car pulling into my driveway and him rushing to my door. I swung the door open and fell into his arms.

He held my crying face up to his. "What happened? Why are you at home and crying?"

We walked into the house and I handed him the balled envelope. He gave me a peculiar look then slowly opened the paper. His eyes grew to the size of frying pans. "She did it! She did it! Damn her."

"The note says they're downsizing, but I know it's because of us, Troy. She found a good way to get rid of me."

"They're not downsizing, it's more like reorganizing. She put me on the night shift. Remember? I went back to head-quarters today to finish the paperwork, drop in and tell you what was going on with me, and didn't see you. So, I called, only to find this out. She can't think this will keep me from you."

"It did for a while."

"But not anymore. I told her everything, Tracey. I told her that I was tired of carrying the relationship alone, tired of not feeling like a man . . . tired of everything, until I met you. She hated that, and retaliated in a way I felt she would, but hoped she wouldn't have."

I wrapped my arms around him, crying. "What am I going to do? I can't live without working, Troy."

"You're going to be fine. My buddies at the fifth precinct are always looking for good workers."

"Really?"

"Don't you dare worry about anything, baby. And you know I will take care of you, Tracey. Anything you want or need, I'll get it, and for as long as you want me to." He kissed my tear-stained lips then slowly parted from me. "You didn't sleep well, did you?"

"I slept in front of the television."

He took my hand into his. "Come on. You need rest. I'll stay with you."

"You have things to do before starting your new shift."

"Screw that. I need to be here with you. I feel responsible for this."

"You didn't do this, Troy."

Without another word, we entered my room. He pulled back the sheets and slid my pink robe from my naked body. "Lay down."

I stared up at him sympathetically. "Will you stay here with me?"

Troy laid his hat on my dresser, removed his guns and shoes and mounted the bed, taking me into his arms. As I rested against his navy blue and silver chest, I toyed with his badge. I had memorized that number, memorized everything on him, and relished in the feel of his clothed body against the bareness of mine.

He smiled down at me. "Better?"

"You always make me feel better."

"You know, you were the only perk down there at that place. I could kill Daisha."

"She's not worth it. Besides, I rather knew she'd pull this. Thank God I saved some money."

He nibbled my ear. "You're a smart girl, Tracey Shane, and I would kill for you in a minute. I'm good with guns, as you can tell."

My teary eyes smiled into his. "You're especially good with one."

"The one that's always cocked and loaded whenever you're near?"

My hands trailed to his tenting pants, playing with an engorged tip. "That's the one."

"You want to see how well it works?"

I moved farther into him. "Well, I have always wanted to make love to a man in uniform." I slid on top of him, lowering my juicy core onto his clothed scrotum. "I really shouldn't mess up this uniform. It's so clean and dark. You look so good in it."

"You can give me a taste. That way I can stay nice and clean. Right?"

Our lips met lavishly. Our tongues coiled in exquisite unison, nibbling one another until both of us were ready to erupt. Daisha was but a vague memory, and that darn letter was dust in the wind.

He rolled me to my back and parted my thighs. "I love you so much, girl, that I can't take my hands off you." He moved me to the foot of the bed and bent to his knees. His tongue quickly mated with my folds, licking and manipulating me until I truly didn't know any name but one: Troy, Troy, Troy. My body squirmed as his mouth continued to latch onto me. His arms coiled around my thighs, pulling me into him with rugged force—and I loved it, loved him. He made me forget the real world, and I was happy to reside in his for as long as he would have me.

My slick sex pushed against him, wanting him to take me through the roof if possible. That's what he did, and my clit hummed to precision as his tongue sweet-talked its way into my body. My eyes closed tightly and my body rode the wave of ecstasy that only Troy could take me on. My fingers played in his hair, along his ears and around to lips that were still working magic on me. He was no mere mortal. He had to be a magician in cop's clothing.

Troy took what I knew he needed. I helped him unearth his massive rod and watched in amazement as it wavered in mid air—so full of love, so full of hot lava that could fill me to my rim. I wanted it bad! He positioned my legs around his waist and entered me over and over for a good ten minutes. My baby was hungry and needed the love Daisha just wasn't capable of giving him. But I was.

I watched him tense, stroking me in heavy thrusts. His throat bobbed as he called my name. Then he poured every single drop he possessed into my small frame. I could feel him filling, spewing, satisfying me. There was something about watching a cop in a navy suit, fully clad with badges and medals, nail me. The best part: he was mine and I knew it.

My naked body still quivered from his attentions, so he laid next to me, rubbing my skin, showing me the love I knew he had for me. His seductive voice mellowed in my mind. "You okay, baby?"

"I am now."

"Don't worry about a job. I've got you covered, but I think you need to take some of that money you tucked away and go on a small vacation. It'll help clear your mind."

"Maybe I will. I've always wanted to go to Vegas. Wanna come?"

He stood and took his cap from my dresser. "I would love to, but I have to settle into this night shift thing. I've never worked nights before." He checked his watch. "I had better get outta here before Daisha fires me, too."

"She could do that?"

"No. The state of Michigan is my employer. Knowing her she'd try it, however."

"You want me to walk you to the door?"

"You stay there and rest. I've kept you from real sleep long enough. The important thing is don't worry. Things will work out. I'll use my key and lock up."

I watched Troy leave my bedroom, but knew he'd be back after his shift. The thing to do, plan a vacation and give my mind a rest

Troy hadn't taken me up on my offer to go to Vegas so I sat in the airport alone thinking of how much I already missed him. Even the travel magazines featuring exotic places I knew my ass couldn't afford couldn't take my mind from him. Daisha finally left us alone, realizing she had not won, so we were free from that bull at least. But I wanted Troy right there with me.

I continued to thumb through the travel brochures when a black carry-on landed next to mine. I looked up and saw Troy smiling down at me. "See, I took your advice and put in for an early vacation."

I stood and my arms automatically wrapped around him, hugging him so tight with a strength I didn't know I had. "I'm so glad to see my baby. What's a vacation without a lover?"

"A boring one."

"Not anymore. What made you decide?"

"I'm so damn tired of everything—that night shift, Daisha, her brother who's now my direct boss. I'm just so tired of it all." He took my hand and kissed it. "Then I thought about you, and spending time alone with you in a hotel in some nice, exotic place. It was so tempting I went right for it."

I looked into his tired eyes, eyes ready to sleep as soon as the plane taxied. That was exactly what he did, and slept practically the entire way to Vegas. Daisha had found yet another way to keep stressing him out. But that was about to end if I had anything to do with it.

Once we landed in Vegas, we went directly to the hotel to catch some z's before venturing out to explore. He sat our luggage inside the door, then moved into my arms. As he moved into me, I could feel his already stiff shaft pressing into my stomach. It felt so luscious that I almost came right there within his arms. He was so thick and stiff, practically pushing into me. My core started throbbing and getting wetter by the second. All I could think about was how it would feel to have him pushing that hot, hard erection all the way through me.

I knew I had to get Troy out of my arms, because he was tired. But what I really wanted was to move all over him and let him eat me out like I was a Big Mac with a side order of fries. My juices would be all over him; he would be drenched in my ocean so well that he wouldn't be able to wash my scent from him.

I moved my hands through his hair and it felt great. It was so silky between my fingers that I almost came from that alone. I cleared my throat and pushed back a bit, saying, "Troy, you need to go to sleep. You're tired."

He moved in closer, not letting me go. His lips were at my ear and each time he spoke it tickled. That just made my center slick, and my g-spot throbbed even harder. I tried pushing him away from me again but he moaned, "Let me just stay a little longer in your arms."

"Troy."

He held me tighter. "Please, don't make me leave."

What could I say to him? I was so crazy in love with him that I would have walked a tightrope for him had he asked. "Okay, but let's get out of this door before everyone in the place sees us."

He stepped back and looked into my eyes. "I just need to be with someone who cares about me."

"You know I love you, Troy."

"Yes, I can count on you when the chips are down, and they

are always down lately. Thank God the hearing for the divorce is coming up soon."

I took him by the hand and led him to the bed. Troy lay across it and buried his face into my pillow. Moments later, I hadn't heard anything and assumed he was sleeping. As I watched him, I imagined how deep his tongue had entered my mouth so many times before. I imagined him between my thighs; how well he caressed me until I spilled all over him. I swear I was getting so hot that I thought I was going to have to move to the other side of the bed and do it to myself.

That was exactly what I did. He had fallen asleep, and the minute I heard deep breathing, I slid the zipper of my jeans down, pulled the panties aside and slid two fingers so deeply into myself that I instantly moaned, "Oh, God, rock me, Troy . . . take me." I had such an enormous orgasm that I rocked the bed. It was marvelous, yet frustrating at the same time. I wanted him so badly because my own fingers were a sorry excuse for what he had for me. I kept my tempo up and gave myself a third orgasm just as he awakened.

I quickly fixed my clothes as he rolled over smiling at me. "Why did you let me go to sleep, Tracey?"

I was so glad that he didn't catch me in the act that I was glad to answer any of his questions. "You were very tired, sweetie."

He stretched and yawned. "I'm still tired." Then he looked at me with this strange expression. "Could you do something for me?"

"What?"

"I could really use a back massage. Would you?"

I patted the bed. "Roll over on your tummy." I started slowly stroking his shoulders and moved down to his middle back. I swear, just touching his back gave me chills beyond reason.

He couldn't get comfortable for some reason, then he said the ultimate to me. "No, don't do it like that. Pull up my shirt."

I pulled his shirt up past his shoulders and wanted to drool. He was killing me and didn't even know it.

I sat on his butt and massaged his shoulders, sides and the middle of his back. I silently came so many times that I was about wore out, and he hadn't even touched me. The band of his jockeys were showing, torturing me even more. My hands moved back down to his lower back and delicately massaged around the band of his underwear, pinching him, raking my nails across him. I was losing it. He had to give it up before I died of rapture from my own lover.

His voice brought me back to reality. "Do my chest now."

He turned over, sat up, pulled the polo over his shoulders, and returned to my pillow. His dark hair shone so brightly against the stark white pillow, and his chocolate nipples stood to attention. Everything on him looked like it was begging to be loved.

I slowly mounted him and sat on his crotch. I had to cover my mouth because I was about to let out a scream brought on only by a raging erection. I covered my mouth and slowly sank onto it. He opened his eyes. "What's wrong?"

I quickly said, "Nothing."

He smiled a sly smile and closed his eyes again. He knew what was going down, but just didn't admit it. Fine, if he was going to be that way about it, so was I. I was about to nail his sexy self and make him beg for me like he did just about every night.

I rubbed my hands together to get them nice and warm, and started in on his pecs. My hands slowly moved up and down his chest and stomach, massaging, rubbing, squeezing everything in sight. I looked down at him and realized just how much I wanted him because my nipples were hard and poking through the material. I quickly unbuttoned my blouse and let it fall to my sides. The demi bra I had on covered barely anything. I think he could sense my top was off because his eyes slowly opened and zeroed in on my breasts. "What are you doing?"

"I was hot, so I shed a few things."

He smiled and moved both thumbs tenderly across my nipples, shooting me straight to Venus. While he rubbed them between his fingers, he looked at me. "Your nipples are so sexy. Before I met you, I actually dreamed of touching them."

He slid my shoulder straps down my arms. My breasts were fully exposed to him by the time he finished, and he cupped both within his hands. Though his hands felt so good squeezing them, I couldn't help but think about Daisha. She would blow a gasket if she had seen us doing what we were about to do in Nevada.

He murmured, "I love you so much, girl. I never thought I would love anyone the way I love you."

"I've always loved you, Troy, from the first day I saw you. Remember the day you gave me that ticket?"

"How could I forget? Now I have something bigger to give you."

"Let me guess, your gun?"

"You know I'm famous for my gun tricks." His eyes lowered to the loaded erection ripping his pants open. He stroked it up and down, then replaced his hand with mine, massaging it to maximum length. It was so hard and stiff within my hands. I could feel all those thick veins pressing and struggling to be set free and invade me once again. His eyes met mine. "Go on, take it out."

I moved my hand inside his pants, immediately feeling his heat, and I couldn't wait to slide it out. My hands wrapped around it, and I could feel it pumping power to his tip; it was the prettiest thing imaginable. I slowly kissed him and licked my way down his chest and stomach, landing back at his tip. My eyes met his again. "Take me, Troy. Take me now, deep, hard and all night long."

He stood from the bed and I watched that delicious cock bounce around as he removed his pants. He stripped me of my clothing and started kissing each and every part of me. I moaned and screamed as he licked my bare flesh until it was almost raw. When he reached my core, it was already wet for him. He wasted no time kissing it, then slid three fingers inside of me. He stroked me several times. "You are so incredible, Tracey."

I stroked his cheek. "Take it."

He moved to my breasts, licked and tugged ferociously on the tender tips while I cradled him in my arms. The idea of Troy on top of me made me burn even more for him. He must have sensed that because his moist lips left my nipples. "Let me come inside, sugar. Let me play around and make you explode all over me."

"How do you want it this time?"

"In all positions, baby. Let's start like this." He put me on my knees and moved behind me. I heard him unwrap his protection. I felt incredible pressure as he pushed that marvelous rod into me. I tightened my muscles to add depth and excitement . . . he gladly accepted. He rocked his body so smoothly up and down on mine that I came two more times. I screamed and moaned to his satisfaction the entire night. The feel of his chest slamming against my back made me yell uncontrollably. I liked that position. I thought we had done it all, but this was yet a new one to master. We did it in every thinkable position, from missionary to 69 and everything in between, all night long, as the television played porn movies. He had secretly ordered them at the front desk.

We changed positions, and I slid him into my mouth. I lay between his thighs and partook of his cream until he collapsed in my arms. I stroked his tip with my tongue over and over again, then moved slowly down his shaft, kissing every inch of him. When I got to his scrotum, I feasted like he was a four-course meal: nibbling him until he boiled over and spilled onto me. He was spent, and so glad to be that way, because he had been missing out on his love for way too long with Daisha. I spent the rest of the trip making sure I was his dream come true. As for what I got, it boiled down to three simple things, and in this order: a man I was crazy about, a great vacation, and a new job when we returned to *our* house, together.

Like hot sex? Double your pleasure with Evangeline Anderson's out-of-this-world cops in TAKE TWO, coming in November 2006 from Aphrodisia . . .

And here's what *New York Times* bestselling author MaryJanice Davidson had to say . . . "Kept me up all night . . . sexy and funny and, hidden beneath the wisecracks, a tender love story. TAKE TWO hooked me from page one. I literally could not put it down until I got to the end and it was well worth the ride. Sadie is charming and funny, the heroes (yes, there are two!) are handsome and gruff and sweet. You'll be rooting for all three of them!"

"We'll take that one."

Sadie knew she was in trouble when the dark, curly haired man pointed straight at her, despite her attempt to hide behind the cybernetic prostie-borg in front of her. Pasting a blank look on her face, she tried to remain calm and look like all the other girls in the lineup.

There were prosties with small breasts, some with large, and some sported racks any porn-vid queen would be proud of. Some were so short they were practically dwarf size and some were so tall they could have played for any Zero-G team in the league. Their measurements ranged from anorexically slender to downright Junoesque. They sported skin tones from ebony to golden tan to peaches and cream pale, and hair ran the gamut from blond to redheaded to brunette and every shade in between.

Every face was plastically perfect and completely blank. *A Girl For Every Taste—Cybernetic Sex Made Delightfully Easy* was the motto of the Prostie Palace. Every possible combination of attractive female features and attributes was represented in the silent ranks of the assembled prosties and this joker had to pick *her*.

Hidden inside her outrageous scarlet wig she could feel the bargain Overlook-Me chip flicker for the last time, fizzle, and die. The noninterference field she'd been wearing like a protective halo for the past two weeks faded into nonexistence. Damn it, she'd known it was a bad idea to buy her main protection from Big Bob's Bargain Basement Chips, but what was a girl on a budget supposed to do?

It was hard enough financing the ticket from Io to Titan in the first place. In the end she'd had to ride on an ore transport that was far from luxurious. Insinuating herself into the Pleasure Dome Prostie Palace had required several bribes to the right people, both to get inside in the first place, and to add herself to the database of resident prostie-borgs. Add that to the cost of her outfit, makeup, and wig, and she barely had any credit left at all.

My whole life savings spent paying for this trip and now I'm screwed. Literally and figuratively. She stared blankly, as the man pointed her out to the mechanical madam who nodded in her direction. It was the same panicky feeling she had experienced when she first walked into the Prostie Palace and saw the kind of outrageous sexual practices that went on here. Having been raised in the morally uptight colony of Goshen on Io, the scene at the prostie brothel was an education to Sadie in more than one way.

She had financed the trip on her own for the ultimate payoff, a juicy scoop on the nitty-gritty, hardboiled life of a prostie-borg in the Outer Rings.

Prostie-borgs were cybernetic organisms grown in flesh tanks on Mars. They were a variation on the more common fleshbots that were used for manual labor all over the solar system but instead of being fitted for heavy lifting and tasks no human laborer could do, prostie-borgs were crafted specifically for sex. Despite a simple synthetic brain that put them on the mental level of a ten-year-old child, they were very popular, especially with the sex-starved men who mined the outer rings of Saturn. Intellectual stimulation wasn't high on the must-have list of female attributes for most Ring miners, and real women were few and far between at this cold, dark end of the solar system.

Sadie was tired of covering joining ceremonies, baby showers, golden anniversaries, and all the other human interest crap that a junior reporter got saddled with at the *Io Moon Times*. Problem was, her senior editor, a grouchy, chauvinistic man by the name of B. F. Fields, thought that was all she could do. Sadie had set out to prove him wrong.

Taking all of her yearly vacation in one big lump, she had hopped an ore transport to the most notorious prostie brothel in the System, located on Titan, Saturn's largest moon. There she had planned to spend her free time gathering facts for a blistering exposé that would blow the top off the barely legal prostie-borg industry. She even had a title for her article all picked out: Pain and Suffering in the Pleasure Dome: A Prostie-Borg's Daily Life in the Outer Rings.

When she got back to Io, Fields would *have* to recognize her reporting prowess and promote her out of the human interest section once and for all. Hell, she might even go freelance and sell her story to one of the intergalactic news vids.

Her plan had been working like a charm, too, until the bargain Overlook-Me chip began to die. When the other prosties began noticing her, Sadie knew she was in trouble, but she kept hoping the chip would last just one more week until her transport for Io left. Now the chip was good and dead and she didn't even have a repair kit to try and get it working again. She was about to find out exactly what the prosties went through and she was afraid it wasn't going to be a pleasant experience.

At least he looks cleaner than most of the clientele you see around here. Sadie eyed the dark man carefully. He had very tan skin and his hair was the color of bitter chocolate, curly and thick, cut short but not too close to his scalp. Any woman she knew would kill for that kind of natural curl, she thought absently, taking in the indigo eyes fringed thickly with black lashes and the narrow but sensual mouth of the man pointing her out. Broad shoulders covered in a black leather jacket tapered to a narrow waist and powerful legs. There was a heavy bulge outlined by his tight black pants that made Sadie bite her bottom lip nervously as she felt those deep blue eyes sweep over her body.

"That one," he said again, and Sadie had no choice but to step forward. *Maybe it won't be so bad. Maybe it'll add realism to the story,* she thought desperately, trying to nerve herself up for the act. She felt horribly exposed in the tiny gold mesh dress that showed her breasts and sex plainly, but, after all, she'd been wearing it and outfits like it for two weeks. While the Overlook-Me chip had remained functional, no one had really *seen* her in them. From the look in the dark man's eyes, he liked what he saw.

Sadie was suddenly aware that her nipples were erect with fright against the scratchy gold mesh fabric. She squeezed her thighs tightly together, trying to keep her knees from shaking.

"Which one for the other gentleman?" the silver-skinned, mechanical madam asked, giving a jerky nod to the man's right. Standing beside him, hidden partially by the dark man's broad shoulders was another client. He stepped out from behind his friend with a nod to the madam and Sadie could see he was almost the exact opposite of the other man.

Tall and muscular with a runner's build, he had hair the color of beaten metal and the clearest sapphire eyes she had ever seen. The dark man wasn't short, but the blond was at least two inches taller with a full mouth that seemed naturally red against his pale golden skin. He was dressed in the same style as his colleague in tight black pants and a white shirt with the ubiquitous mining company symbol stitched in red on the collar. He was also wearing an identical black leather jacket.

Sadie couldn't help noticing that the bulge outlined by his pants was no less impressive than the dark-haired man's. Did they work for some mining company that only hired well-hung men? What was their motto—*less than nine inches need not apply?*

These two were so different from the typical grimy, disheveled specimens who usually patronized the Prostie Palace that they might have come from Stud Miners R Us. Sadie felt a hysterical bubble of laughter rise in her throat at the thought and forced it back down. Prostie-borgs did not laugh.

"My friend and I prefer to share," the blond man said, to Sadie's horror. "That one will do fine."

Two at the same time...? She couldn't stop her eyes from widening. Merciful Goddess, she didn't have all that much experience in the first place and she'd never done anything even remotely kinky. Certainly nothing like this...

"Excuse me? Would you mind not talking about me like I'm not in the room?" Sadie had to raise her voice to be heard. Their eyes turned in her direction. "Look, I can *help* you." She stood and shrugged off the jacket, leaving it on the chair and began pacing as she made her point. "I'm good undercover," she pointed out. "I've survived on my own out here for two weeks and I would've been fine until my transport showed up except for the rotten luck with my chip. I can get you information you couldn't get otherwise. I'm sure you're both very good detectives, but you're *men* and most prostie-borgs are female. And *I* have extensive experience impersonating a prostie; I know what I'm doing." Sadie took a step toward them, hands on her hips and breasts thrust out, showing all her flesh through the golden mesh of her skimpy dress. She knew what she looked like—hot, wild, and wanton. She normally wouldn't act so brazenly but there was a big story on the line. A once-in-a-lifetime chance.

"Hmmm." With the mesh dress back in view and most of her considerable assets on display, the blond detective seemed to be rethinking his position. He exchanged an unreadable look with his dark-haired partner.

"She's got a point, Holt," Blakely murmured. "I bet she'd be real good under the covers."

"Undercover," the blond man corrected him, a sardonic grin curving his full lips.

"That, too," Blakely agreed, smiling back.

The mood in the tiny metal room had changed. Sadie could sense it like a new weather pattern, the heat from both sets of blue eyes raking over her body and pulsing against her nearly naked skin. She blushed from the tips of her toes to the roots of her hair, but she held her ground. *Think Solar Pulitzer,* she told herself. This kind of story could make or break her career.

Holt looked at her appraisingly. "So you're up for a little *undercover* work, hmm?" The blond man's tone was mocking, but interested.

Sadie felt her cheeks grow hot but refused to drop her eyes. "Absolutely. I won't lie to you; a story like this could make my career. I—I'd be willing to do almost anything to get a first hand exclusive."

"*Almost* anything?" Holt drawled, rising with catlike grace from the rickety bed and circling her. He didn't touch her in any way, but he was so close she could smell a faint hint of masculine musk that clung to his big frame. Sadie looked to the dark-haired detective for help because he had been so sympathetic to her earlier; but Blakely seemed content to watch the byplay between her and his partner without saying a word.

"Y—yes." She hated the stupid tremble that came into her

voice when she was nervous. She had no doubt what he was implying. Men like Detectives Christian Holt and David Blakely didn't give you a free ride and an exclusive scoop on a story this big for nothing. There was bound to be a price, a mutual exchange of favors involved. *Sexual* favors. It looked like she was right back where she had started when Blakely picked her out of the prostie line-up.

Trying to control the tremble in her tone and sound sophisticated, maybe even a little bored, Sadie asked, "What do you say, boys?" What would they think of her in Goshen right now if they could see her using her body as a bargaining chip to get an exclusive scoop? She pushed the thought away.

Holt sat back on the bed and looked at Blakely. The look they shared seemed to convey something—some form of nonverbal communication that Sadie couldn't begin to decipher, but at last the blond turned back to her and spoke for both of them.

"Fine. You can come with us on the condition that you *stay out of the way.*"

"And promise to behave yourself." Blakely looked up at her from under the fringe of tangled black lashes and Sadie thought she had never seen a blue so deep.

"I'll be a perfect angel," she promised, trying to regain her composure. "Cross my heart, officer. If I'm not you can put me in cuffs." She held out her slender wrists, miming a set of restraints and then blushed. What had made her say such a thing? She was definitely going too far.

From the look in his eyes, Blakely liked the idea. "I'll hafta keep that in mind, baby," he drawled, obviously enjoying the mental image of Sadie in a pair of handcuffs.

Trying not to think about what she had just let herself in for, Sadie attempted to get back to business. "Well then it's all set. You two bring your ship around by the back of the far dome,

I'll palm a sample of the evening injection, and we're home free." She smiled brightly and stepped away to go for the door, but a large, warm hand encircled her wrist, keeping her from completing the motion.

"Wait a minute, sweetheart. Aren't you forgetting somethin'?" Blakely's eyes were a sleepy-hot blue in his dark face, and Holt was looking thoughtfully at her as well.

"What?" Sadie quavered, all of her self-possession momentarily gone. "You said you weren't here for sex." *At least not yet . . .*

"We're not." Holt's voice was calm and he reached up to hold her other hand in a large palm, pulling her down to sit between them on the squeaky bed. Both men put an arm around her and despite the skimpy mesh dress, or maybe because of it, Sadie felt truly warm for the first time in weeks. In fact, she was beginning to feel distinctly overheated. "But I think what my partner is trying to say is, don't you think we'd better make it look real? I mean, you've been in here for over half an hour, supposedly with two sex-starved miners who haven't seen female flesh for a lunar year. Don't you think you'd be a little, shall we say, *roughed up* if that were really the case?"

"Oh, well . . ." Sadie flashed on the usual appearances of post-clientele prosties, *the ones that were able to walk out under their own power anyway*, and swallowed hard. "I guess you're right. I could, um, mess up my hair." She ruffled the scarlet wig with one hand and looked hopefully from sapphire to indigo eyes.

"Not quite what I had in mind." Blakely's voice rumbled in his chest and Sadie noticed that with his jacket off, she could see a hint of black, curling hair peeking from the neckline of his plain white shirt. The scent of sandalwood soap was stronger and Holt also gave off that appealingly masculine scent of musk and something else she couldn't quite name. Something fresh and sharp . . . The scents seemed to mix in her brain making her dizzy.

"What did you have in mind?" She kept her voice steady by force of will.

"Just this." Blakely leaned toward her and Sadie drew back until she realized it almost put her in the blond detective's lap. She turned to look up at Holt and he was smiling, a look of cool condescension in his ice-blue eyes. On the whole, she thought she preferred the dark-haired detective's openly predatory attitude to his partner's sarcastic one.

"Don't worry, sweetheart. I'll keep my hands to myself. Just gonna give you a little love mark on the side of your neck, okay?" Blakely raised his hands, palms up to show his intentions were honorable.

"Well . . . I guess. As long as that's *all* you do. Make it quick." Tilting her head, she offered him the side of her throat and gave an involuntary sigh when the sensual mouth descended, licking delicately along her slender neck before settling in the sensitive area beneath her ear to mark her. Blakely's breath smelled like cinnamon. "Mmmm," she moaned involuntarily, feeling the brush of his coarse curls against her tender flesh as he worked. *What's wrong with me?* she wondered, even as she responded to the searing mouth on her throat. *I shouldn't be acting like this.* Blakely did something hot with his tongue that made her gasp, but she didn't try to pull away.

"Like that, huh?" he whispered. Raising his head for a moment, he looked over at Holt. "You joinin' the party, babe?" he asked his partner, his voice low and sensual.

"One for each side?" The fair-haired detective raised a silvery-blond eyebrow. "How does the lady feel about that?" He looked at Sadie and the sapphire eyes were filled with the same sleepy sensuality that lit Blakely's.

"Well, I . . ." To tell the truth, Sadie was pretty far gone. It was obviously wrong to be enjoying something that was simply a necessity, but she couldn't quite seem to help herself.

"Good for your cover," Blakely explained reasonably, his hot breath blowing against her ear. When she turned to look at him, the indigo eyes were dark and intense, and Sadie got the distinct feeling that he wanted his partner to do this with him. To *share* this with him for some reason. She wondered why, but somehow it didn't seem important. He was right, after all—it was important that she look the part of a recently rented prostie and another love mark could only help that impression. She decided not to worry about it for now.

"When you put it that way . . . I guess so," she heard herself saying.

With a low laugh, Blakely returned to the spot under her ear and then she felt another hot mouth—Holt's—kissing lightly along the heavy pulse on the other side of her throat until he stopped to suck gently at the sensitive place where her neck met her shoulder.

At that moment, something strange happened. When Holt's mouth opened and his tongue touched her flesh it was as though the sensation from both sides had not just been doubled, but infinitely multiplied. Sadie stiffened between them and then melted helplessly into the embrace. Her nipples felt like two hard pebbles at the tips of her breasts and she pressed her thighs together tightly, trying to deny the heat and moisture that was gathering between them. It was hard to believe that this simple act when the two men weren't touching her in any other way that was remotely sexual could make her respond so blatantly, but her arousal was undeniable.

"Goddess . . ." she breathed softly, drowning in the hot sensation of both mouths tasting her, sucking her, marking her. Involuntarily she reached out and gripped their legs, one in each hand, feeling the bunching of heavy thigh muscles under her palms as she did. Both men were excited, as excited as herself if not more so; she could feel it in the tension that thrummed through the big bodies on either side of her like an electric current. *And I'm the conductor between them,* she thought faintly. The strange thought was enough to bring her back to herself and she pushed suddenly, convulsively, away from them, using their legs as a prop to propel herself off the rickety bed.

"I think that's enough, gentlemen." Her voice shook as she stood in front of them and tried to catch her breath. She placed her hands on either side of her neck protectively, feeling how tender the flesh was.

"I guess." Blakely looked disappointed, but Holt still looked amused.

"You look fairly *roughed up* now, I would say," the blond detective drawled, annoying Sadie even as he agreed with her.

Sadie felt herself flush and forced herself to speak calmly. "Take me back to the common room now and I'll meet you with the injection the new prosties are receiving at the back of the far dome at eight tonight. Be sure you're on time."

"We'll be there, sweetheart," Blakely assured her, rising from the rumpled bed and retrieving his jacket.

"Wouldn't miss it." Holt agreed.

Someone's in the kitchen with the sexy chef of DELICIOUS. And the action is *hot*. Don't miss this scorching excerpt from Jami Alden's Aphrodisia debut, coming in November 2006 . . .

Reggie shifted restlessly on the bed. Despite the wine at dinner, she was too wired to sleep. She'd hoped the hot shower would help her wind down. But as she'd rubbed her own soapy hands over her wet skin, she'd found herself wishing Gabe would ignore his professional code of ethics and walk through that door and join her. Flustered, she'd finished with a quick, cold rinse and made a beeline for the bedroom before she did something stupid. Like try to jump him.

She flipped over on her back, trying to ignore the awareness that made every nerve ending tingle. She could feel him through the paper-thin walls, his heat, his masculinity, surging over her, overwhelming her with memories of the single, sultry night they'd shared.

As though with a will of its own, her hand trailed down her belly, lifting the hem of her pajama top so she could feel her own smooth skin. She remembered Gabe's callused fingertips sliding over her, drifting up her ribcage to capture the soft weight of her breasts. His dark, fathomless eyes had flared with heat as he'd pulled her dress off her shoulders, revealing her to his gaze.

"Your nipples are the same gorgeous pink as your lips," he *murmured, sucking and licking one into his mouth. His thumb slid inside the lace edge of her panties, brushing over her clit in a matching rhythm. "I wonder what color these beautiful lips are." His thumb traced the dripping seam of her sex, teasing the entrance of her body with shallow thrusts of his fingers.*

Reggie's thumb and forefinger pinched at her own nipple as wet heat pooled between her legs. God, it had been so long since she had been touched, since she had been fucked. Her other hand slid into her panties, fingers sliding into her damp, swollen folds. Her clit was a firm, throbbing bud, dying for the touch of the man sleeping on the couch less than twenty feet away.

Her breath hissed at the first touch of her sensitive skin, and she nearly came at the first brush of her finger. But as much as she needed the release, she wanted to slow down, savor it. It was pathetic, masturbating while the man she craved was so close by, but she couldn't face another rejection. So for the first time since Gabe had reappeared in her life, she allowed herself to relive every look, every touch, every stroke.

He gazed down at her as she lay sprawled on the bed, eyes gleaming in the dim light. "Damn darlin', you're about the sweetest piece I've ever seen." His drawl thickened with every syllable. "But I'll never forgive myself if I don't treat you properly."

From what she could tell, there was nothing "proper" about their behavior, but she wasn't about to argue as he started dropping soft, moist kisses down her neck and across her collarbones.

She twined her fingers in his hair, tugging insistently until his mouth hovered over her rock-hard nipple. The harsh, hungry sound he made as his lips pulled firmly sent a jolt of heat straight to her pussy. *The hot, rigid length of his cock burned against her inner thigh, and she squirmed in anticipation of feeling his thick length buried inside her.*

"Sweet thing, you taste so good I hardly know where to start." *He lavished attention to her breasts, alternating almost rough sucking with gentle, teasing lashes of his tongue. Oh God, she wanted—needed—to feel that skillful tongue on her pussy. Tugging at his hair, she guided his head down her belly.*

"You read my mind." *He landed a wet, sucking kiss just below her belly button and slid her panties down her legs.* "Mm, you smell like peaches." *With a purely male sound of satisfaction he stroked his thumbs against her plump lips, spreading her wide for his hungry mouth.*

Reggie circled her clit with her middle finger, wishing it was Gabe's tongue flicking against the turgid flesh.

She nearly came at the first touch of his tongue, lapping at her clit before slipping down to probe her drenched slit.

She dipped her finger inside her throbbing pussy, imagining it was his thick cock pressing deep.

He soaked the plump head of his cock in her juices, stretching her wide as he sank into her with one powerful stroke. "Honey, you're so tight and sweet," *he moaned, increasing the pace of his thrusts as she hitched her legs over his hips, opening herself more fully.* "Your pussy feels so good, squeezing me like a tight little fist."

No on had ever talked to her like this, in such graphic terms, and she would have been embarrassed if she hadn't been so turned on. Sharp moans erupted from her chest in tandem with his thrusts. He reared up and grabbed her hips, driving into her in a hard, circling rhythm that made her thrash against the sheets and claw at the slick skin of his back.

Her fingers stilled on her clit as she sought to hold her orgasm at bay, just for few more seconds. She wanted to draw it out, relive the memory of him fucking her deep and hard for just a little longer.

He stilled his thrusts, watching her with hot, dark eyes as he traced his thumb against her lower lip, pressing it inside her mouth for her to suck. Then he settled that moist thumb in the slick folds of her pussy, right where they were joined. He held himself deep, impossibly deep inside her, grinding as his thumb circled and pressed against her throbbing clit.

"Open your eyes, Gina." A long slow slide, a stroke of his thumb. *"Open your eyes and look at me when you come."*

Her finger increased the pressure on her clit, every nerve pulsing as she imagined him watching her again. Her eyes drifted closed and she bit her lip against the cry working its way up her throat. She was coming, but it wasn't enough, it wasn't the same without his thick cock driving inside her.

But unless Gabe walked through the door, it would have to do. As the last tremors of her climax receded, she rolled to her stomach, willing herself to sleep.

Gabe had nearly drifted off when the soft noise penetrated the haze of near sleep. He slipped off the couch and padded toward Reggie's door. There it was again, a soft, high sound, a hitch of her breath carrying through the thin plywood door. His cock went instantly hard as he remembered her making a similar sound, only louder, when he had sucked her clit into his mouth for the first time.

Easy there, big boy, he admonished his cock, *she's most likely having a bad dream.* But her door had only been closed for about five minutes, hardly enough time to go into REM sleep and dream. He put his palm against the door, applying the lightest of pressures. It opened a few inches.

Moonlight spilled over the bed, and Gabe nearly fell to his knees at the sight that greeted him. Reggie's eyes were closed, her teeth clamped down on her lower lip as she fought to stifle the little sounds working their way out of her throat. One hand had disappeared up her shirt, the other down the front of her pajama bottoms, and from the way she was squirming around, she was showing herself a very good time.

He held his breath, afraid he'd groan if he let it out. He wanted to dive on the bed, strip off her clothes and replace her hands with his own. Her movements stopped, and he froze, half afraid, half hoping she'd realized he was watching. Then she'd beckon him over to the bed, spread her legs wide to show him how wet she'd made herself, all in preparation for the real thing.

Then she started again, her hand moving in sure, deliberate strokes. She arched up into her hand, fucking herself with a steady rhythm, his cock pulsed a matching beat. His fingers itched to feel her soft, slick flesh, to feel the tight, muscular grip of her pussy closing around him like she couldn't get enough. She uttered a stifled cry and stiffened, and his heart pounded in his ears. He was so hard he hurt, wanting with every cell in his body to join her in that bed, to see if fucking her could possibly be as good as he remembered.

Instead he watched her get herself off. Her body relaxed in post-orgasmic satiation. Gabe knew he should move, should walk away before she saw him standing in the doorway. Instead he stared, cock aching, as though willing her to open her eyes. If she turned those big brown eyes on him, he had no faith in his ability to practice self restraint. He'd be a dead man.

His stomach curled in anticipation as she shifted to make herself more comfortable. Instead of turning toward the door, she rolled onto her stomach without opening her eyes, completely oblivious to his presence in the doorway.

Muttering a vicious curse, he slunk back to the foldout couch, his hand wrapped around his aching cock. He flopped back on the foldout bed, wincing as a metal bar nearly severed his spine through the flimsy excuse for a mattress. He'd thought the training he'd gone through for Special Forces was hard. But tailing Reggie Caldwell without touching her was going to be the longest month and a half of his life.